J. Kenner (aka Julie Kenner) is the *New York Times*, *USA Today*, *Publishers Weekly*, *Wall Street Journal*, and No. 1 internationally bestselling author of over seventy novels, novellas, and short stories in a variety of genres.

Though known primarily for her award-winning and internationally bestselling erotic romances (including the Stark and Most Wanted series) that have reached as high as No. 2 on the *New York Times* bestseller list, Kenner has been writing full-time for over a decade in a variety of genres, including paranormal and contemporary romance, 'chicklit' suspense, urban fantasy, and paranormal mommy lit.

Kenner has been praised by *Publishers Weekly* as an author with a 'flair for dialogue and eccentric characterizations' and by *Romantic Times* for having 'cornered the market on sinfully attractive, dominant antiheroes and the women who swoon for them'. A five-time finalist for Romance Writers of America's prestigious RITA award, Kenner took home the first RITA trophy awarded in the category of erotic romance in 2014 for her novel, *Claim Me* (book two of her Stark Trilogy). Her books have sold well over a million copies and are published in over twenty countries.

In her previous career as an attorney, Kenner worked as a lawyer in Southern California and Texas. She currently lives in Central Texas, with her husband, two daughters and two cats.

Visit J. Kenner online at **www.jkenner.com**. Or connect with her via Twitter **@juliekenner** or through Facebook at **www.facebook.com/ JKennerBooks**.

By J. Kenner

Just some .... **sensual
and erotic** ...

'Kenner may very well have cornered the market on sinfully
attractive .... for
them ... Her characters' scorching, scandalous affair explore
very nature of attraction and desire, redeeming and changing them
beyond measure' *Romantic Times*

'The plot is complex, the characters engaging, and J. Kenner's
passionate writing brings it all perfectly together' *Harlequin Junkie*

'Another J. Kenner masterpiece ... This was an intriguing look at
self-discovery and forbidden love all wrapped into a neat little
action-suspense package. There was plenty of sexual tension and
eventually action ... But can we expect anything less from J. Kenner?'
Reading Haven

'The heat practically radiates from the page ... This book is sexy,
romantic, steamy and thrilling all wrapped into one extremely well
written package' *Books & Boys Book Blog*

'J. Kenner's evocative writing thrillingly captures the power of physical
attraction, the pull of longing, the universe-altering effect one person
can have on another ... *Claim Me* has the emotional depth to back up
the sex ... Every scene is infused with both erotic tension, and the
tension of wondering what lies beneath Damien's veneer – and how
and when it will be revealed' *Heroes and Heartbreakers*

'A toe-curling smokin' hot read, full of incredible characters and a
brilliant storyline that you won't be able to get enough of. I can't wait
for the next book in this series ... I'm hooked!' *Flirty & Dirty Book Blog*

'I do believe that I just found my newest guilty pleasure' *Hooker
Heels Book Blog*

'Kenner definitely knows how to write steamy love scenes and how
to push the pain/pleasure envelope with her characters' *Harlequin
Junkie*

'PERFECT for fans of *Fifty Shades of Grey* and *Bared to You*. *Release
Me* is a powerful and erotic romance novel that is sure to make
adult romance readers sweat, sigh and swoon' *Reading, Eating &
Dreaming Blog*

'[A] sexy and exciting ride' *Fresh Fiction*

'This is deeply sensual and the story packs an emotional punch that I really hadn't expected ... If you enjoyed *Fifty Shades* [and] the Crossfire books, you're definitely going to enjoy this one. It's compelling, engaging and I was thoroughly engrossed' *Sinfully Sexy Blog*

'Once again Kenner has written a book that reaches into your soul, pulls out all your emotions and leaves you with a smile' *The Book Reading Gals*

'I am in the "I loved *Fifty Shades*" camp, but after reading *Release Me*, Mr Grey only scratches the surface compared to Damien Stark' *Cocktails and Books Blog*

'It is not often when a book is so amazingly well-written that I find it hard to even begin to accurately describe it ... I recommend this book to everyone who is interested in a passionate love story' *Romancebookworm's Reviews*

'Delivers both scorching hot scenes along with the evolution and unpeeling of emotional barriers built by past dark secrets. Moreover, the characters are complex, the passion is intense and the ultimate message that love can heal all is inspiring' *The Romance Reviews* (five stars)

'The story is one that will rank up with the *Fifty Shades* and Crossfire trilogies' *Incubus Publishing Blog*

'Be prepared for a roller coaster filled with twists and turns, ups and downs, hope, heartbreak and cliffhangers' *Book Boyfriend Blog*

J KENNER

Wicked GRIND

HEADLINE
ETERNAL

First published in Great Britain in 2017
by HEADLINE ETERNAL
An imprint of HEADLINE PUBLISHING GROUP

1

Cataloguing in Publication Data is available from the British Library

ISBN 978 1 4722 4692 9

Typeset in 11/14 pt Minion Pro by Jouve (UK), Milton Keynes

Printed and bound in Great Britain by CPI Group (UK) Ltd, Croydon, CR0 4YY

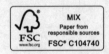

MIX
Paper from
responsible sources
FSC® C104740

Headline's policy is to use papers that are natural, renewable and recyclable
products and made from wood grown in well-managed forests and other
controlled sources. The logging and manufacturing processes are expected
to conform to the environmental regulations of the country of origin.

HEADLINE PUBLISHING GROUP
An Hachette UK Company
Carmelite House
50 Victoria Embankment
London EC4Y 0DZ

www.headlineeternal.com
www.headline.co.uk
www.hachette.co.uk

For Melissa.
Because she's the boss.

Prologue

I'd thought he was out of my life forever. That all that remained of him was a memory, sharp and forbidden. Terrifying, yet tempting.

The one man who changed everything.

The one night that destroyed my world.

I told myself I was past it. That I could see him again and not feel that tug. Not remember the hurt or the shame.

That's what I believed, anyway.

Honestly, I should have known better . . .

He was surrounded by naked women, and he was bored out of his mind.

Wyatt Royce forced himself not to frown as he lowered his camera without taking a single shot. Thoughtfully, he took a step back, his critical eye raking over the four women who stood in front of him in absolutely nothing but their birthday suits.

Gorgeous women. Confident women. With luscious curves, smooth skin, bright eyes, and the kind of strong, supple muscles that left no doubt that each and every one of them could wrap their legs around a man and hold him tight.

In other words, each one had an erotic allure. A glow. A certain *je ne sais quoi* that turned heads and left men hard.

None of them, however, had *it*.

"Wyatt? You ready, man?"

Jon Paul's voice pulled Wyatt from his frustrated thoughts, and he nodded at his lighting director. "Sorry. Just thinking."

JP turned his back to the girls before flashing a wolfish grin and lowering his voice. "I'll bet you were."

Wyatt chuckled. "Down, boy." Wyatt had hired the

twenty-three-year-old UCLA photography grad student as a jack-of-all-trades six months ago. But when JP had proved himself to be not only an excellent photographer, but also a prodigy with lighting, the relationship had morphed from boss/assistant to mentor/protégé before finally holding steady at friend/colleague.

JP was damn good at his job, and Wyatt had come to rely on him. But JP's background was in architectural photography. And the fact that the female models he faced every day were not only gorgeous, but often flat-out, one hundred percent, provocatively nude, continued to be both a fascination to JP and, Wyatt suspected, the cause of a daily cold shower. Or three.

Not that Wyatt could criticize. After all, he was the one who'd manufactured the sensual, erotic world in which both he and JP spent their days. For months, he'd lost himself daily inside this studio, locked in with a series of stunning women, their skin warm beneath his fingers as he gently positioned them for the camera. Women eager to please. To move however he directed. To contort their bodies in enticing, tantalizing poses that were often unnatural and uncomfortable, and for no other reason than that he told them to.

As long as they were in front of his camera, Wyatt owned those women, fully and completely. And he'd be lying to himself if he didn't admit that in many ways the photo shoots were as erotically charged as the ultimate photographs.

So, yeah, he understood the allure, but he'd damn sure never succumbed to it. Not even when so many of his models had made it crystal clear that they were eager to move from his studio to his bedroom.

There was just too much riding on this project.

Too much? Hell, *everything* was riding on his upcoming show. His career. His life. His reputation. Not to mention his personal savings.

Eighteen months ago he'd set out to make a splash in the world of art and photography, and in just twenty-seven days, he'd find out if he'd succeeded.

What he hoped was that success would slam against him like a cannonball hitting water. So hard and fast that everybody in the vicinity ended up drenched, with him squarely at the center, the unabashed cause of all the commotion.

What he feared was that the show would be nothing more than a ripple, as if he'd done little more than stick his big toe into the deep end of the pool.

Behind him, JP coughed, the harsh sound pulling Wyatt from his thoughts. He glanced up, saw that each of the four women were staring at him with hope in their eyes, and felt like the ultimate heel.

"Sorry to keep you waiting, ladies. Just trying to decide how I want you." He spoke without any innuendo, but the petite brunette giggled anyway, then immediately pressed her lips together and dipped her gaze to the floor. Wyatt pretended not to notice. "JP, go grab my Leica from my office. I'm thinking I want to shoot black and white."

He wasn't thinking that at all, not really. He was just buying time. Talking out of his ass while he decided what—if anything—to do with the girls.

As he spoke, he moved toward the women, trying to figure out why the hell he was so damned uninterested in all of them. Were they really that inadequate? So unsuited for the role he needed to fill?

Slowly, he walked around them, studying their curves, their angles, the soft glow of their skin under the muted lighting. This one had a haughty, aquiline nose. That one a wide, sensual mouth. Another had the kind of bedroom eyes that promised to fulfill any man's fantasies. The fourth, a kind of wide-eyed innocence that practically begged to be tarnished.

Each had submitted a portfolio through her agent, and he'd

spent hours poring over every photograph. He had one slot left in the show. The centerpiece. The lynchpin. A single woman that would anchor all of his carefully staged and shot photos with a series of erotic images that he could already see clearly in his mind. A confluence of lighting and staging, of body and attitude. Sensuality coupled with innocence and underscored with daring.

He knew what he wanted. More than that, somewhere in the deep recesses of his mind, he even knew *who* he wanted.

So far, she hadn't wandered into his studio.

But she was out there, whoever she was; he was certain of it.

Too bad he only had twenty-seven days to find her.

Which was why he'd stooped to scouring modeling agencies, even though his vision for this show had always been to use amateur models. Women whose features or attitude caught his attention on the beach, in the grocery store, wherever he might be. Women from his past. Women from his work. But always women who didn't make a living with their bodies. That had been his promise to himself from the beginning.

And yet here he was, begging agents to send their most sensual girls to him. Breaking his own damn rule because he was desperate to find her. That elusive girl who was hiding in his mind, and who maybe—just maybe—had an agent and a modeling contract.

But he knew she wouldn't. Not that girl.

No, the girl he wanted would be a virgin with the camera, and he'd be the one who would first capture that innocence. That was his vision. The plan he'd stuck to for eighteen long months of squeezing in sessions between his regular commercial photography gigs. Almost two years of all-nighters in the dark room and surviving on coffee and protein bars because there wasn't time to order take-out, much less cook.

Months of planning and worrying and slaving toward a goal. And those sweet, precious moments when he knew—really knew—that he was on the verge of creating something truly spectacular.

He was exhausted, yes. But he was almost done.

So far, he had forty-one final images chosen for the show, each and every one perfect as far as he was concerned.

He just needed the final nine. That last set of photos of his one perfect woman. Photos that would finally seal his vision—both of the girl in his mind and of what he wanted to accomplish with this solo exhibition.

He'd sacrificed so much, and he was finally close. So damn close . . . and yet here he was, spinning his wheels with models who weren't what he wanted or needed.

Fuck.

With a sigh of frustration, Wyatt dragged his fingers through his thick, short hair. "Actually, ladies, I think we're done here. I appreciate your time and your interest in the project, and I'll review your portfolios and be in touch with your agent if you're selected. You're free to get dressed and go."

The girls glanced at each other, bewildered. For that matter, JP looked equally puzzled as he returned to the studio with Wyatt's Leica slung over his shoulder and a tall, familiar redhead at his side.

"Siobhan," Wyatt said, ignoring the trepidation building in his gut. "I didn't realize we had a meeting scheduled."

"I thought you were going to shoot a roll of black and white," JP said at the same time, holding up the Leica in the manner of a third grader at Show-and-Tell.

In front of Wyatt, the girls paused in the act of pulling on their robes, obviously uncertain.

"We're done," Wyatt said to them before turning his attention to his assistant. "I have everything I need to make a decision."

"Right. Sure. You're the boss." But as JP spoke, he looked sideways at Siobhan, whose arms were now crossed over her chest, her brow furrowed with either confusion or annoyance. Quite probably both.

But Wyatt had to hand it to her; she held in her questions until the last model had entered the hallway that led to the dressing room, and the door had clicked shut behind her.

"You got what you needed?" she asked, cutting straight to the chase. "Does that mean one of those models is the girl you've been looking for?"

"Is that why you're here? Checking my progress?" *Shit.* He sounded like a guilty little boy standing in front of the principal.

Siobhan, thank God, just laughed. "One, I'm going to assume from the defensive tone that the answer is no. And two, I'm the director of your show first and foremost because we're friends. So take this in the spirit of friendship when I ask, what the hell are you doing? We have less than a month to pull all of this together. So if none of those girls is the one you need, then tell me what I can do to help. Because this is on me, too, remember? This show flops, and we both lose."

"Thanks," he said dryly. "I appreciate the uplifting and heartfelt speech."

"Screw uplifting. I want you on the cover of every art and photography magazine in the country, with your show booked out on loan to at least a dozen museums and galleries for the next five years. I couldn't care less if you're uplifted. I just want you to pull this off."

"Is that all?" he asked, fighting a smile.

"Hell no. I also want a promotion. My boss is considering moving to Manhattan. I covet her office."

"Good to have a goal," JP said, tilting his head toward Wyatt. "I covet his."

"Go," Wyatt said, waving his thumb toward the dressing room. "Escort the girls out through the gallery," he ordered. The space was divided into his two-story studio that boasted a discreet entrance off the service alley, and a newly remodeled gallery and storefront that opened onto one of Santa Monica's well-trafficked retail areas.

"So you're really done?" JP pressed. "That's it? Not even a single shot?"

"I don't need to see anything else," Wyatt said. "Go. Chat them up so they don't feel like they wasted their time. And then I'll see you tomorrow."

"That's your subtle way of getting rid of me, isn't it?"

"Don't be ridiculous," Wyatt retorted. "I wasn't being subtle at all."

JP smirked, but didn't argue. And with a wave to Siobhan, he disappeared into the back hallway.

"So how can I help?" Siobhan asked once he was gone. "Should I arrange a round of auditions? After all, I know a lot of really hot women."

That was true enough. In fact, Siobhan's girlfriend, Cassidy, featured prominently in the show. And it had been through Cass that Wyatt had originally met Siobhan, who had both a background in art and a shiny new job as the assistant director of the Stark Center for the Visual Arts in downtown Los Angeles.

Originally, Wyatt had envisioned a significantly smaller show staged in his studio. The location was good, after all, and he anticipated a lot of foot traffic since folks could walk from the Third Street Promenade. He'd asked Cass to model about eight months ago, not only because she was stunning, but because he knew the flamboyant tattoo artist well enough to know that she wouldn't balk at any pose he came up with, no matter how provocative. Cass didn't have a shy bone in her body, and she was more than happy to shock—so long as the shock was delivered on her terms.

Siobhan had come with her, and before the shoot, Wyatt had shown both of them three of the pieces he'd already finished so that Cass would have a sense of his vision. It was the first time he'd laid it out in detail, and it had been cathartic talking to Siobhan, who spoke the language, and Cass, who was an artist herself, albeit one whose canvas was skin and whose tools were ink and needles.

He'd explained how he'd originally just wanted a break from the portraits and other commercial photography jobs that paid the bills. And, yes, he was beginning to make a name for himself artistically with his landscapes and city scenes. That success was gratifying, but ultimately unsatisfying because those subjects weren't his passion. There was beauty in nature, sure, but Wyatt wanted to capture physical, feminine eroticism on film.

More than that, he wanted to make a statement, to tell a story. Beauty. Innocence. Longing. Ecstasy. He wanted to look at the world through the eyes of these women, and the women through the eyes of the world.

Ultimately, he wanted to elevate erotic art. To use it to reveal more about the models than even they were aware. Strength and sensuality. Innocence and power. Passion and gentleness. He envisioned using a series of provocative, stunning images to manipulate the audience through the story of the show, sending them on a journey from innocence to debauchery and back again, and then leaving them breathless with desire and wonder.

That afternoon, Wyatt spoke with Cass and Siobhan for over an hour. Showing them examples. Describing the emotions he wanted to evoke. Listening to their suggestions, and taking satisfaction from the fact that they obviously loved the concept. They'd ended the conversation with Cass posing for another hour as he burned through three rolls of film, certain he was capturing some of his best work yet.

Then they'd walked to Q, a Santa Monica restaurant and bar known for its martini flights. They'd toasted his project, Cass's pictures, and Siobhan's career, and by the time they ended the evening, he was feeling pretty damn good about his little pet project.

The next morning, he'd felt even better. That's when Siobhan had come to him with a formal offer from the Stark Center. He'd said yes on the spot, never once thinking that by doing so he was tying another person to his success—or, more to the point, his potential failure.

"I'm serious," she pressed now, as his silence continued to linger. "Whatever you need."

"I'll find her," Wyatt said. "I have time."

"Not much," she countered. "I need the prints ahead of time for the catalog, not to mention installation. Keisha's already getting twitchy," she added, referring to her boss. "We don't usually cut it this close."

"I know. It's going to be—"

"Twenty-seven days to the show, Wyatt." He could hear the tension in her voice, and hated himself for being the cause of it. "But about half that before you need to deliver the prints. We're running out of time. If you can't find the girl, then you need to just find *a* girl. I'm sorry, but—"

"I said I'll find her. You have to trust me on this."

Right then, she didn't look like she'd trust him to take care of her goldfish, but to her credit, she nodded. "Fine. In that case, all I need today is to see the latest print so I can think about the promotional image. And you'll email me a file for the catalog?"

"Sure. This is it," he added, walking to a covered canvas centered on the nearest wall. He pulled down the white drape, revealing a life-size black and white photograph of a woman getting dressed. At first glance, it wasn't the most titillating of his images, but that was because it was such a tease. The woman stood in a dressing room, and hidden among the dresses and coats were at least a dozen men, peering out to watch her.

The woman, however, was oblivious. She was bending over, one foot on a stool, as she fastened a garter. The view was at an angle, so at first glance the audience saw only her skirt, a hint of garter, and the woman's silk-sheathed leg.

Then they noticed the mirror behind her. A mirror that revealed that she wasn't wearing panties under the garter belt. And even though absolutely nothing was left to the imagination, it still wasn't a particularly racy or erotic photograph. But then you noticed the reflection in the mirror of another mirror. And another. And another. Each with an image of that same woman, and each slightly more risqué, until finally, as the mirror approached infinity, the woman was nude, her head thrown back, one hand between her legs, the other at her throat. And all those men from the closet were out in the open now, their hands stroking and teasing her.

Most important, the mirror was so deep in the image that you had to stand practically nose-to-print to see it.

Wyatt couldn't wait to see how many people did exactly that at the showing.

"This is fabulous," Siobhan said with genuine awe in her voice.

"It was a hell of a photograph to set up and then develop. Lots of work on the set and in the darkroom."

"You could have set it up digitally."

He scoffed. "No. Some of the images, sure. But not this one." He turned his head, regarding it critically. "This one had to be hands-on. It's as much about the process as the product."

"I get that." She met his eyes, and the respect in hers reminded him of why he didn't just take photos for himself. "I want to take it back with me right now and show Keisha," she added.

"Soon." Although Siobhan and Keisha had wanted him to deliver each print upon completion, Wyatt had balked, explaining that he needed the art surrounding him in order to ensure the continuity of story in the overall exhibit. And the size of the canvas and the particulars of the way he handled the image in the darkroom were such that duplicates weren't adequate.

That meant that when Siobhan needed to see a piece, she came to him. And now that she was not only putting together the official catalog, but also doing promotional pieces from the images, she was coming a lot.

Wyatt was adamant that the images not be revealed prior to the show, but Siobhan's team had promised him the rapidly expanding catalog mockup would be kept under lock and key. More important, the pre-show promotion wouldn't reveal any of the artwork—while at the same time, teasing the art's sensual and daring nature.

So far, they'd not only managed to do just that, but the campaign was already a success. The gallery had been releasing one image a month—one of his photographs, yes, but only a sexy snippet shown through a virtual barrier laid over the image. Once, it was yellow *caution* tape. Another time, it was a keyhole in a hotel room door. Clever, yes, but also effective. Wyatt had already been interviewed and the exhibit pimped out in no less than five local papers and magazines. And he was booked on two morning shows the day the exhibit opened.

Not bad, all things considered, and he told Siobhan as much.

"If you really want to see a bump in our publicity," she replied, "we should get your grandmother on board."

"No." The word came swift and firm.

"Wyatt . . ."

"I said no. This exhibit is on my shoulders. I can't hide who I am, but I don't have to advertise it. If we trot my grandmother out, book her on morning shows, make her sing little Wyatt's praises, then everyone is going to come. You know that."

"Um, yeah. That's the point. To get people to your show."

"I want them to come for the show. Not because they're hoping to get Anika Segel's autograph."

"But they'll see your art. They'll fall in love then. Who cares what brings them through the door?"

"I do," he said and was relieved to see that she didn't seem to have an argument against that.

She stood still for a moment, possibly trying to come up

with something, but soon enough she shook her head and sighed. "You're the artist." She made a face. "And you have the temperament to go with it."

"See, that's how you wooed me into doing the show with you. That embarrassingly sentimental flattery."

"You're a laugh a minute, Wyatt." She hitched her purse further onto her shoulder, then pointed a finger at him. "Don't fuck this up."

"Cross my heart."

"All right then." She leaned in for an air kiss, but caught him in a hug. "It's going to be great," she whispered, and he was surprised by how much he appreciated those simple words.

"It will," he agreed. "All I have to do is find the girl." He glanced at his watch. "An agency's sending someone over in about half an hour. Nia. Mia. Something like that. Who knows? Maybe she'll be the one."

"Fingers crossed." Her grin turned wicked. "But if she's not, just say the word and Cass and I will dive into the search."

"A few more days like today, and I'll take you up on that."

"A few days is all you have," she retorted, then tossed up her hands, self-defense style. "I know, I know. I'm leaving."

She headed for the front door, and he turned back to the print, studying it critically. A moment later he reached for the drapes that covered the prints on either side of the first image, then tugged them off, revealing the full-color photos beneath.

He took a step back as he continued his inspection, ensuring himself that there were no more refinements to be made. Slowly, he moved farther back, wanting all three in his field of vision, just like a visitor to the exhibition would see. One step, then another and another.

He stopped when he heard the door open behind him, cursing himself for not locking up as Siobhan was leaving. "Did you forget something?" he asked as he turned.

But it wasn't Siobhan.

It was *her*.

The girl who'd filled his mind. The girl who'd haunted his nights.

The woman he needed if he was going to pull this exhibit off the way he wanted to.

A woman with the kind of wide sensual mouth that could make a man crazy, and a strong, lithe body, with curves in all the right places. Eyes that could see all the way into a man's soul—and an innocent air that suggested she wouldn't approve of what she saw there.

All of that, topped off with a wicked little tease of a smile and a sexy swing to her hips.

She was a walking contradiction. Sensual yet demure. Sexy yet sweet.

A woman who one minute could look like a cover model, and the next like she'd never done anything more glamorous than walk the dog.

She was hotter than sin, and at the same time she was as cold as ice.

She was Kelsey Draper, and he hadn't spoken to her since the summer before his senior year, and as far as he was concerned, that was a damn good thing.

Her eyes widened as she looked at him, and her lips twitched in a tremulous smile. "Oh," was all she said.

And in that moment, Wyatt knew that he was well and truly screwed.

2

Oh.

The word seems to hang above us inside a cartoon bubble, and I mentally cringe. Ten years at an exclusive girls' school, an undergraduate degree in early education, minors in both dance and English, and the best I can come up with is *Oh?*

And, yes, I know I should cut myself a little slack. After all, I was caught off guard. Not by the stunning and sensual art displayed in front of me, but by the man who created it. A man who's the reason my palms are sweaty, my nipples tight, and my pulse beating a staccato rhythm in my neck.

A man I once knew as Wyatt Segel.

A man I was completely unprepared to see.

Which means that Nia has some serious explaining to do. *"Just some photographer looking for models. My agent says the pay is awesome, and considering how much cash you need by the end of the month, it's worth a shot. He goes by W. Royce, but I've never heard of the guy. Then again, who cares so long as he pays?"*

Never heard of the guy? Oh, please. Nia's a model; Wyatt's a photographer. She must have known he'd taken a stage name. And then she went and set me up.

Honestly, I just might have to kill her.

First, though, I have to get this job. My brother Griffin's a fourth-degree burn survivor, and I have less than a month to come up with fifteen thousand dollars in order to enroll him in trials for an innovative new clinical protocol. Not an easy task on my kindergarten teacher salary, and even the additional dance classes I've added to my summer teaching schedule don't come close to taking up the monetary slack.

Which is why when my best friend Nia told me about the audition, it seemed worth the shot. Granted, I took some convincing. And I wasn't entirely comfortable with the idea of putting myself on display. But I psyched myself up. Desperate times, and all that.

"My agent booked me for a lingerie shoot," she'd told me over drinks on the balcony of her beachfront condo yesterday. "A last minute gig. I guess the photographer's pushing up against his deadline. Anyway, I think you should go in my place. His name's W. Royce, and I can text you the address and time."

My stomach lurched at the thought. "Are you crazy? I can't do that!"

Nia sighed dramatically. "Why? Because it would be *wrong*?" She put finger quotes around the last word.

"Actually, yes," I said adamantly. Nia constantly teases me about what she calls my elevated sense of scruples. She's convinced that I'm too staid and regimented. That I need to deviate from my safe little routine and cut loose sometimes. But she's one hundred percent wrong about that.

I know better than anyone the price you pay when you break the rules.

"He'll be expecting a drop-dead gorgeous woman who oozes sensuality," I said pragmatically. "And that's really not me."

"Oh, honey, please. We both know you're gorgeous. And where else are you going to get that kind of money so quickly? Especially since you're too stubborn to borrow from me."

"You're assuming I'll get the job." Unlike Nia, who's been modeling since she was seven, I have absolutely zero experience.

"Did I mention you're gorgeous? Just because you never flaunt it, doesn't mean it's not true."

I crossed my arms to hide an involuntary shudder. She's wrong, of course. Not about me being pretty—I am. And that's a cross I've had to bear my entire life.

No, she was wrong about the rest of it. Because I did flaunt it. Maybe not much—and only once—but that was enough, and I opened a Pandora's Box of badness that I'm still trying to close.

I licked my lips, my thoughts turning to my brother. That photographer might be pushing a deadline, but so was I. And if there was even the tiniest chance that this job could get me the cash I needed, then didn't I at least owe it to Griffin to try? Maybe under normal circumstances, lingerie modeling would be too racy for my sensibilities. But these weren't ordinary circumstances.

"I can't do sexy photos. I wouldn't have a clue how to pose," I said, but my protest lacked oomph, and I saw from the way Nia's eyes lit up that she knew I'd taken the bait, and all she had to do was reel me in.

"It's just commercial lingerie photos," she shrugged as if to say that was no big deal. "Just pretend you're at the beach in a bikini."

I considered that, then nodded. It's not like I've never displayed a little skin. And I do own a bikini. I even wear it on the beach. In public. Sometimes.

And after everything that happened back then, wasn't there some sort of karmic justice in me stripping down to my underwear for a good cause? I didn't know, but it sounded like a solid justification to me.

"Besides," Nia continued, "a professional photographer's going to have an excellent bedside manner."

"Nia!"

"Oh, for fuck's sake, Kels. It's a figure of speech."

"Language."

"Fuckety, fuck, fuck, fuck," she retorted. And I couldn't help myself—I burst out laughing. "Love me, love my potty mouth," she said.

"I do love you," I admitted. "*Despite* the potty mouth."

"That's because I'm so damn, fucking lovable." She flashed a wicked grin before taking another sip of wine while I tried hard not to laugh again. Best not to egg her on.

"Seriously, Kels, it'll be easy. It's a lot like dancing. Form and position and movement. In a lot of ways modeling is like choreography. And I've seen the outfits you rehearse in. Not a lot left to the imagination, right?"

"That's different." When I dance, I dress for comfort and ease of movement. More to the point, I let myself become someone else, someone in tune with the euphoria of the music. Someone willing to let go of control, because the thread of the music is always there to pull me back and keep me safe.

"Quit arguing and just go for it. Trust me, this job will be good for you. You can get your naughty on in a baby step kind of way, and all the while you can tell yourself you're only doing it because of Griffin. It's perfect."

"First of all, I *am* only doing it for Griffin. I'm not looking for excuses to wear a tiny bikini or flash my breasts. I like me. I like my life. I'm happy. I'm comfortable with who I am."

"Methinks the lady doth protest too much."

"Oh, give me a break," I snapped, feeling unreasonably defensive. "I don't need to hop in bed with a guy on the first date or—"

"First date? Try fifth. Or never. And for that matter, when was the last time you even went on a date?"

"That's not the point," I said, because it really wasn't. "There just aren't many guys out there that interest me. And why should I go to dinner or drinks with a total dud, much less sleep with him? And you're getting off the subject," I added.

She held up her hands. "You're the one who started talking about dating. My point was only that you should take the job because you need the money—but that you should try to have a good time, too."

I took a long swallow and finished off my wine. "All I care about is getting enough money to enroll Griffin in the protocol."

"Sure. Right. You justify it however you want. The point is, this is a rock solid deal. At the very least, you owe it to yourself—and Griffin—to go to the audition."

I think about that conversation now, as I stand in Wyatt's studio in the shadow of these sensual, shocking photos. Photos that terrify me, taken by a man who excites me.

I think about it, and I want to run.

But I can't. Because Nia was right. I have to do this. I have to land this job.

All of which means that I have to ace this audition, Wyatt or no Wyatt. And that will probably go a lot better if I can actually conjure words. Which, considering how many times I've imagined bumping into him, is turning out to be surprisingly difficult.

In my head, I'm always clever and amusing during our imaginary encounters in bookstores and restaurants. And when we're assigned as seatmates on the long journey from Los Angeles to Australia, I'm not the least bit tongue-tied.

Not that I've ever actually flown to Australia, but I've spent the better part of my life playing out a variety of fantasies in my head. And what's the point of fantasy if you can't fix past mistakes? If you can't be someone a little different than who you are? Especially if there's no way in hell you'd take the leap in real life?

Over the last twelve years, I've spun infinite variations on my Wyatt fantasy. Sometimes we barely speak two words. Sometimes, I'll let him buy me a drink. Once or twice, I let it go a little bit further. But even in my fantasies, I can't bring myself to give us a happily ever after.

Because between Wyatt and me, the story is a tragedy, not a romance. Considering everything that happened, how could it be anything else?

Now, Wyatt is nothing more than a pushpin in the map of my life. A reminder of how horrible things can get, and why bad choices are, as advertised, *bad*.

He's not a man, he's a concept. A talisman. Fantasy mixed with memory and topped with a sprinkle of loss.

Unfortunate, maybe, but at least *that's* a Wyatt I can handle.

But this Wyatt? The one standing in front of me with golden-brown hair and whiskey-colored eyes that can see all the way into our past. The one whose lean body I can still imagine pressed against me, and whose strong arms once made me feel safe. The one with the impudent grin that used to make my heart flutter, but who now isn't smiling at all.

The boy who once made my breath catch in my throat whenever I caught a glimpse of him. Who's now a man who walks with confidence and grace and commands a room simply by standing in it.

The boy who made me break all the rules. Who made me lose control.

The man who nearly destroyed me.

That man isn't manageable at all. On the contrary, that man terrifies me. And right now, I can't help but think that coming on this audition was a mistake of monumental proportions.

Yup. Definitely going to have to kill Nia. A pity, really. Because when am I going to find the time to go shopping for a new best friend?

More important, how else am I going to earn fifteen grand by the end of the month?

As I stand there like a dolt, he crosses his arms over his chest and tilts his head just slightly. That's when I realize that he's been watching me all this time. Not saying a word. Just waiting. As if this is all on me.

I guess maybe it is.

I swallow, forcing myself not to dry my sweaty palms on my gray pencil skirt as I smile tentatively. I watch his face, hoping for an answering grin. For some hint that he's thought of me over the last twelve years. A sign that he remembers the things we said, the way we laughed. The way we touched.

I wait for even the tiniest inkling that I have lingered in his mind the way that he's lingered in mine. Because he has. Even when everything was screwed up and horrible. Even after I ruined everything. Even when I knew I shouldn't, I still thought of him.

And now, like a damn beggar, I'm searching his face for some sign that he's thought of me, too.

But there's nothing to see.

Right. Fine. Okay.

I let my gaze shift to the walls, but that's a mistake because I'm immediately drawn to the three uncovered photographs hanging behind him. They're raw and titillating, disturbing and honest. I can feel them resonate inside me, firing my blood and causing a flurry of pleasant-yet-terrifying sparks to zing around inside me.

I quickly turn my attention back to Wyatt and clear my throat. "So," I say, trying to speak normally. "Usually I'm auditioning to dance, not model. What do you want me to do?"

A heat so quick it could be my imagination flashes as his eyes narrow more, and I see a subtle tightening in his jaw. "Kelsey," he finally says, and the sound of my name on his lips sends a wave of relief coursing through me. At the very least, I know he remembers me.

"Yeah." I smile brightly, then remember that this is supposed to be an audition. I've been clutching a headshot with my email address and cell number on it, and I scurry forward and thrust it at him. "It's me."

He doesn't even look at it.

"It's been a long time." His voice is flat. Even.

"It has," I agree, my voice so sing-song I feel like an idiot. But he doesn't seem to hear me. Instead, he's looking me up and down, the slow inspection as sensual as a hand moving leisurely up my body. I draw in a breath and feel it flutter in my throat. My skin tingles with awareness, and I can feel small beads of sweat rise at the base of my neck, thankfully hidden under my shoulder-length chestnut waves.

I force myself not to shift my weight from foot to foot. It's hard, because right now I feel as exposed as the models in the photographs gracing the walls behind him. And when Wyatt's eyes finally meet mine, and his inspection ceases, I'm positive that my cheeks have bloomed a bright, revealing red.

I draw another breath in anticipation of his words. I expect him to say something about our past. At the very least, to say that it's good to see me after so much time.

I couldn't be more wrong.

"What the hell are you doing here?" he demands, and it's as if he's tossed a bucket of cold water all over me.

I sputter. I actually sputter as a chill runs through me, and I struggle to recover my thoughts, my power of speech, my pride. "I—I just . . . well, the job."

I stand straighter, fighting a fresh wave of vulnerability. Because Wyatt is dangerous to me, and I really need to keep that little fact at the forefront of my mind. "I'm here about the job," I repeat, and this time my voice is crisp and clear.

He pulls out his phone, taps the screen, then looks back at me with a frown. "Nia Hancock. Twenty-seven. Mixed race female. Her agent called yesterday and said he was sending her over."

I lick my lips. "She, um, couldn't come. And since I could use the job, I came in her place."

"You came?" he repeats, and I watch as a series of expressions crosses his face, starting with surprise, then moving into confusion, and settling on something that looks remarkably like anger. "You?" His voice takes on a bland tone that is more than a little disconcerting.

I open my mouth to answer, but he continues before I can get a word in edgewise.

"You expect me to believe that Kelsey Draper wants to be a model. One of these models?" he adds, waving a hand behind him to indicate the three uncovered paintings, larger than life in so many ways.

I lick my lips, then immediately regret the unconscious action. Because I'm not sure. I'm really not sure at all.

Then I remember Griffin. And the money. And the fact that I'm desperate.

And, yes, I think about those scary-but-tantalizing sparks that are zinging around in my bloodstream. I shouldn't want it. In fact, I should hightail it right out that door before everything crashes down on me again.

But I don't. Instead, I glance down at the floor and murmur, "Yes. That's exactly what I want."

He's silent, so I lift my chin, hoping he can see my resolve, but there's nothing warm or welcoming in his expression. On the contrary, what I see on his face is anger. And when he scoffs and says, "What the hell kind of game are you playing this time?" I know that I've made a terrible, horrible, awful mistake.

"I'm not playing a game," I protest, but my voice comes out shaky instead of strong. "It's just that I need—"

"What?" he demands. "What could you possibly need from me?"

The harshness in his voice slices through me, and I cringe. I want to explain myself, but when I feel the tears well in my eyes, I know that there's no way I can hold myself together. "I'm sorry," I whisper as I turn to flee. "I should never have come here at all."

3

I slam through the door to the alley just as my tears start to flow in earnest. And as the steel door clangs shut, I lean against the brick wall and force myself to simply breathe while my blood pounds in my veins, and images of those photographs—and the man who took them—fill my head.

Honestly, this is my own fault. What was I thinking? I should have turned around the moment I realized the audition was for Wyatt. I should have run far and fast and not even thought twice.

Instead, I lingered, craving recognition from a man who clearly wants nothing to do with me.

Which should be just fine with me. After all, if anyone can throw my carefully constructed life out of whack, it's Wyatt. He's temptation personified, and when I'm around him, my self-control vanishes.

And nothing good ever comes from that.

Nothing that lasts, anyway. He made me feel good, that's for sure. So much so that the memory of his touch still fuels my fantasies, as potent now as it was more than a decade ago.

But those touches were forbidden, our moments together

stolen. I knew I was breaking the rules, but I didn't care. What good was the threat of punishment against the reality of his kisses? His soft caresses?

He eviscerated my control. Made me forget my objections. Turned my willpower to mush. And though I want to blame him, I know that in reality, it was all on me.

I wanted to be bad—more specifically, I wanted to be bad with Wyatt.

Even then, I knew I'd have to pay. Of course, I would. There's always a price when you break the rules. Hadn't I been raised on that mantra? Hadn't it been drilled deep into my soul?

But until Wyatt, I never really tested it.

Maybe I didn't believe it.

Maybe I thought I could outwit fate.

But Karma is a nosy, invasive bookie, and when you try to cheat her, she takes what she's owed.

I've been scrambling for years to pay that debt. And fifteen thousand will go a long way to repairing the biggest mistake of my life.

Or it could have. But I bolted, and in the process I destroyed my only chance to get that much money in so short a time.

My stomach churns and bile rises in my throat as that simple reality settles over me. *I bolted.*

I didn't just walk away from the chance to earn that money, I sprinted.

Am I really so lame? So fragile that I'll shatter under the chill in his voice or the ice in his eyes?

After all, what did I expect? That we'd both look at each other with wide-eyed surprise and then leap across a daisy-strewn studio into each other's arms while orchestral music played in the background?

That our past would be magically erased, and bluebirds of happiness would ring our heads while tweeting a chipper melody?

Not hardly.

I should have stayed. I should have looked him in the eye, told him I'd come about the job, and steadfastly repeated that the past didn't matter. Over and over and over for as long as it took for him to ignore everything that happened before and simply hire me.

Because I hadn't come to Santa Monica to see Wyatt Segel or W. Royce or whatever name he wanted to go by. I hadn't come because I have some deep hidden desire to strip my clothes off in front of a camera. And I most certainly hadn't come for the fizzle and pop that fills me every time Wyatt is near.

I came solely for the money. For Griffin.

And there is no way I'm letting Wyatt's Arctic glare send me scurrying away.

I need this job, and he needs a model. So I'm doing this. I can, and I will.

With my pep talk still ringing in my ears, I turn and pull open the heavy steel door. It creaks, and as I step over the threshold, Wyatt turns once again to face me.

He's standing like a sentry in front of a wall decorated with dozens and dozens of white-draped photographs. I know what's hidden behind the drapes—images of women just like me, their bare bodies posed provocatively. And for one tiny moment, I breathe easier. Soon, those women will be on display for anyone in the world to see, but until then, Wyatt's covered them. He's protecting them. Guarding their honor.

And surely a man who does that will protect me, too.

I clear my throat and flash a tentative smile. "I shouldn't have run."

Immediately, the guarded expression in his eyes fades, replaced by something that looks almost like hope.

Encouraged, I rush on. "It's just that I really need this job, and you made it so clear you didn't want to see me, and—"

"I see." He'd been walking toward me, but now he stops, his

hands sliding into his pockets. His posture stiffens. He's no longer hopeful; if anything, he's hostile.

A wave of embarrassment crashes over me, and I want to kick myself for being such a fool. My apology was for running away twelve minutes ago. But Wyatt obviously thought I was apologizing for what happened twelve *years* ago.

I expect him to order me out. To tell me firmly and plainly that I have no business being there.

But he says none of that. All he does is look at me so deeply I'm certain he can see all the way to my soul.

I shift under his inspection, feeling raw and naked and exposed. I want to explain. To tell him how confused I was. How much he meant to me. How badly I screwed up. How many people I hurt.

But I can't. The words just don't come. Instead, I can only manage a breathy little gasp before I force out his name, "Wyatt, I—"

"I'm not hiring you, Kelsey. Did you really expect that I would?"

"I—I didn't know it was you," I admit.

"And now you do." He starts to pivot, dismissing me.

"Dammit, Wyatt!"

He stops. His eyes are wide, and I think he's as surprised as I am that a curse escaped my lips. The teenager inside me actually cringes, but my father isn't here. It's only Wyatt, and my outburst has at least snagged his attention.

"You need a model," I say. "I need the work."

"This isn't the job for you, Kelsey. We both know that."

I lift my chin. "You don't know me at all."

"No, I don't. I thought I did," he adds, his harsh words making me cringe. "But I know enough to know this isn't you." He indicates the three photographs without drapes. "Or this," he adds, yanking more drapes to the ground to reveal two riveting photos of women who are entirely nude, yet staring out at the camera without an ounce of shame, as if they owned the world and everything in it.

"And certainly not her," he continues, uncovering another, this one in virginal white bridal lingerie, her wrists and ankles bound with red ribbons, her face alight with ecstasy. "Or am I wrong? Is that really what you want, Kelsey? Or are you just here for another piece of me?"

Another piece of me? I have no idea what he means by that, but I don't ask him. I can't. I'm too distracted by the way my heart is beating wildly, and not just in reaction to the waves of restrained anger pulsing off this man, but because of the images he's revealed. Bold women. Brash women.

Fearless women who ask for—and get—what they want. But that isn't me. It never has been. How can it be when I know only too well the price I'd have to pay?

"Well?" Wyatt demands, and when I remain silent, he makes a scoffing noise. "Like I said, that's not who you are."

I bristle. "Did you really just say that? Are you actually telling me that I ought to be ashamed for wanting to pose for you? That those women should be ashamed of their bodies? Their emotions?"

"Ashamed?" He sounds genuinely surprised. "Hell no."

"Then what?"

With a soft chuckle, he saunters toward me. He stops only inches away, his proximity making my head spin.

When he reaches out, I start to take a step back, but force myself to stay perfectly still. This is a test, I'm certain of it. And it's one I'm determined to pass.

Even so, I can't stifle the soft exhale of breath when he gently brushes my hair off my face, his fingertip grazing my ear in the process. I feel that touch all the way in my core, and I have to forcibly press my lips together in order not to whimper.

Slowly, he traces his fingertip down the line of my jaw, then down my neck, lower and lower until I'm not breathing, and it's taking all of my strength to stand perfectly still and not run.

"What I'm saying," he says as his fingertip rises with the curve of my breast, "is that I don't think you can handle it."

"I can," I say, though my voice comes out shaky and not firm at all.

"Is that so? The kindergarten teacher has a wild side? The dancer's abandoning beginning ballet and tap for more exotic pursuits?"

"How do you know what I've been—?"

But he continues speaking as if I hadn't said a word. "You're willing to do this?" he asks, putting his hands on my shoulders as he steps behind me, so that we are both facing the wall of exposed photos.

"You're actually going to reveal yourself to the camera? To me?" His hands graze down my arms as he speaks, making it difficult for me to concentrate on his words, which are drowned out by the pounding of my blood.

"And it's not just your body on display, but what's inside you. Are you willing to show that fire? That heat? To expose yourself like that, open and vulnerable, to whoever stands in front of those photos? And to me, too, Kelsey. Can you handle knowing I'll see you raw and vulnerable? And not just *see* you. Do you understand that I'm the one who's going to take you there?"

The thought terrifies me—and yet I can't deny that the terror is tinged with something else. Something scary and exciting all at the same time. "I can do it." I force the words out past dry lips. "I'm not the same girl I was when you knew me."

"Aren't you?" His hands move to my hips, his fingertips resting on the edge of my pubic bone. My skin beneath his fingers warms, but it is the heat that pools between my thighs that has put me at a distinct disadvantage, and though I try to focus, I know with absolute certainty that if this showdown is going to be decided by cool minds and clear heads, I am going to lose.

It's not a pleasant thought, and I force myself to think about Griffin. About the past. About the money I need to earn. Even my grocery list. Anything I can think of to block out the way that Wyatt's touch is making me feel. Because what I'm thinking is that there could still be something between us.

What I'm thinking is that maybe I want there to be.

And those are thoughts that I really shouldn't be having.

"My models have to be exceptional. To not just display passion, but to feel it. And this final woman that I'm casting has to be honest with her emotions. With her desire. She's the centerpiece. The strongest and the most vulnerable."

"I can handle whatever I need to," I say, hoping I sound more confident than I feel.

"So you say, but I'm not convinced."

He's still behind me, and I whip around to face him, surprised and angered by his casual indictment.

"Is this how you auditioned those women?" I demand. "Did you touch them? Did you stroke their skin and whisper to them? Because I'm thinking no."

"You'd be right," he says, surprising me.

"So you're punishing me."

His gaze never wavers as he says, "Maybe I am."

My chest tightens, and I immediately regret poking the beast. I'd never expected him to admit it, and now I'm staring straight into a past that I don't want to think about, much less discuss.

I draw a deep breath. "Then you're being an idiot. I need a job. You need a model. You're only hurting your show by turning me away."

His left eyebrow arches up, a trick I used to find bone-meltingly sexy. Now, all I feel is panic. And not just because I need this job and fear that he's going to send me away. No, the real source of my panic is something much deeper. Much more unexpected. And much, much scarier.

It's Wyatt. It's the girls on the wall. And it's this whirlwind of emotion swirling inside me that I don't understand and refuse to examine.

I square my shoulders, forcing myself to keep my eyes on the prize. The job. The paycheck. "Fine. Punish me all you want. Just give me a chance. I can do this."

He drags his fingers through his hair, and he no longer looks angry. Instead he looks wounded. Defeated. And I know that's all on me. Because he put his heart on the line once for me, and I know I ripped it to shreds.

"I can do this," I say again, as if repetition will persuade him. "I just need—"

"Can you? Sweet Kelsey Draper? You practically sank into the floor when you let out a curse a few minutes ago. I don't believe there's any way you can put yourself out there the way I need."

"I can. You just have to believe me."

"I don't."

"Then let me prove it to you."

"How?"

That is a really good question, and one I don't have an answer to. Then I remember a bachelorette party I got dragged to last year. "Do you know X-tasy?"

"The strip club in Van Nuys?" Something like amusement sparks on his face. "It's crossed my radar."

"Tonight. 9 o'clock."

"Why—"

"Just be there. And bring a pen. Because you're going to want me to sign your contract right then."

"Don't hold your breath," he says as he takes a single step toward me, and a pleasant but unwelcome warmth floods my body.

I take a step back in a vain effort to keep my wits about me, but he matches my movement. "I'm under the gun here, Kelsey," he says, leaning in even closer. "I need someone I can depend on."

I force my expression to remain bland. He's right in front of me, and if I take another step back, he'll have me caged in against the wall.

"I'm dependable," I say, but instead of sounding firm and determined, I sound breathy and overwhelmed.

"History would suggest otherwise."

His harsh word lands on me like a punch in the gut, and I fight the urge to cringe. Or, worse, to escape through that door again.

Except I did that already, didn't I? I left. I ran. And I never looked back.

"It's been twelve years," I snap, not sure if I'm more angry with him or with me. "I don't owe you an explanation."

"Fair enough," he replies coolly. "I don't owe you a job."

"No, you don't. But you need a model. And I can do the job. You're an idiot if you don't let me prove that to you."

"I've been called worse."

I draw a calming breath. "Please," I beg. "Tonight. Nine. I won't let you down."

He cocks his head, silently studying me. "You already did that, Kelsey. A long time ago."

4

Twelve years ago

"That's him," Grace whispered. "The tall guy in the dark green swim trunks. Isn't he the finest thing you ever saw?"

"Oh my God! He's so hot. Did you really talk to him?"

"He let me cut in line when I went inside to get a Diet Coke," Grace said, her tone suggesting she'd just been anointed by the Pope.

"No way!" Marsha squealed.

"Way!"

Two tables over, Kelsey Draper kept her head down, hoping that Grace Farmer and Marsha Greene wouldn't look over and notice that she was eavesdropping when she was supposed to be wiping down the poolside tables.

Normally, she ignored the members' kids. After all, she was staff, and in the world of the Pacific View Country Club, staff and members simply didn't mix. But Grace was talking about the new guy—the one Kelsey had noticed when she'd worked the coffee bar that morning. For that matter, *everybody* was talking about the new guy and his family, but Kelsey hadn't managed to learn any of the details yet.

There was something about him, though. She'd met his eyes when she was filling a Thermos for one of the golfers, and he was standing against the window, probably waiting for his father. The moment lasted barely a second, but she'd felt a *zing* shoot all the way through her.

It had filled her up, and the sensation had lasted for hours. Warm and comforting, like a freshly baked loaf of bread. But also biting and exotic, like the Indian food her stepmother adored, the kind that tasted so good, but had such a kick.

All in all, he'd ignited a storm of sensations inside her. Nice, yes, but unsettling, too.

And definitely not the kind of thing that she was used to experiencing. Not by a long shot.

So she wanted to know. And since Grace and Marsha made it their business to know everything about everybody, Kelsey couldn't simply walk away. Not and miss the chance to learn whatever she could about whoever he was.

She lifted her head just long enough to take another look at him. He'd recently emerged from the deep end of the pool, and he was standing in line for the high diving board, his tan body glistening in the Santa Barbara sun. As she watched, he reached up and ran his fingers through hair that looked dark now, but that she knew would glisten golden-brown in the sun once it dried.

She guessed he was a year or so older than her—sixteen, maybe seventeen—and she'd never in her life experienced the kind of jolt she'd felt after that one shared look with him.

For just a moment, she closed her eyes and let the memory sweep over her once more, sweet and tantalizing and scary and awesome. She wanted to savor it, because she knew with one hundred percent certainty that as far as she and this boy went, one look across the coffee bar was all they would ever share.

"Draper!" Her manager's voice cut through her reverie and she jumped, embarrassed to realize she'd stopped cleaning and was simply leaning on the table, lost in thought. "What? Is it nap time?"

"Sorry! Sorry!" She spritzed the table again and started scrubbing enthusiastically, as if working on a particularly tough stain. And with her eyes focused on the tabletop, she tuned back in to the girls' conversation.

"You really don't know who he is?" Grace was saying.

"Oh, come off it, already. Just tell me."

"He's Wyatt Segel. Can you believe it?"

Kelsey glanced up in time to see Marsha shake her head, her mouth curving down into a frown. "Who's that?"

"Oh, my God! Do you live under a rock? He's like totally famous. Or, at least, his family is."

Marsha's nose wrinkled. "Well, he's cute and all, but I've never seen him in anything."

"Not him, his grandmother. Well, his mom, too. She writes screenplays or something. But it's his grandmother who's really huge. She's freaking Anika Segel."

"Um?"

"You really do live on another planet. You honestly don't know who that is?"

Kelsey didn't get to hear Marsha's answer because a couple sitting on the far side of the dining area called her over to wipe up some spilled wine. Not that she needed to hear. She knew all about Anika Segel, her stepmother's favorite star, and one of Hollywood's greatest actresses from the Golden Age. Kelsey had seen her dozens of times on the television, but she'd never thought about the woman as a real person. Someone who had a home and a family and maybe a dog.

She was still thinking about families as she carried the wine-soaked rag over to the bus trays. Kelsey had never known either of her grandmothers, and her own mother had passed away when she was two. She wondered what it was like for Wyatt having a famous grandparent. Hard, she supposed. Even on his first day at a new place he couldn't be anonymous. But easier, too, because at least people would talk to him, and they already found him interesting.

No one ever found Kelsey interesting. Why would they? She was a teenage girl who woke up, went to work with her dad, then went home. Three nights a week she went to dance class, but she was the only one in the class who was serious about studying dance. The other girls were just there to check themselves out in the mirror.

Kelsey couldn't understand how they could be so cavalier. She'd had to fight to go to class. To convince her father that the leotards and tights served a purpose. Even then, she'd had to promise to wear a skirt over her outfit when she practiced, since that was the only way he'd let her go. "A woman shouldn't show off her form like that," he'd insisted. "Mischief can happen."

"It's just me in a room with a bunch of girls."

"It's making a habit."

"A habit of dancing, Daddy. There's nothing wrong with dancing."

"You see there, sugar? You say I treat you like a little girl, but when you say those kinds of things it just proves that you're still too young. There are all kinds of things wrong with dancing, and you'll learn about them soon enough."

"Then why do you let me go at all?" She'd immediately regretted the question, terrified that he'd rip her beloved lessons out from under her.

"How else will you learn what's the good, and what's the bad? You have to know. You have to be clear. You can't grow up to be like your mother. A woman like that . . . well, people get hurt. But I love you, baby girl. I love you so damn much, and I'm watching out for you. So don't you worry, sugar. Daddy will always be here to help you."

A fat tear rolled down her cheek, surprising Kelsey out of the memory. Her whole life, she'd wished she knew her real mother, but Kelsey had been two when Annie Draper died, and in a lot of ways she seemed like a mythical person. Someone faraway and imaginary.

Leonard Draper had married Tessa only two years later, bringing a baby boy into the family with her. As far as Kelsey was concerned, Tessa was her mom and Griffin was her brother. After all, she'd only been four when Tessa and Leonard had put Griffin into her arms and told her that she was now a big sister, with all the responsibility that came with it.

Griffin!

She glanced up at the clock, saw that she was late, then bit her lip to prevent the curse that wanted to fly from her mouth. Her father would have a fit if she cursed, and even though she was almost sixteen, there were some offenses that he'd probably still spank her for.

"I'm off the clock," she yelled as she ripped off her apron and handed it to a startled bus boy. "See you tomorrow!"

Her dad was working as a temporary landscaper at the club this summer, which meant she'd been able to land a job in food services. Tessa didn't work—her dad said a man should provide for his woman—but even though she was home, Leonard didn't want Griffin staying in the house all summer. "He's twelve now. Can't be some sissy-boy who spends all his time with Mommy. Not my son."

Which was why Griffin was enrolled in the club's tennis camp, even though they really couldn't afford it. And since Kelsey's shift ended twenty minutes before Griffin's camp did, she'd been charged with collecting him and getting the two of them home safe.

Work for her. Camp for him. She knew she ought to be annoyed by that, but at least she got out of the house. And at least the money she earned was hers, not that she ever spent it. She was saving it to go to a New York dance academy when she graduated. She was going to be on stage. She was going to be remarkable. And in the end her dad would see that she was creating beauty, and there was nothing wrong with that.

So how could she resent Griffin's tennis class when she was working toward her future? Besides, she adored Griff, even when he was being an annoying little brother. And seeing his excited face every day was one of the things she most looked forward to.

Now, she sprinted through the gate that surrounded the pool area, then ran the length of the recreation building. She was just rounding the corner so she could head up the path to the tennis courts when she slammed into something hard, stumbled back, then collapsed in a pile of limbs and embarrassment on the concrete sidewalk.

"Oh, man! I'm so sorry." The low, melodic voice came from somewhere above her, soothing her without touching her. "Are you okay?"

She glanced up, at first seeing only the hand stretched out in front of her. She took it, and the shock of connection would have knocked her over if she hadn't already been on the ground.

Him.

She knew it even before she tilted her head the rest of the way up. Even before she saw the light in his eyes, the hesitant smile on his lips.

He gave her a little tug, and she rose to her feet, then gasped as he placed his free hand on her waist to steady her.

"You work at the cafe?"

"I—I'm sorry, what?"

His eyes narrowed. "You sure you're okay?"

I don't think I'll ever be okay again.

"Sure. Yes. I mean, my ego's more bruised than my rear." She stepped back, out from under his touch. She regretted the loss of contact, but had to cheer the return of rational thought. "I wasn't watching where I was going. I was in a hurry."

"So I noticed. You must have somewhere to be."

"I do. I have to fetch my brother."

He nodded. "Too bad."

"Too bad?"

A dimple flashed with his quick smile. "That means you don't have time to grab some French fries with me."

"Oh. I—" She swallowed her words as panic started to rise. She didn't know how to talk to him. She didn't know how to talk to boys at all, especially boys who made her feel like this, the way she shouldn't feel. The way she knew her father would say was dangerous for a girl.

"I'm sorry," she finally mumbled to her shoes. "I'm late. I really have to go."

And then she took off, making it a point not to look back. Not to think about him.

But that smile—and that dimple—lingered in her mind.

5

The sharp blare of a horn startles me from my reverie, and I jerk the steering wheel to one side, barely missing the BMW that had been approaching on my right as I tried to change lanes.

I clutch the wheel tighter, my heart pounding in my chest as I carefully maneuver my 1969 Mustang convertible across two lanes and into the parking lot of a Ralph's grocery store. I pull into a spot, kill the engine, and drop my face into my palms.

What the devil is wrong with me? I'm a careful driver, I always have been. I don't text, talk on the phone, or get lost in thought while I'm driving. I went to the classes. I saw the Driver's Ed videos. I know what can happen if you're not careful behind the wheel. And I'm most definitely not one of those people who believe that the bad stuff will never happen to them.

I know better, after all. I've pissed fate off once already; I'm not inclined to do it again.

Not to mention the fact that Griffin rebuilt this car himself and gave it to me for my twenty-fifth birthday. With its sky blue paint, shiny chrome trim and white leather interior, it's about the prettiest car I've ever seen. So there's no way I'd risk scratching her, much less wreck her. I named her Blue, and I totally baby her. Regular maintenance. Monthly detailing. And absolutely no reckless driving.

Griffin's always telling me I'm not letting Blue live up to her full potential, although he usually says that after a couple of drinks and with his narrowed eyes laser-focused on me. I ignore him, though. Both the blatant statement about the car and the more subtle indictment of my life.

So despite Griffin's repeated protests that the engine is a dream and I should take Blue out to the desert, put a scarf over my hair, and open her up, I think Blue and I are doing just fine.

Or at least we were until I almost drove her into the side of a silver Beemer. But that wasn't my fault. Not really.

That little near miss is all on *him*.

Wyatt.

Once again, he's filled my head. Once again, he's made me lose control.

He's dangerous. To me, to my heart, and to everyone around me.

With a sigh, I let my head fall back against the leather. I've turned the AC off, and the sun beats down on me, making my mind drift back to the summer before I turned sixteen.

I'd been happy—so ecstatically happy. At least until the moment I wasn't.

And now here I am, putting all my hopes in the hands of a man I know only too well I should run from.

But I can't.

And the secret, horrible, deep-down truth is that I'm not even sure I want to.

"Kelsey," I say to the sky. "You're a mess."

I frown. To be more specific, I'm a mess who's about to take her clothes off in front of who-knows-how-many gawking men.

Clearly, I'm a crazy person.

Determined. But crazy.

I sit up straight and grab my phone to call Nia. Not only do

I need to chew her out for not telling me that W. Royce is Wyatt Segel, but I also need her wardrobe advice. Because despite umpty-billion dance recitals over the course of my life, I don't have a clue which of my costumes I should wear with an eye to removing it.

Unfortunately, I only get her voicemail, and after leaving a message, I slide my phone back into my purse.

Am I really going through with this?

The question echoes loudly through my head, and the answer comes just as swiftly on its heels. I am.

And Wyatt better show up. Because if he's not in that audience, I'm out of luck.

With a grimace, I reach for the keys still hanging in the ignition. Time to get home, plan my dance, pick a costume, and hyperventilate.

If my dad could see me now . . .

The thought shoots through my mind, an unwelcome irritant that's been in my head ever since I blurted out my plan to Wyatt. Like a pebble in a tennis shoe. Always there, but sometimes more painful than others.

But Daddy can't see me. Daddy's in Georgia doing landscaping work for the same commercial development company that's employed him for over a decade now. So he has no way of knowing what I'm doing, much less that I'm stripping. And if he ever does find out . . .

Well, by that time, I'll already have the money and Griff will be enrolled in the protocol and I'll weather the storm of his disapproval.

Not that lying sits well with me—that's another one of those things I never do, because I can still feel the sting of Daddy's belt all too well. But in this case I'm not lying. I'm just not telling.

I roll my eyes, annoyed with myself. My dad's not even in the state, and I'm making up excuses. Not that I'm surprised. I'm nervous about tonight, and my mind is jumping to all sorts of places. Anything at all to keep from settling on my sexy dance—or the man I'll be performing it for.

I'm about to back out of the space and head home when my phone rings. I shift into park and reach for my purse, certain it's Nia.

It's not, though. It's a number I don't recognize, and since I recently applied for teaching jobs at three different dance studios in the Valley, I answer the call with a chipper, "Kelsey Draper."

"I don't know if this is a good idea," Wyatt says, as if we're already in the middle of a conversation.

"It's probably not," I admit. "But I need the money, and it's the best idea I have."

"Hmm," he says, though it's more of a sigh and seems a little sad.

I try to stay quiet, expecting him to continue, but I can't keep my mouth shut. "You're coming tonight, right? You're going to give me a chance?"

"Why did you run? Back in Santa Barbara. Why did you run away?"

The question is so unexpected, it pushes me back against my seat. I sit stunned for a moment, then answer quietly, "Does it matter? I already apologized."

He laughs, a harsh sound in his throat. "Even now, you can't own up to it. Or are you still playing the same damn game."

"What game?" I ask, recalling his quixotic statement from earlier. "What are you talking about?"

"Let's not go there, Kelsey. If we're going to do this, let's at least try to be honest."

"Do this?" I retort, my temper flaring. "Does that mean you're hiring me? Because if it doesn't, I'm not sure what *this* is."

He doesn't answer, and this time it's me who makes the hard scoffing noise.

"You know what?" I demand, the ferocity in my voice fueled

by irritation. "You're being an unfair son-of-a— well, you're a jerk." I rush on before he can squeeze in an argument. "Maybe I screwed up back then, but you weren't exactly innocent. You screwed up, too."

He's completely silent. No sounds of disbelief. No laughter. No breathing.

I pull the phone from my ear and check the display, wondering for a moment if he's hung up on me. But the connection is clear, and there are four bars of service.

"Hello?" I press.

His answer is a single word that seems fragile against the weight of this conversation. "How?"

I shouldn't say anything. I know that. But now that I've seen him again, it's all so fresh. So painful.

But against my better judgment, I whisper, "When I left. You didn't even try to come after me."

I hear him draw a breath, but he doesn't speak.

"Wyatt?"

"Nine o'clock? That's what time you said, right?"

"Does that mean you're coming?"

"I guess we'll find out," he says, and then the line goes dead.

6

I guess we'll find out.

Hours later, his words still ring in my mind as I pace the cramped dressing room backstage at X-tasy. There are five of us squeezed in together, surrounded by fogged mirrors, dim lighting, and the stale miasma of sweat, body oil, and desperation. Behind a black curtain, music blares as the first contestant is out there shaking her groove thing.

I've been here only once before, but never backstage. Nia's friend Gerrie—a struggling fashion designer—was about to marry the lawyer who'd negotiated her deal with one of the home shopping channels. Since Nia was in charge of the bachelorette entertainment, we'd all been dragged to X-tasy for the Naughty Girls Amateur Hour, where Gerrie was goaded into signing up to perform, with the aid of about five Cosmopolitans and three test tube shots.

She'd put up a protest, but ultimately conceded, saying that the cash prize would come in handy during their honeymoon in Monaco. And because she'd promised her husband-to-be that she'd act out some of the dances she saw on her girls' night. "And maybe it sounds a little fun, too," she'd added, before scurrying off to cull together a costume from the bag of lingerie that Nia had brought for that very reason.

I'd watched, a little bit jealous, telling myself that I was only envious of the fact that she was dancing, the thing I love most in the world and have so little time for except when I'm teaching it during the summer.

But it was more than that. It was the way the audience responded, and the buzz that I knew she must be feeling because of their energy. It was the sensation of moving through space, and of controlling that space and your own body, and creating something that other people find sensual or thought-provoking or enticing or just plain lovely.

Most of all, though, I'd been jealous of the fact that she'd owned what I couldn't. That she'd stood up and admitted that it would be fun to dance on that stage. To be a little drunk and a little wild and just have a good time. To be raw and let loose.

To dance for the express purpose of getting a man hot and bothered.

The music fades, giving way to catcalls and clapping. The voice of the bartender-turned-emcee blares out through the sound system, encouraging the men in the audience to cast their vote in hard, cold cash deposited into the buckets that the club's waitresses were bringing around.

Normally, the men would show their approval by tucking a bill into a dancer's G-string, but that's against the rules during amateur hour. Each girl has an assigned bucket, and whoever has the most money at the end wins the entire pot.

I intend to win, of course. Even though I came here to audition for Wyatt, until Griffin's officially on the protocol, I'm scrounging every penny I can.

And, also, as far as dancing goes, I might be a teensy bit competitive.

The amateur hour theme music starts up—an unpleasant

electronic tune—and a moment later the curtains flutter as the girl who just finished slips backstage.

Her skin glistens with the sweat of exertion, but she's smiling, so I have to assume she thinks she's done well. She has long, lean thighs and a dancer's body that's pretty similar to mine, and I frown, because she might be real competition for me.

I also can't help but notice that she's essentially nude, having stripped down to nothing—seriously, *nothing*—but a pair of black thong panties.

The butterflies that have been pirouetting lazily in my stomach for the last hour morph into badgers, clawing and twisting and fighting.

I don't think I can do this. How the heck can I do this?

I take a deep breath. And then, for good measure, I take another. Because I *can*. I can, and I will. It's for Griffin. It's for the money. And I just need to keep my eyes on the prize.

The emcee announces the name of the next girl, and as she struts onto the stage to the blare of Madonna's *Like A Virgin*, I peek through the gap in the curtain, searching for Wyatt in the audience.

If he's there, I don't see him, and a fresh wave of emotion floods through me.

Disappointment.

It settles in my veins, twisting me up inside. I bend over, stretching out my quads as I tell myself that I'm only disappointed because if he doesn't show, that means I don't get the job. So my disappointment is about the money. About Griff and the protocol. And about the fact that my last ditch plan to get him here didn't work.

I tell myself that, but of course it's a lie.

In reality, I'm disappointed that I won't feel his eyes on me again. That I won't experience that tingle of awareness when he's near, the way I did back when there was nothing dark between us.

I move to a reasonably clean spot on the floor and sit,

stretching my legs wide and bending at the waist until my fore-head is on my knee and my hands are cupping the ball of my foot. I hold the stretch, feeling the pleasant tightness, the mild burn as my muscles come alive, ready to perform.

I've already warmed up, of course, but I need the distraction now. Because no matter how much I wish I could pretend that this is just about the money and the dance, it's about Wyatt. Of course it is. And instead of running from that uncomfortable little fact, I need to be like Gerrie. I need to just own it.

Own that it excites me to be around him. That I miss the way he made me feel. The way we used to laugh.

Maybe it was nothing more than a teenage summer fling, but it didn't feel like it back then. And it doesn't feel like it now.

So I'm dancing tonight for him. For the Wyatt I used to know. For the boy I might have loved.

I'm dancing for the memory. The way he'd looked at me with a mix of heat and tenderness when I'd slowly unbuttoned my sun-dress. The way he'd made me feel beautiful and exotic and terribly sexy even in white cotton panties and a plain, unlined bra.

Admit it, Kelsey, I order myself. *You're here for the memory—for the man—as much as for the money.*

And it's true. It really is.

And that's *so* not good.

Nia had said pretty much the same thing when she called me back and I started to chew her out for not telling me that W. Royce and Wyatt Segel are one in the same.

"The guy from the Santa Barbara country club? The one you were with that night when—"

"Yes. Who else? I can't believe you didn't tell me."

"Whoa, whoa! Hold on, girlfriend. I swear, I didn't know. Do you really think I'd blindside you like that?"

I frowned, because she was right; I didn't really believe that. Of everyone in my life other than Griffin, Nia is the person I trust the most.

We met when we shared a dorm my freshman year of college. She dropped out in the middle of our first semester when her modeling career took off, but it didn't matter. We'd already spent too many long nights sharing each other's secrets, and you just can't put the brakes on that kind of a friendship.

She's the only one who knows what really happened between me and Wyatt. I'd told her after I'd dodged her third attempt to set me up with a random guy from one of her classes.

"Wow," she'd said when I'd finished laying out the story. "No wonder you're such a neurotic mess."

No wonder, indeed. But at least she's always understood why I keep myself in check, not pushing the envelope. Not taking risks.

And, honestly, I like my life the way it is. It's uncomplicated and ordered, and I know what to expect.

Or, rather, I like the way it *was*. Back before I set my sights on earning fifteen grand. Before I walked into that studio, and Wyatt fell back into my life.

"I mean, come on, Kels," she continued during our call this evening. "Just because I think we need to shove your OCD into a box and slam it tight, doesn't mean I'm going to throw you to the wolves."

"I know. I'm sorry. It's just been a crazy, freaky day."

"I get that," she said. "But the real question is, did you get the job?"

"Undetermined," I'd told her, then explained about tonight.

"X-tasy? I know I've been saying that you need to let go, but are you sure about this?" I heard genuine concern in her voice. "I mean, think about it, Kels. What kind of door are you opening? And can you handle whatever's on the other side?"

I knew the answer then, and I know it now: I'm opening a door that should stay closed. But what choice do I have?

I need this job. I need to help my brother.

Besides, I'd kicked that door wide open the moment I agreed

to go to the audition in Nia's place. I hadn't known it at the time. I hadn't planned it. But now that it's open, I can't go back.

All I can do is hope that he'll help me.

All I can do is try to protect my heart.

I exhale slowly, then shift my torso to stretch out my other side, trying to concentrate on my body instead of the mish-mash of thoughts in my head. I'm successful for about seven seconds, then Madonna's voice starts to fade out and the audience applauds and shouts a few catcalls. Moments later, the girl bounces back into the dressing area. I hadn't been watching, but from the way she's smiling, I'm guessing she did okay.

That's two so far I have to beat.

The girl who's performing immediately before me wrings her hands as she stands in front of the curtain, then turns and looks in my direction, her eyes wide with fear.

I smile sympathetically, but the truth is that I don't under-stand that kind of stage fright. The fear of making a mistake, sure. But being on stage is like being alive, but in a world that's perfect and beautiful, and where I'm always in control.

Her music starts, and she makes a little squeaking noise before bounding onto the stage when her name is called. As soon as she's through the curtain, I hurry over to the dressing area and sit at the sticky, stained dressing table I'd claimed. I know I have time. The staff already told us that after she dances, there will be a ten-minute break for the audience to order fresh food and drinks. Then I'll perform, followed by the rest of the girls.

I dig in my purse for my lip balm, and as I do, I see my phone light up with a call. It's on silent, and I consider letting it ring through to voicemail, but it's Griffin.

I press the button to connect, "Hey, make it fast. I'm in the middle of something."

"No prob. I was just hoping you could come over tonight. There's noise on the tracks during the chase scene."

"Really? That sucks. We nailed that scene." Griff's a voice

actor. Or, at least, he's a struggling part-time voice actor, although he's starting to get more work as his reputation grows. But my brother's also scrappy, and so he's written and is producing his own podcast. Kind of a modern day *Beauty and the Beast* meets *The Count of Monte Cristo*. I've read all the scripts, and it's brilliant.

He hasn't aired any of the episodes yet; he wants to have the entire season finished before he puts it out. He says it's so that he won't lose steam if it sucks and gets no subscribers. I say it's smart because he's going to be doing so many media interviews and fielding so many job offers that he won't have as much time to spend in the studio.

His cast is made up primarily of other voice actors he's met over the years, but he really wants me involved. So he's given me a bit part in every episode. In the one he's talking about, I'm a homeless girl with three scenes. I'm not an actress, but I can't deny it's fun, and I love the idea of having been a part of something I'm sure is going to put my brother on the map.

"We'll nail it again," he says cheerfully, because nothing ever gets Griffin down. Well, almost nothing. "But I want to get it redone now so I can edit it tomorrow night after that cocktail party. You're still going with me, right?"

"Honestly, I should bail. You ought to take a date."

He sighs, then repeats. "You're still going with me, right?"

I roll my eyes and mimic his sigh. "Of course. Do you honestly think I'd miss a party where there's free food and alcohol? I'm totally there."

I'm joking, of course. Well, mostly. The salary of a kindergarten teacher is not a shiny treasure chest of gold, and that's even when you throw in the extra money I earn teaching dance during the summer. Which means I pinch pennies as a matter of course. Only now that I'm saving for Griffin's treatment, I've been pinching them so hard the little copper devils are practically disintegrating between my fingers.

"Anyway, I can't come tonight," I continue. "I'm tied up for a while. But I'll come over tomorrow after I teach my Zumba class. I'll just change at your place and we can leave for the party after we redo the recording."

"Sounds good."

"Great. I'll be there. Unless you decide to take a date in the meantime."

"Give it a rest, Kels."

I know I should shut up, but my brother is awesome, and if he'd just put himself out there more, I know he'd find someone. "There are a couple of girls taking my Wednesday Barre class who I think you'd really like."

He mutters something I can't make out, which is probably a good thing. "Tell you what, when you come over, you can give me a list of all the dancers you think are perfect for me, and then I'll tell you the reason why they're not. There's just the one reason, Kels. And we both know what it is."

I grimace, knowing I'm poking his one sore spot, but I can't seem to help it. "Griff—"

"Don't even start."

I want to argue, but the intro music starts up, meaning the break is almost over. "Fine. As a matter of fact, you're in luck, because I can't. I have to go. I'm trying—"

I cut myself off, realizing this really isn't the time to get into it.

"What?"

"Nothing. I really have to run. But I'll see you tomorrow."

"Is that music? What? Are you auditioning? Is it for a show? At this hour?"

"No, it's a—doesn't matter. I have to go. Seriously, they're calling for me."

"Right, right. Tell me about it tomorrow. And break a leg, okay?"

I'm grinning as I hang up. Griffin has always encouraged

my dancing, telling me I need to audition more and get out of the teaching grind and into performing. Somehow, though, I don't think this is what he had in mind.

I draw a deep breath and step up to the curtain as the emcee announces me. The pounding beat of Def Leppard's "Pour Some Sugar On Me" fills the club. The music swells inside me, and I travel across the floor in time with the beat, then leap onto the pole, hooking one leg around it and holding on loosely so that I spin around, my back arched and my breasts high.

It's a move designed to grab attention, and from the rising applause, I know that it worked. I hold the pose for a moment, then rise back up until my breasts rub the pole and my feet are firmly on the stage. I plié down, the pole rubbing between my legs as I add in a few sensual gyrations for good measure.

The men applaud, and I can only assume that they're imagining me doing that very move with them. But it's not anonymous men I care about. It's not even their vote or the money they might put in a canister for me to win.

It's Wyatt. And not just the job, but the man.

That simple truth twists inside me, as raw and wild as the music I'm dancing to, and I straighten up, then hold on tight as I slide one leg up until I'm in a sideways split. I search the crowd for him, arcing my body as if that's part of my dance, when really all I'm trying to do is see the crowd.

But he's not there, and a bone deep disappointment rushes through me. He's the reason I'm here. The reason I'm dressed in a filmy skirt made of four different colored scarves stitched loosely to a ribbon tied around my waist. The reason I'm wearing a fragile silk blouse that I fully intend to sacrifice as part of my dance.

I've come here ready and willing to put my whole body on display for strangers to prove to him that I have the gumption to handle his job, and yet he's not here.

He's really not here.

I'm still lost in the dance, though. Lost in the performance—because a true dancer doesn't let her emotions stall her. Doesn't let real life interfere with either the movements or the fantasy world through which she's moving.

He's not here, I think again. *And the truth is that I don't care.*

It's a heady realization—and a scary one. But in that moment at least, I'm exactly where I want to be. I'm dancing. Wildly. Provocatively. Seductively.

That basic reality overwhelms me, and I gasp, then cover my unexpected reaction by dropping to the ground and starting my floor routine early. A series of overtly sexual moves that perfectly match the music, and end with me arching my back as I face the ceiling, then ripping open the shirt, sending buttons flying. The shirt slips off, baring my shoulders while my arms remain in the sleeves.

I'm on my back on the stage, my hands pushing me up so that my torso is elevated and my back arched. My arms are bound behind me by my own shirt. For a moment, I'm vulnerable, both on this stage and in the fantasy of the dance where I am bound and helpless in my lover's bed.

I roll my head as I improvise a struggle, my dance comprising both movement and a story.

And that's when I see him.

He's standing at the back of the club, leaning against a pillar. The dim light from a nearby fixture illuminates his face, so that I can't escape the weight of his gaze—or the intensity of his attention. He's watching me.

He's entranced by me.

The power of that moment flows through me. *I've captured him.* For this moment at least, he's mine.

That's when something shifts inside me. I'm no longer dancing for my own pleasure. And I'm certainly not dancing for the anonymous men in the audience.

Now I'm dancing for Wyatt. For *only* Wyatt.

I roll over, and as I do, I let the shirt slide off, freeing my arms. I place my palms on the ground in front of me in child's pose, then lift my rear until I'm in a pike position. Now my body forms a triangle, with my butt at the apex. I hold that pose for a moment, then rise up, my movements always in time to the music.

I'm almost bare on top now, something that is obvious to the audience now that I'm standing in front of them wearing only a tiny flesh-colored bra. I kick up a leg and twirl, thankful the stage is polished. With each rotation, I pull off a scarf from my makeshift skirt, holding onto it long enough so that it flutters beside me for dramatic effect. I release it after a full rotation, letting it pool on the ground beside me.

When all the scarves are gone, I'm left wearing nothing but a pink ribbon around my waist and a G-string that matches the bra. I pull off the ribbon and let it fall to the stage with the scarves.

The song starts to wrap, and I draw a breath. I'm lost in the dance, but somewhere deep inside me, I know I ought to be nervous. I'm revealing myself. I'm being bad, getting my naughty on. It's scary stuff, and yet I'm really not scared.

On the contrary, I want it to go on and on. I'm on stage—a real stage—and I'm not only dancing for an audience, I'm dancing for Wyatt.

I tell myself that the only reason I can do this is because there's a good cause behind it, but that's just not true.

It's everything. It's the way the music fills me. The way the audience watches me.

Mostly, though, it's the heat in Wyatt's eyes. The desire I see on his face. The memory of his touch.

I remember everything—and I'm fantasizing about even more. I don't want this feeling to end. This exultant thrill. This wild ride.

I look out into the dark of the club, and the men at the nearby tables seem to fade away. I'm seeing only Wyatt now.

I slide my hands over my hips, my waist, my breasts. I do that, and I imagine it's his touch. His seduction.

I'm dancing for him, and only him.

I'll get the job, I think. I'm certain of it.

But as I look in his eyes, I can't help but wonder if that's really a good thing. Because now I'll be seeing him every day.

And in the end, that's just going to hurt all the more . . .

7

She was driving him crazy.

The way she held his eyes while she moved, so bold and flirtatious, as if she was just daring him to pull her into his arms and kiss her senseless.

Daring him? No, strike that. She wasn't just daring him, she was throwing down a goddamned gauntlet. But was she challenging him to claim her? Or was she goading him that he couldn't have her?

Damned if he knew. Right then, Wyatt was certain of only one thing—his body was tight, his cock was hard, and he wanted to be somewhere other than here. Someplace without other people.

Someplace with a bed.

It was the dancing that did it. Because Kelsey Draper and her dancing had always been his downfall. After all, that was what had started everything all those years ago. He'd seen her dancing to a bouncy pop song, her interpretation elevating the music and lyrics. He'd seen passion and precision, sensuality and seduction. She'd enchanted him. Cast a spell over him.

He'd seen the magic in her, so much larger than the quiet,

subdued girl he'd met before. The Kelsey he'd watched dancing had surprised him. She was vibrant. Alive. Unexpected.

He'd fallen hard, and then she'd broken his heart.

He wouldn't make the same mistake again.

He might want her—hell, he *did* want her. For his bed. For his show.

But he damn sure wasn't going to trust her. He'd already learned that lesson, and he really didn't need a refresher course.

As he watched, she dropped to the floor, then used one hand to rip open her shirt before letting it fall down her arms. She writhed on stage, her seductive movements making him ache inside, all the more when he imagined taking it further. Her wrists bound not with a tattered blouse, but with silk ropes. And not just her wrists, but her legs as well. Red ropes, the only color in an otherwise black and white image. Her body twisting, and the audience unsure if she was fighting the bonds or reveling in her own rising passion.

She was exactly what he needed for the show. The complete package. Hell, he'd known that from the moment she'd walked into his studio.

So why was he hesitating?

Because he wanted her?

Or was it because he wanted to punish her?

Or maybe it was even more insidious than that. Maybe it came down to how much was riding on this show. It was his shot, after all. The apex of all his work and sacrifice. The chance to escape from under the black cloud his father had left hanging over him.

The chance to prove himself to his family.

To live up to the goddamn Segel name.

But that would only happen if the show was a success.

So maybe that was why he was hesitating. Because the moment he committed was the moment the truth crept toward him on little cat paws, and it would either curl up and purr, or rip his heart out.

On stage, Kelsey rose, then did some sort of pirouette, twirling as she pulled off one of those transparent, colored scarves that served as a barely-there skirt. Wyatt imagined his hands on her waist, the brush of her skin against his palms as she spun. He could imagine her heat. The way she shivered under his touch.

So help him, he wanted that. Wanted to hear her sighs. Those little moans he remembered.

Another scarf went flying, and he straightened so that he was no longer leaning against the pillar. Instead, he shifted his weight from foot to foot as he tried to tamp down the rising lust. The violent need. To not only have her, but to have her in his show.

He wanted her, yes. But she was an indulgence he couldn't justify. An indulgence and a risk, because he knew damn well that she'd run if things got too intense.

And damn but his show was intense. That was the point, after all.

He couldn't take a chance on her, no matter how much he might want to. Couldn't even bring her in only long enough to test her out. Not on such a tight schedule. Not when there was no way to ensure that she wouldn't bolt.

Kelsey was a risk he simply couldn't take. He had to get it right. There was too much at stake for him to be wrong about her.

The final scarf fluttered to the ground, and Wyatt's pulse pounded in his throat as he moved closer, his mouth going dry as she reached for her bra, pulled it over her head, then tossed it aside.

The music faded out, and the dim, colored stage lights made the flesh-colored G-string blend into her pale skin, enhancing the illusion that she now stood before the entire room not just topless, but one hundred percent, birthday-suit naked.

She took a bow as the lights came up, and the men in the

audience actually stood to applaud her. She'd blown away the competition, and even though Wyatt wanted to rush the stage and wrap his jacket around her, he couldn't deny the swell of pride he felt for her victory. There might be two girls still to follow, but everyone in that room knew who deserved to win the kitty.

"Baby doll, you sure can move," one guy yelled to her.

She crossed her arms over her chest, her eyes darting to the guy, and then immediately away.

He saw the familiar innocence, and he saw a hint of fear.

A fierce protectiveness welled up inside of him, and he took a sideways step toward the guy, who was standing now, a twenty dollar bill waving in his hand.

"Sir?" A waitress stood in front of the prick, one of the contest collection buckets thrust out in front of her. "You'll want to put that in here. That's how you vote for your favorite."

"Screw the contest," the prick said, as Kelsey hurried to put her shirt back on. "I wanna give this to that little piece of ass personally."

"What the hell did you call her?" Wyatt asked, taking another step toward the bastard.

But the guy either didn't hear or chose to ignore. He was drunk—that much was obvious—but he moved with remarkable alacrity as he clambered up onto the stage, then grabbed Kelsey's wrist and yanked her toward him. He slipped the twenty into her G-string, despite the fact that she was tugging away from him.

He jerked her back, making her cry out as she stumbled toward him.

Then he started to slide his arm around her waist, but he didn't get that far. Wyatt had already leaped onto the stage, and as the bartender came rushing from the opposite direction, Wyatt grabbed the drunk's shoulder and pushed him back, forcing him to get his filthy paws off Kelsey.

"What the fuck's your problem, man?"

"I don't have a problem," Wyatt said. "Keep your hands off the lady, and I have no problem at all."

"Ain't no lady. And I gave the bitch a twenty." He looked over Wyatt's shoulder. "I want a lap dance, sugarbuns. Do it good, and I got another twenty for you."

Wyatt didn't turn. Didn't look at Kelsey. Didn't even think about what he was doing.

Instead, he simply lashed out, his fist saying all the words he didn't bother to articulate. One punch and the drunk went down.

The bastard looked up at Wyatt from his new perspective, his eyes wide with surprise, a trickle of blood oozing from the corner of his mouth.

"What the fuck, man?" He started to sit up. "You hit me over a goddamn whore?"

Whore?

That was the last straw. Wyatt launched himself, practically falling down onto the guy, who cowered back, real fear shining in those beady, bloodshot eyes. Wyatt grabbed his arm, then twisted it back and up, putting pressure on the joint, pushing it almost to the breaking point.

"Apologize to the lady," he demanded as Kelsey yelled for him to stop, and the bartender made noises about kicking them both out of the club.

Wyatt tuned it all out. "I said apologize, you worthless piece of shit."

"Dammit, Wyatt, stop!" Kelsey called. "You're going to break his arm."

At the moment, Wyatt didn't care. But he looked at the guy's face, saw that he was turning green, and backed off. The guy sucked in air, his face a mask of fury so greenish-red it seemed like Christmas.

Wyatt climbed to his feet, then hauled the drunk up beside

him. The guy wobbled, unsteady on his feet. Wyatt didn't much care about that either. "Get the fuck out of here," he insisted, as he gave the guy a push. For a moment, it looked like the drunk would fight back, but then the vigor seemed to drain out of him, and he backed away, pausing only long enough to shoot Wyatt the finger.

"And you," Wyatt continued, pointing at Kelsey. "You're coming with me."

Her eyes went wide. "The hell I will." She lifted her chin, obviously digging her heels.

He took a step toward her, so damn frustrated he was seriously considering scooping her up over his shoulder and hauling her the hell out of there.

The bouncer was on the stage now, and he stepped in front of Wyatt. "You need to leave, too, sir."

"Not a problem. I just need the lady to come with me." He looked past the bouncer, his eyes hard on Kelsey's. "Now."

The bouncer shifted his attention toward Kelsey. "You with this guy?" he asked, then stood silently, obviously waiting for her answer. Honestly, Wyatt wasn't sure he wanted to hear it. She looked ready to explode. Her cheeks were red, and when she opened her mouth to answer, Wyatt wasn't sure if she was going to let out a howl of fury or actually answer the question.

Finally, she spoke. "My stuff's in the dressing room."

"Then go get it and meet me at my car."

"I've got my own car."

"Dammit, Kelsey, quit arguing."

The bouncer took a threatening step toward him. "The lady says she has her own car."

Wyatt ignored him, his attention on Kelsey. "Will you just do this? Please?"

For a moment, he thought she was going to keep up the fight. But then she nodded, and relief flooded through him, so potent it almost knocked him over.

"Good," he said. "Fine." He swallowed, then added, "Thank you."

She nodded, then turned her back on him. He lingered a moment, watching her walk away. And hoping that, unlike twelve years ago, this time she'd come back to him.

8

Twelve years ago

Wyatt watched her leave, the pretty girl with the dark hair that flashed sparks of red when the sun hit it just right.

He'd noticed her earlier when he'd been at the pool. She'd been cleaning some tables, and he'd pretended like he was watching the other kids climb the diving board. But he'd really been sneaking glances her way.

Something about her had captured his attention. Her looks, sure. But it was more than that. She had a sweetness about her. A purity. But he couldn't help thinking that her wholesomeness was marred by a few rough edges. As if she were a little girl in a pristine white Easter dress who couldn't wait to slosh through the mud.

In other words, she was a contradiction. Someone different from the girls he usually met. And he made up his mind right there on the sun bleached pool deck that he was going to ask her out.

So when he'd literally bumped into her as she rounded the corner of the rec center, it was like he'd been handed a gift. Not that it had worked out the way he'd hoped. The bad news was that she'd flat out turned down his offer to buy her some french fries.

The good news was that she seemed to genuinely regret having to leave to go get her brother.

Which meant he had a shot. And considering he was stuck there for the summer, and all the other girls looked like clones of the girls he knew from LA, he figured that was a good thing.

He spent the next few days trying to get her attention, but he never seemed to manage. He'd see her wiping a table and try to talk, and she'd blush and mumble that she was on the clock. He'd fall into step beside her and ask where she was headed, and she'd reply easily enough. But then she'd duck her head, tell him she was in a hurry, and take off in a jog to wherever she was supposedly going.

Mostly, he thought she was just trying to get away from him.

The thought bothered him. He was seventeen years old and about to move to New England to enroll in one of the most prestigious private photography programs in the country. *And* he'd gotten in on a merit scholarship. Not because his parents had written the Trustees a check.

He could talk about pop culture, but also liked sports. He knew his way around any art museum, modern or classic. And he was well-versed enough about ballet and the opera to impress girls who were into that kind of thing. He was a halfway decent surfer. He'd had a string of girlfriends from the time he was eleven, mostly because they'd pursued him, and the female attention made him cool in the eyes of his friends.

And even though he suspected that some of that attention had been directed more at his family name than at him, he also knew that he wasn't a complete dud.

So why the hell was Kelsey running from him?

"Her," he said one day, pointing her out to his friend Patrick, whose father was the general manager of the country club. "What's her story?"

They sat at a table by the pool, eating burgers and fries. Directly across from them, Kelsey was working the cordoned off adult section, delivering dry towels and magazines to a cadre of women who showed up daily at the club to sun themselves, drink fruity cocktails, and gossip. She moved with an enchanting grace, and her lips were perpetually curved up at the corners, like she had a delicious secret that she wasn't telling.

"I don't know much," Patrick admitted, as Wyatt's thumb stroked the edge of the Ricoh camera that was his constant companion. He itched to pick it up and capture her on film, and it was taking all of his effort not to be the kind of invasive ass who started snapping pictures of people without their permission. He saw enough of that breed around his grandmother and sister, and his mom to a lesser extent. He really didn't need to join their ranks.

That didn't change the desire, though, and so instead of capturing her in his camera, he tried to burn her image into his mind. A mental picture of beauty and grace that he could keep with him always.

"—this summer."

Wyatt shook his head, realizing he'd zoned out. "Sorry. What?"

Patrick shot him a look that was both irritated and amused. "I said, her dad's heading up the landscaping crew this summer."

"Just the summer?"

"Our old guy quit, and the new guy they hired can't start until September. And Draper was available. My dad said something about how he's between jobs. I guess he has a gig starting in LA in the fall."

"Yeah, but what about her?"

"She's shy. I met her at one of the staff meetings. I said hello, and she stared at her shoes. Probably because I'm so intimidating."

"Probably," Wyatt agreed ironically. Patrick was pretty much the least intimidating guy on the planet, which was why he worked the member relations desk three times a week even though he was barely eighteen. "But why's she working at all? What are her hours? Do you know what she likes?"

"Because her father insisted that my uncle give her a job, too," Patrick began, counting his answer out on his fingers. "Pretty much eight to five. And I really don't know." He cocked his head as he considered something. "I know she watches her brother play tennis sometimes when she has free time. So she either likes him or she likes tennis."

"Tennis," Wyatt muttered, nodding thoughtfully. "Okay. That's good to know."

"Good?" Patrick said. "I don't know about that. Because if *good* means you're thinking about asking her out, I think you should just back away slowly and find someone else. She's not worth the trouble."

"Yeah? Why?"

Patrick shrugged. "You've seen her. The girl's too shy. It's the summer, dude. You'll barely get to first base before she moves back home and you head to Boston."

"It's not just about sex."

"Yeah? Then you're doing it wrong."

Wyatt rolled his eyes. Patrick might like to talk big, but he was more bluster than action.

"Besides," Patrick continued, "from what I've seen, her dad's pretty strict. Like he walked out of a nineteen-fifties TV show. Probably why she doesn't talk to the guys. Or really to the girls, for that matter. Just forget about it. Seriously."

It was good advice, and Wyatt even tried to follow it for a few days, forcibly pushing her out of his thoughts and going out of his way to not be anywhere that she might be working. It even worked. Sort of. But then he'd catch a glimpse of her out of the corner of his eye, and she'd enchant him all over again.

Soon, he realized that he was finding ways to be around when she was finishing her shift. He'd offer her a ride, and she'd repeatedly turn him down. Politely and sweetly, but also firmly.

He also found ways to be around when she was starting her shift. That's when he'd offer to bring her a coffee. Again, she always said no.

He tried again and again, sometimes suggesting a coffee, once even asking if she wanted to play a game of tennis after her shift. "I can't," she said. "I have to get home. Besides, I'm horrible at tennis."

"Right," he said. "Me, too." That was a blatant lie—he was actually pretty good at the game—but she'd rattled him. And he crossed tennis off the list.

After a full week of trying, he started to give up. She hadn't said as much, but considering what Patrick had said about her dad, Wyatt assumed she wasn't allowed to date. Or maybe she just didn't want to date him. Maybe that was even what he found so attractive, the fact that she didn't seem to care in the least who his family was.

The day she said, "no thanks, really," before he'd even asked her about a coffee was the day he started to worry that he was crossing into stalker territory, which was really not the vibe he wanted. He made a point of backing off. No sense acting like a douchebag, after all.

He started spending more time with Patrick. And then Grace joined them, and she was most definitely interested in him. She sat a little closer than necessary. She brushed his arm when she laughed at his jokes.

She also talked incessantly about his family. His sister and her cooking show. His mother, with her screenplays and novels. His grandmother, with her Hollywood pedigree and all those lovely award statues. The family mansion in Beverly Hills. The twenty-thousand square foot summer house in Santa Barbara.

The chalet in St. Moritz. The family legacy. The studio Wyatt's great-grandfather had founded. And on, and on, and on.

All stuff that had nothing to do with *him*.

All stuff he really didn't want to talk about.

But at the same time, he was a guy, wasn't he? A seventeen-year-old guy with all the raging hormones that came with it. And maybe he had more discipline than some of his peers, but he wasn't a saint, not by a long shot.

So when Grace came to him when he was leaving the club one Friday night and told him her car wouldn't start, he did the gentlemanly thing. He offered her a ride. And when she offered to use her fake ID to buy some beer as payment for the lift, that seemed the polite thing to do. And when she offered to go down on him . . . well, he was a *guy*, after all.

Or rather, he was guy enough to enjoy it in the moment, but afterwards, he felt like shit. He didn't want Grace, and all he'd done was lead her on. And when she started hanging around him more—obviously believing that they were sliding into coupledom—he manned up, told her he didn't think it was going to work, and ended it.

To say she didn't take it well would be the understatement of the century. She called him a stuck up prick who thought he could just skate by on his family name and didn't have to be nice to anyone. Which was ridiculously unfair since he'd always felt like his family name was an albatross. But unfair or not, it stung.

"That's the price we pay," his father had said when Wyatt decided to bite the bullet, swallow some pride, and ask his dad for advice. He'd always had a good relationship with his father, but lately Carlton Royce had seemed distracted. An accountant, Carlton had met Wyatt's mother, Lorelei, when they were both attending the same charity function. They'd each come with other dates, had met at the dessert table, and had married four months later.

"Price?" Wyatt asked.

"Of celebrity."

"Yeah, but I'm not a celebrity. That's Grandma. And Jenna," he added, referring to his sister who owned three restaurants and starred in her own Manhattan-based celebrity cooking show. "Mom, too, sort of." Considering all his mother's work was behind the camera, she wasn't as recognizable. But she'd grown up on studio lots and at star-studded premiers. So that definitely put her in the celebrity bucket.

But Wyatt had avoided all that stuff. Not because he was shy, but because he just didn't get it. If the spotlight wasn't actually shining on him, why would he want to be standing in its glow?

"Comes with the territory, kid," his dad had said. "Just because you never escort your mom down the red carpet doesn't mean the world doesn't see you as one of them. You're Hollywood royalty, son. We both are. Whether we want to be or not. Whether we deserve it or not. And most of the time, that's all anyone cares about. They want that piece of you. That shiny anointed part. They don't see you. They see the family."

Wyatt frowned, not used to hearing such harshness in his father's voice.

He started to ask about it, but his dad continued. "Even on the inside," he said. "It's everywhere. Permeates everything. It's like dry rot, and it eats away at the foundation."

"Dad? What are you talking about?"

Carlton drew a breath and shook his head. "Sorry. Just rambling. Don't listen to me." He sighed, the sound long and mournful. "You know I love you, right?"

"Um, sure," Wyatt frowned, worried by his father's tone and uncharacteristic sentimentality. "I love you, too."

"And God knows your grandmother thinks you hung the moon."

"Sure, Dad," Wyatt said. The fact was, Anika Segel was a

force of nature, and although Wyatt was firmly convinced that she was one of the most incredible women to ever walk the earth, he had no freaking idea what she really thought about him. Or anybody, for that matter, other than his mother and sister. With those two, she'd hole up for hours talking career and how to position themselves, and on and on and on.

There were times when Wyatt felt invisible.

So while his dad's words were nice to hear, Wyatt wasn't at all sure he believed them.

His dad clapped him on the shoulder. "Just forget about Grace, son. She'll move on. Another girl will come along soon enough."

He thought of Kelsey and cringed as he felt his cheeks heat. Was he actually blushing? How lame was that?

His dad chuckled. "So she's come along, already? All right, then. Tell me about her."

"I dunno. She's pretty. She's different." He lifted a shoulder. "And she's not interested in me at all."

"You sure about that?"

Wyatt shrugged again.

"But you like her?"

"Yeah. I like her a lot."

"So tell her."

"I tried."

His dad nodded thoughtfully. "Fair enough. But maybe you need to try harder. Deep down, nobody's that different."

"She is," Wyatt said firmly. Because Kelsey *was* different, with her shy and quiet ways counterpointed by a light that burned inside of her. He'd only seen flickers, so far. But what he wanted was for it to shine on him. He wanted to bask in her glow.

His father's mouth curved down thoughtfully. "Maybe she is. But don't be blinded by a pretty girl," he said. "Or a sweet one, or a charming one. Sure, there are girls out there who aren't as obvious as Grace, but in the end, everybody's drawn to fame. Everybody. Even the people who say they don't want it themselves, they're still drawn to the light. We're a culture of moths, Wyatt, and you'll be a happier man if you remember that."

Disturbing words, but he pushed most of them aside, focusing only on the *try harder* part of the equation. Because something told him that Kelsey was worth the effort. He just hadn't found the way in yet. She was a sweet girl, and instead of trying to really get to know her, he'd given up and gone out with Grace instead.

God, he was an idiot.

He spent the next few days avoiding Grace and trying to get close to Kelsey, something he never quite managed to do. They shared a few words, and every time, he'd see a spark of interest in her eyes. She liked him—he was certain of it. But she stayed behind her wall.

That reality frustrated the crap out of Wyatt. He wanted to get to know the real Kelsey, because he was sure there was another girl living behind that wall of sweet shyness. But the most he ever saw was that tiny glimmer of light, and he had no idea how to break through the wall to let the fullness of her shine through.

Try harder, his dad had said, but isn't that what he'd been doing? How long should he keep trying? Wasn't it crazy to keep on and on, expecting her to suddenly smile brightly and slide into his arms? Wasn't that the definition of insanity? Doing the same thing over and over and over and expecting a different result every time?

It was. Which meant Wyatt was certifiable. Because he just kept at it, trying to think of different ways to catch her attention even while avoiding Grace, who was determined to go out with him again even though he'd politely told her that he didn't think it was going to work out between them.

Grace, however, wasn't the kind to take no for an answer, and maybe that was a good thing. After all, Grace was the reason he was finally able to find a way over Kelsey's wall.

He'd been pacing outside the rec center, planning to grab Kelsey when she came out. But then he heard Grace approaching with a group of her friends, and since he really wasn't in the mood to see her again, he ducked inside, then pressed himself against the wall as he breathed hard, hoping that the girls weren't planning to come into the center.

He peered through the windows, waiting until they'd safely passed. When he saw them disappear around the copse of trees near the picnic area, he exhaled and started for the door. He was about to go back outside when the music that had been playing in the background suddenly grew louder. He paused, confused, then realized that someone must have opened a door to one of the studios.

For just a few moments, pop music flooded the hall, the sound steamy and seductive and a little bit familiar. He moved that direction, curious to see why a provocative current chart-topper was front-and-center in a dance class filled with little kids.

Except there were no little kids. That much was clear as he got closer. The music was coming from the largest studio, the one at the end of the hall. The door was open, and Mrs. Hinson was leaning casually against the door frame. A fifty-something former Broadway chorus dancer, Sarah Hinson had moved to Santa Barbara to open her own studio, and had ended up contracting with the club to teach all the dance classes from toddler all the way up to ballroom dancing for seniors.

He paused in front of the door to the men's room, the slight offset from the wall helping him to stay out of sight should she look his way.

"Honey, you are too good to waste your time spritzing tables," Mrs. Hinson was saying. "You should be in New York going to auditions. I still have a few contacts. At the very least, you should be spending your days dancing. Goodness knows I could use your help teaching. And you'd have all the studio time you wanted between classes."

Wyatt cocked his head, trying to hear the response from whoever was in the room, but the voice was too low and the music—even though the volume had significantly diminished—drowned it out.

"Well, that may be so," Mrs. Hinson said, "but that doesn't mean your father is right. I don't doubt that man loves you, but he's not doing right by you."

Wyatt took a step closer, not sure why, only knowing that he was curious.

"Fine." Mrs. Hinson threw her hands up dramatically. "I know better than to try to convince you. But you just remember that the offer stands. And if you ever need a letter of recommendation, I'll—well, of course I mean it," she said after a pause, during which the girl she was talking to had obviously said something. "And now I've got to run. No, no. You stay as long as you want. There aren't any more classes today. You enjoy yourself. Just be sure to lock up."

The girl must have agreed, because Mrs. Hinson waved, then turned and headed down the hall toward Wyatt. She had her head down as she rummaged in her purse, and he slipped quietly into the men's room until he heard her footsteps pass.

He counted to ten, then counted again just to be sure. Then he slipped out into the abandoned hallway. The music was back—louder now—and he headed toward the still-open door. He was curious to see who was in there, although when he thought back on it later, he was certain that some part of him already knew.

It was her, of course. *Kelsey.*

She wore tights and the bottom half of a leotard that looked like it had been cut in two with hedge shears. On top, she wore a sports bra with a collarless T-shirt over it, cut off at the midriff. He could see the taut muscles of her back and abs as she soared across the room. Because that's what it was—*soaring*. Not dancing. Hell, not anything he'd seen before. She was magic, her movement and power elevating what used to be a simple pop song into something absolutely transcendent.

This was it, he thought. *This was her. This was Kelsey, and he was seeing her for the very first time.*

He'd only seen hints of the core of her before. That spark. That vitality.

But he'd seen it now, and he knew it lived inside her.

She wasn't shy; she was extraordinary. Alive. Vibrant.

Real.

More than that, she was going to be his.

Somehow, he was going to win this girl.

9

Somehow he was going to win the girl.

As plans went, Wyatt had to admit it was a little vague. Not so much a plan, but a hope. An intention.

Somehow, though, he was going to see it through. At least he knew more about her now than he had before. And he pursued her like he'd never pursued a girl before. Flowers in her locker. Compliments whenever he saw her. Lattes in the morning, which he left for her even if she said no. And, best of all, tickets to the final round of a ballroom dance competition being held right there in Santa Barbara.

"I don't know if you're into dancing," he lied, thrusting two tickets into her hand as they stood outside the tennis center. "But someone gave these to me, and I thought you might want to go. With me, I mean." He gave himself a mental kick. He sounded like a douche. Not a confident seventeen-year-old.

But from the way she was smiling, it didn't look like she thought he was lame. On the contrary, her entire face glowed.

"I love dancing," she admitted. "It's—well, it's what I want to do. The only thing I want to do."

"Then this works out great," he said, the feeling that he was an idiot morphing into something much more pleasant.

"Except—well, it's just—" She held the tickets back out to him, and it felt like a punch in the gut. "It's just that I can't accept this."

"You don't have to." The words tumbled out of his mouth. "I mean, I already accepted. They were a gift to me." Not exactly a lie since his grandmother gave him the tickets. "I just need someone to tag along so I don't have an empty seat beside me. Looks pathetic, you know."

She bit her lower lip. "Really?"

"You'd be helping me out a lot."

"Thursday?"

"It's in the afternoon. You don't have to work, do you?" He knew she didn't; he'd already checked her schedule.

She shook her head. "That's my day off."

"Great. Your parents will let you come, right?"

"I don't—" She cut herself off, then lifted her chin. For the first time, she looked him straight in the eye, and he felt the reverberations all the way through him. "I mean, I don't think that would be a problem. Thank you," she added, then drew a deep breath. "I'd love to go with you."

Those tickets turned everything upside down, switching his world from just okay to absolutely perfect. He and Kelsey started walking together regularly, taking the long way from the snack bar to the tennis center. They snuck in more time, too. Breaks at the edge of the golf course. Hours stolen during weekends.

He learned that she danced whenever she could sneak in the time, and that she adored her little brother. "I try to stay mad at him," she admitted. "But then he'll make up a story in these crazy voices he does, and whatever irritated me just sort of fades away. Griffin's great."

"I want to meet him." They'd paused on the main walking path at the turn-off to the tennis center. "Why don't I just come with you?" Every day, this is where he left her. But every day, he didn't want their stolen time together to end.

"Someday. But I—"

"Ashamed of me?" he quipped.

She bit her lower lip, looking younger than her fifteen years. "It's just that Griff's only twelve, and if he says something . . . I mean, I'm not allowed to date—"

"We just went to the competition together."

"Yeah, well, that wasn't really a date. I was doing you a favor filling that seat, right? And, um, my parents were out of town. They took my brother to LA for an appointment, and I knew they wouldn't be back until late."

"So you didn't tell them."

Her cheeks bloomed pink. "I don't usually sneak around," she admitted. "But I—you know." She met his eyes, then looked at her shoes. He thought her shyness was adorable. Hell, he thought *she* was adorable.

She drew a breath. "I guess I told myself it was like going to a movie. Only with live dancers. But seriously, Wyatt, if my dad—"

He held up a hand, then pressed his finger to her lips. "It's okay. Really. I get it." He flashed a grin. "I'll meet Griffin some other time. Once your dad approves of me," he teased.

"Yeah?" Her smile was like sunshine. "You don't mind?"

"I want to hang out with you," he said. "All the rest is no big deal."

With every day that passed, they managed to sneak in more and more time. He took photo after photo of her. By the pool, on the walking path, anywhere he could. Mostly, they talked incessantly, learning everything they could about each other. He learned she liked salted chocolate, but hated nuts. That she loved pink in her dance outfits, but hated it in her regular clothes. That her favorite author was Mark Twain, but that she had a weakness for Nancy Drew books, and that even though she stopped reading them years ago, she had her entire collection packed neatly in plastic boxes she kept stacked in her closet.

He confessed that he generally despised fast food but had a weakness for In-N-Out Burger. That he'd accidentally blown up the garden shed in middle school when he was trying to come up with a project for the science fair, and that he'd once played Pac-Man for twelve hours straight on the free-standing machine that his grandmother kept in the game room.

The last revelation led to an even bigger one, because he hadn't realized that she knew about his family until she asked him, point blank, if it was hard growing up around so many famous people.

"Wow," he said, thrown by the question. "I didn't think you knew about my family."

"I overheard Grace and Marsha talking that first day you came to the pool."

"Really?" He cocked his head as he looked at her, then realized he was grinning so wide he must look like a fool.

She laughed. "Why are you looking at me like that?"

"No reason." He was still grinning, but how could he not? He thought back on all the days he'd been pursuing her, and it gave him a nice, warm feeling in his gut to know that all that time she knew who he was.

"No reason?" she repeated, then laughed. "Come on. Tell me."

"Maybe I like you," he said, though the simple words did nothing to capture the euphoria he felt from just being around her. From knowing that she wanted to be around *him,* and not the Segel boy. He reached out and took her hand, then twined his fingers with hers.

She ducked her head, then gently hip-butted him. "Maybe I like you, too."

They walked, hands swinging, toward the little copse of trees between the eighth and ninth greens. Wyatt had discovered it when he was wandering the grounds taking landscape shots, and now they were heading that direction so that he could take photos of Kelsey sitting on the massive, low-lying limb.

"I felt a little sorry for you that day," she said softly. "That first day, I mean." She glanced up at him, then almost immediately back down at the grass.

"You did?" He couldn't remember the last time someone said they felt sorry for him. Oh, wait. Yes, he could. That would have been the fourth of absolutely never ever. "Why?"

"I guess because it must be hard, and a little lonely, too. Because you never really know why someone wants to be your friend, do you?"

They were still walking, but now he tugged her to a stop. He wanted to tell her she was right. That he didn't think anyone else understood that, at least not anyone who wasn't born into a celebrity family. Mostly, he wanted to just look at her. To feel the warmth inside him turn into a raging blaze of longing for this girl who got him. Who really and truly got him.

"Wyatt?"

He blinked, realizing suddenly that he was staring. "Sorry. Sorry, it's just—well, it's just that you're right. It is hard."

She nodded, but frowned a bit, too.

"What?"

"I was thinking that your last name makes it even more hard. It's so well known. But then I was wondering why it's your name at all. Shouldn't you have your father's name?"

"You've obviously never met Anika Segel. My grandmother is the head of a wide and vast matriarchy. No way was my dad going to win that battle."

Her mouth twisted a bit. "Guess it's hard for your dad, too, huh?"

He nodded, thinking about the conversation he'd had with his father back when he was still trying to get Kelsey's attention. "Yeah," he admitted. "It is."

She took his hand and they started walking again. They'd

veered off the path and were now walking on the green toward the cluster of trees. "At least people see you and talk to you," she said. "They notice you because of the name and your family. I'm invisible."

He pulled her to a stop again, then searched her face, his heart breaking a little at the truth he saw there. A truth he didn't understand, because she was amazing. Sweet and smart and funny and talented. He could spend days talking to her, sitting with her, or just quietly holding her hand. He *could*, and yet he couldn't, because her parents kept her on such a tight leash.

"You're not invisible to me," he said, and he almost kissed her right then. Instead, he brushed her lips with the tip of his finger.

She sighed with more passion and longing than he'd ever heard from any of the girls he'd dated.

That's when he knew. He wasn't just Wyatt anymore. He was Wyatt and Kelsey.

And damned if that didn't feel nice.

"Have you ever been kissed?"

Her eyes shot up to his, and he wasn't sure if it was excitement he saw there, or terror.

She swallowed, then shook her head. "No," she whispered.

That little word made him happier than it should. "I'm going to be your first, Kelsey Draper."

"Oh." A pink stain flooded her cheeks. "Okay."

"But not today."

"Oh." Now the word was laced with disappointment, and damned if that didn't make him feel good, too. "When?" she added.

But he only smiled, released her hand, and said, "Race you to the trees."

The next day, he brought her tickets to the ballet. He pulled her around the rec center to the service doors because nobody ever went there, and handed her a small, flat box. Then he had to fight not to smile like an idiot as he watched the awe on her face when she opened it and drew out the two printed pieces of paper.

"Wyatt. This is amazing. You got me tickets to *Swan Lake*?"

"You like?"

"It's one of my favorite ballets ever. This is incredible."

"*You're* incredible," he said and was surprised when she frowned.

"It's in Los Angeles," she said. "My father's never going to let me go."

"Really? Not even to the ballet? It's cultural."

She lifted her shoulders, and it killed him the way she seemed to be sinking into herself. He hadn't met her dad, but she'd told him enough. And Wyatt had seen the man, too. Leonard Draper worked ten-hour days at the club, so even though he was usually out on the golf course or overseeing the maintenance of the shrubs and flowers in the various public areas, he was around enough that Wyatt had managed to pick him out. A lean, lanky man with a hard face and the leathery skin of someone who'd worked outside his whole life.

Only his eyes reminded him of Kelsey. But where hers were as blue as the Caribbean, his seemed as distant and cold as a glacier.

Wyatt watched her face, now drained of the joy that had lit her from within only a few moments before. *Bastard.* He didn't know what Leonard Draper's problem was, but he knew it pissed him off. And that if the rules he made regarding his daughter denied Kelsey access to all the things she loved, then the rules were stupid.

And Wyatt didn't have a problem breaking stupid rules.

"We don't have to tell your dad," he said.

Her eyes went wide. "If he ever found out . . . I mean, the dance competition was here. And he was out of town. And I could have just told him I got a ticket all on my own because I wanted to see the dancing. I would have gotten in trouble, but not for being with a boy. But this? If he finds out. . . ." She shuddered. "Not telling him would be as bad as going to the ballet in the first place."

"What does he have against the ballet?"

"He . . . he just doesn't think it's right for me. Watching it is okay. But not watching it with a boy all the way in Los Angeles."

"Do you have any girlfriends here?"

For a moment, she looked at him blankly. Then her eyes went wide, and she hugged herself, then looked at her watch. "I need to run. I've got to get Griffin."

"No, you don't," he said, with a quick glance at his own watch. "You've got at least five more minutes." But he was saying the last to the air. Kelsey had already sprinted away.

Damn.

He kicked himself for even suggesting it. He should have known she wasn't the kind of girl who'd go against her parents, even if the law her parents set down was stupid.

He told himself he'd apologize when he saw her the next day, and then the next day he had to kick himself even harder, because she managed to avoid him altogether.

He'd screwed it up. He'd gone and completely screwed it up.

Two entire days later he still hadn't seen her. He spent the afternoon swimming laps, and realized that she must have asked to switch her schedule around, because she didn't wipe down one single table the entire time he was there.

He finally gave up and headed to his car, all the while wondering as to the best tactic for groveling his way back into her good graces. But when he arrived at the parking lot and saw her leaning against the BMW he'd borrowed from the fleet his grandmother kept in Santa Barbara, his heart skipped a beat as a flicker of hope settled in his chest.

Maybe—just maybe—he hadn't screwed this up too bad.

"Hi," he said, half-afraid he was hallucinating.

"My friend Joy lives here during the summers." She drew a breath as if for courage. "I could say I was staying with her next Friday."

"You'd be okay with that?" His heart was pounding so loud he was certain she could hear it. "You're not exactly the rule-breaking kind, Kelsey Draper. And I don't want—"

"What?"

It was his turn to suck in air. "I don't want you to resent me if you get in trouble. Or even if you just feel guilty."

She shoved her hands in the pockets of her shorts and nodded. "That's sweet." She looked down at the pavement. "And—and well, I probably will feel guilty. But I think you're worth it," she added, tilting her head up to look at him.

"Yeah?"

She nodded, her entire face lighting up as she smiled.

"You can trust this girl?"

"Definitely. We go to school together. Brighton," she said, referring to an exclusive girls' school in Los Angeles. "I'm on scholarship."

"I'm impressed. Brighton's got a hell of a reputation."

"I guess. I got in based on academics, but I applied because they offer dance for PE credit. It's not a dance academy, but they support the arts, and so at least I get to study, you know?"

"And your dad's okay with that?"

"Technically, my dance class is a gym class. So he copes. Mostly he likes being able to say that his little girl goes there on scholarship. And—" She cut herself off with a shake of her head.

"What?"

"I don't know. Nothing. It's petty," she added when he lifted a brow and stared her down.

"So? I'm not going to think less of you."

"He doesn't let me dance—you know, not at a real studio. And he knows it bugs me. So I think in his mind I can't complain since he's letting me go to Brighton."

Wyatt nodded, hoping she wouldn't see the way he was clenching his fists to fight back the anger. Her dad was a piece of work, and the sooner she graduated and got out of there the better.

"I never asked where you go," she said.

"Beverly Hills High School," he said, then grimaced. "I fit the profile of a Hollywood cliché, but my mom and sister went there, so no one was going to rock the boat for me. But I'm doing my senior year in Boston," he added. "I got into an exclusive photography academy."

"I'm not surprised. And I bet you're the top in the class. Your work is fabulous."

He'd hooked his camera up to the computer at Patrick's work station once between her shifts and showed her some of the images that were on the memory disk. It wasn't his best work, and it was all raw, without any time spent cleaning up or enhancing at his own computer. Even so, he appreciated the compliment as much as the tone of absolute loyalty and certainty.

"Will you get to study only photography? Or do you have to do the regular school stuff, too?"

"A couple of classes, but mostly I'm done with all my academic requirements."

Her sigh was filled with longing. "I wish I could go to a dance academy."

He started to say something, but she shook her head, cutting him off. He knew her situation—even if she got a scholarship, her dad wouldn't let her go. "Well, at least you have Brighton," he said, lamely. "I can't believe you've been going to school just a few miles from me all this time."

"And now you're going to Boston." She cleared her throat. "I'll miss you."

"I probably wouldn't have applied if I'd known about you. There are excellent photography schools around LA, too."

"Really? Then why didn't you apply to those? Boston's all the way across the country."

He considered giving her his stock bullshit answer about how the Boston program was the most innovative, had the most variety of classes, offered him an amazing scholarship. And all of those reasons were true. They just weren't *the* reason.

And Kelsey deserved the truth.

"I want to get away from my family," he said simply.

"You do? But you love your parents. And you've said yourself your grandmother's amazing."

"She is. And I do. But—oh, hell. I want to be a photographer. More than that, I want to be a successful one. I don't want to be a starving artist. I want to make a real living."

Her brow furrowed. "But you—"

"What?" He snapped the word, then kicked himself when she flinched. But didn't she get it? After all the talks they'd had? All the time they'd spent together? "You think it doesn't matter because I have a trust fund? That I should just live on that and fund my business and not care if it never really earns a penny because what does it matter, I can pay my rent and buy my groceries?"

She crossed her arms over her chest, her expression somehow both stern and sympathetic. "Actually, I was going to say that being a success doesn't depend on where you go to school. You'll be a success even if you teach yourself. You're really talented, Wyatt. Of course, you're going to be amazing."

Everything that had been tightening up in him loosened again, and he basked for a moment in her complete faith in him. Then he kicked himself even harder for assuming that she'd been thinking the worst.

Frustrated, he ran his fingers through his hair. "Sorry. I didn't mean—it's just that it's hard trying to do anything in the arts around my family. My grandmother would want to set me up with a gallery on Rodeo Drive." He paused. "Should we sit in the car?"

She shook her head. "If my dad sees me in your car, he'll

have a fit. Out here, I can say you were asking me about working for the club. Member staff relations or some silliness like that."

"Well, sit on the hood if you want."

She laughed. "I'm fine, and you're changing the subject. Even if your grandmother did set you up with a gallery, it would only stay open if you're talented enough to keep the customers coming in. And you are."

"Except, I'd never know for sure. The circles my family runs in—they can afford to buy bullshit art, just for the social value of saying they own a Segel print."

"Maybe they really like what they buy."

"Maybe they do. But how do I know?" He shrugged, then thrust his hands deep into the pockets of his khaki shorts. "I want to earn it, Kelsey. I see my dad and all the attention he gets just from marrying in to the family. I know it bugs him. He's a CPA, and not even for the entertainment industry. But the paparazzi still hound him. And he feels like a fraud."

"How do you know?"

"Because he said so. Not to me, but I overheard him talking to my mom just the other day. About how nobody sees him for himself. And how my family all expect him to be larger than life. The way they are. He hates it. I mean, he loves my mom, but he hates that he's invisible. All the public sees is the name. Not him."

She nodded thoughtfully. "I get that."

"You're not invisible. I already told you."

"Not to you." Her smile filled him up. "But I understand where he's coming from. And you, too. You want to make a name in photography the same way I imagine dancing on the stage."

"You could do that, you know. Maybe not now," he added as she started to shake her head. "But after you graduate. Move out on your own."

"Maybe. I don't know."

He wanted to press the issue. To tell her that whatever weirdness her dad was holding onto about dancing and dating and anything else, she needed to just ignore it. He'd never even really met the man and he knew that Leonard Draper was sucking the life out of his daughter. He wanted to say all that—to tell her to not let anyone stop her from following her dream—but before he got the words out, she stepped forward and kissed him on the cheek.

"What was that for?" he asked, a little stunned, and very pleased.

"For *Swan Lake*."

He hesitated, because he knew that was her way of changing the subject. But in the end, he let it go. "You're welcome," he said. "And we'll both have to thank Joy."

"True." She laughed. "She's never going to let me forget this. She said you can pick me up at her house, and then after the show you can drop me back as late as you need to. She'll drive me home in the morning so that my dad can see her drop me off."

"And she won't blow your secret?"

"Never."

"Then it's a date."

"My first real date."

A wave of pride swelled inside him, and he swore to himself that not only was Friday night going to be memorable as a first date, it was going to rank for all time as her best date ever, even if he did only have two days to pull it off.

When Friday rolled around, he had to congratulate himself. He met her at Joy's in a Lincoln Town Car with a private driver, and he felt pretty damn sophisticated as he walked up the porch to get her. And then, when the front door opened and she stood there looking stunning and elegant in a simple black dress with a string of pearls, her luxurious hair curling softly around her face, he knew that he'd made the perfect decision.

So he really wasn't expecting her look of confusion, maybe even shock, when she saw the car.

"It'll be more fun," he explained as he led her toward the drive. "We can talk, we don't have to worry about parking, and I won't completely turn you off by cursing like a pirate once we hit LA traffic."

"Oh. I guess that makes sense," she said, even though the little furrow between her brows suggested it didn't make sense at all. "It's just—you know what? Never mind." She squeezed his hand. "I'm really looking forward to tonight."

"Me, too," he said, even though her odd behavior had taken a bite out of his enthusiasm. "Actually, wait," he said, because he really couldn't stand the not knowing. He took her arm and pulled her to a stop. "What's going on?"

She hesitated, then answered. "It's just that I thought you didn't like all of, well, *that* stuff." She waved her hand at the car. "Your grandmother's stuff, I mean. The drivers and the limos and all of the show."

He laughed, so relieved the sound just bubbled out of him. "I like it just fine. What I said was that I want to earn it."

"But—"

"And I did. I have family money, sure. But I also have my own account. I opened it when I was twelve and sold my first print at an art fair in Laguna Beach."

"You used the money you've been saving since you were a kid to rent us a car?" Her smile was so wide she could have advertised toothpaste.

"I want tonight to be special."

She took the arm he offered. "It already is."

And she was right. The night started perfect and only got better. She'd never seen a professionally performed live ballet, and he felt like a superhero, simply from being the guy who gave that to her. They didn't have time for dinner, but they drove through In-N-Out Burger, his favorite fast food place ever, and though he'd been worried that she'd think it was tacky, she was so obviously delighted that they were eating to-go hamburgers in the back of a Town Car that he grinned all the way to the theater.

Best of all, they shared a chocolate milkshake.

She was smart and funny and easy to be with, and the more time they spent together the more she came out of her shell. The only hitch in the entire evening was the rather minor point that he couldn't watch the ballet at all. He pretended to, sure. But mostly he just watched her. The way she moved. The way her dress hugged her body. He wanted to touch her so damn much. To kiss her softly so that he could hear how much she liked it. And then hard, because that's what he wanted. All these feelings inside him, this *need*. It was all because of her, and he was a walking, talking ball of lust with a hard-on, and he really wasn't sure how he was going to hide *that* from her.

He spent the last act of the ballet trying to distract himself by thinking about how he'd photograph the stage if he'd been hired to do the publicity shots. What film speed. What aperture. How he'd place the dancers in relation to the set. How he'd set up the lighting. And maybe he should use a filter to give it a magical quality.

The more he thought about it, the deeper he sank. And, thank God, the more he relaxed. So by the curtain call he could stand beside her and not risk complete and total mortification.

But oh, God, he wanted this girl.

"That was amazing." She took his hands. "*You're* amazing. Thank you."

They were in a semi-private box, and the two other couples filed out first. She started to head that direction, but he tugged her back. "Wait," he ordered when she arched a brow in question. "I still owe you something."

For a moment she looked confused. But when he stepped closer and slid his hand around her waist, her eyes grew wide. His palm rested against her lower back, and he could feel her heat and the little nervous tremble. "I owe you a kiss, remember?"

Her lips parted just a little, as if she was going to speak. But then she swallowed and simply nodded. He leaned in and brushed his lips over hers, a kiss as soft as breath, tentative and easy, because he knew it was her first. But when he heard her soft little moan of pleasure, it was like someone had thrown gasoline on a fire. Need exploded inside him, and he pulled her closer, until her body was flush against his, and her arms locked around his neck as if he was the only safe haven she knew.

With his free hand, he cupped her head, wanting more—everything—and when her lips parted and he deepened the kiss, his tongue tasting and teasing, he thought that if he died right then it didn't matter, because nothing could be more perfect than this.

When they finally broke the kiss, she was flushed and breathless and absolutely beautiful. "First kiss," he said, with a tease in his voice. "How'd you like it?"

"I'm not sure," she said, her words belied by the sparkle in her eye. "Maybe I need a second kiss to compare it to."

He was happy to comply, and gave her lots and lots of comparison kisses on the far-too-short ride back to LA. And when the car pulled up in front of Joy's house, her lips were swollen, her eyes bright, and her hair just a little disheveled.

She looked amazing. More than that, she made him feel amazing.

"Thank you," she said as the driver opened the door. "You showed me the world tonight," she added, and he was certain she wasn't only talking about the ballet.

He kissed her one more time on Joy's doorstep, and felt like the coolest guy in the world.

After that night, they became inseparable, but in an understated, quiet way. Neither of them wanted word to get back to her dad. So they were careful. Very careful. They walked together in the areas of the club that weren't well-trafficked. They spent a lot of time in their copse of trees, where he took photo after photo of her, until she'd hold up her hand and say that she wanted to talk to him, not a lens.

And there were kisses. Lots of kisses. The kind that were a promise of things to come. Things they both wanted, but certainly couldn't ever have. How could they, when they couldn't even go on a real date?

When the end came, he had no clue that he'd started walking down that path. On the contrary, he was actually looking forward to the future. Wondering how they'd make it work with him in Boston and her in LA. But he was sure they *would* make it work. That much he promised himself.

The night of Patrick's party, he knew that her parents were out of town, and he'd called her house and asked if she wanted to come. Just a bunch of kids from the club and a few from the town. It would be fun, he assured her.

"I'm watching Griffin tonight."

"I thought he was almost thirteen. He can't stay a few hours by himself?"

"It's just that—"

"What if I come over to your place?"

"And, what? Rely on Griff to keep a secret? He would—for me, he totally would—but he's just a kid and he might slip up. We've talked about that, Wyatt. Remember?"

"I know. I know. It's okay. I get it." He wanted to mean it, but he couldn't keep the disappointment out of his voice. "It's just that Patrick's family's house is huge. There'd be space for us to be alone, you know? Without feeling like we're in a spotlight at the club."

"I want that, too," she said, with so much sincerity in her voice that he felt like a heel for being irritated that she wouldn't come. "But even if babysitting wasn't part of the equation, should we really be seen together like that? At a party? I mean, we've been so careful. What if my dad—"

"It'll be crowded. Just a group of kids. Worst that happens is he finds out you left your brother for a few hours to go to a party with a bunch of teenagers. He doesn't need to know anything else."

Even as the words came out of his mouth, he couldn't believe he was saying them. Was he really encouraging her to break all those rules? Yeah, he was. Because he was a selfish asshole who wanted to see her. Just for a few hours. What was the harm?

And they had so little time left.

"The summer's almost over," he pointed out. "I'm gone in less than two weeks."

"Wyatt, please—"

"Just write down the address. I'm staying the night with Patrick, so you can come anytime if you change your mind, okay?"

She hesitated, but in the end she relented. "Okay. But I probably won't come."

He gave her the address. "And Kelsey? I'll be waiting."

"Don't count on me." Her whisper was so soft, he barely heard it, and when she ended the call, he felt a little lost.

"You fell hard, dude," Patrick said. "Is widdle Wyatt in wuv?"

Wyatt punched him in the arm. "You're a prick, you know that, right?"

"Bullshit. I'm a great guy. Everyone says so."

Wyatt laughed, but he couldn't get the question out of his head. It was the first time he'd really thought about it, and he knew with one hundred percent certainty that the answer was yes.

That ought to scare him, he thought, but it didn't. It made him feel great. And it made him want Kelsey beside him all the more.

Which, of course, made the party a complete bore, because he didn't want to be there without her.

He wandered the rooms aimlessly, chatting with some of the kids, drinking beer like it was water until the room was spinning just a little.

Which explained why when he first saw her by the big screen TV, he thought he was hallucinating. Then she walked toward him, holding a plastic cup like a good luck charm. She took a sip, then another. Then she downed the rest of the drink and finished crossing the room to him.

"Hi," she said, then kissed him, and from the bourbon on her breath, he had a feeling she'd downed more than the one glass when she'd been searching the house for him.

"Hi, yourself." He pushed back from her. "What happened to being discreet?"

She shrugged. "I missed you."

"Let's get out of the crowd." He took her hand. "Come on. I have something for you."

"Really?"

He led her to the guest room where Patrick had told him to throw his stuff, then shut the door. "You can sit," he said, pointing to the bed, since the room had no chair.

She made a funny little sound, but sat awkwardly on the bed, and he started to rummage through his duffel, finally coming up with the little silver-wrapped box he'd brought for her.

"For me?" she asked, when he handed it to her.

"Open it."

She licked her lips, then slid her finger under the tape and carefully removed the wrapping to reveal a square, white jewelry box.

"Go on," he urged, since she'd hesitated once again.

She did, pulling off the lid and then gasping when she saw the bracelet inside. It was a cuff-style, brushed silver bracelet that was shaped into the sign of infinity, a sideways figure eight. It gleamed in the dim light, and she ran her fingertip over it as if it was the most priceless thing she'd ever seen.

"I found it at this boutique when I was out with my grand-mother last weekend. I thought of you. And, you know, forever."

He would have felt silly saying the word, except it was so damn true.

"Forever," she whispered, then stood up and held it out for him to put on her wrist. He did, then drew his hand back, his fingertips grazing her skin until he closed his hand around hers and pulled her to him. He kissed her then, not asking, simply taking what he wanted. And unlike their first kiss in the theater, this one was wild and deep and familiar.

They'd shared many kisses since that first, and yet this one felt different. Richer. Fuller. Overflowing with promise, ripe with sensuality, laden with desire.

"Kelsey," he murmured when they broke apart, now joined only by their hands. "I want—"

"I know. But I—"

He shut her up with a kiss, not wanting to hear why he couldn't have her the way he wanted her. *All* of her.

He craved her. Needed her. Felt like he'd lose himself if he couldn't find his soul in hers. He was swimming in poetic non-sense that would have seemed sappy and stupid at any other time or with any other girl, but with Kelsey seemed as real and true as gravity.

And since he knew he'd never convince her with words, he set out to convince her with action. He touched her. Teased her. His hands roamed over her even as his mouth tasted. Her mouth, her ear, her neck. He cupped the back of her neck, his other hand finding her breast as his lips kissed down to the tiny bit of cleavage revealed by the simple sundress she wore.

Her heart was beating fast—he could feel it against his hand, against his lips. And he was so hard, so desperate for her. He'd wanted her from the first moment he'd seen her, then more and more with each minute he spent with her. She'd captured him completely, but he knew from the way she surrendered in his arms that she felt the same way. That she was ready.

But then she pushed away, and all of his hopes shattered like so much broken glass.

"Kelsey?"

She stepped back, breathing hard. "I want to—I do. But I can't. I shouldn't."

"You *should*," he insisted, even though he knew he was being a selfish prick. He should be telling her it was okay, it didn't matter. But he wanted. Oh, dear God, he *wanted*. "Kelsey, I love you."

The words escaped before he could think about them, and even though they were true, he hated himself for saying them. He didn't want to force her. Didn't want to use bullshit emotional blackmail. And he damn sure didn't want her to think he was saying pretty words just to get her in bed.

But that's what she thought—he was certain of it. Because she turned away to the back wall as soon as the words were out of his mouth.

Fuck. He'd done it. He'd gone and ruined the best thing ever.

He was in the process of brutally kicking his own ass when she faced him again, a fierce determination burning in her eyes.

And when she started to unbutton her sundress, all he could see was her. All he could imagine was the feel of her skin against his.

All he could think was that she loved him, too.

But he was an idiot, of course. A goddamn fool.

Because he didn't have the slightest clue that a night that looked like heaven was going to end up turning into hell.

10

I see him the moment I step outside the club. He's leaning against the side of a Lincoln Navigator, his arms crossed over his chest as he watches me. His hair is windswept, the gold shining under the yellow-tinted parking area lights, and from his posture it's obvious he's still wound up tight, as if he's on the verge of exploding.

As I get closer, I can see the irritation and impatience on his face as clearly as if it was stamped there. I know it's directed at me—and that knowledge kicks off a swarm of butterflies in my stomach, my reaction one of both anticipation and trepidation. Because even while I fear the explosion, I'm grateful for any reaction from him. This is the man who never looked back, after all, whereas I spent years mourning his loss.

And, while his attack on Drunk Dude may have mortified me, I can't deny that it excited me, too.

What I'm not certain about is why exactly he's annoyed. Is it because of my dance? Or is it because he's getting tired of waiting in the parking lot for me?

The latter wouldn't surprise me. The truth is, I did take my time coming out. In fact, I'd considered staying until the final girls danced, not only because I was in the mood to aggravate Wyatt, but also because I wanted that money.

Based on the chatter backstage as I was changing and packing up my stuff, I know I was in the lead by a huge margin. And everyone was speculating who would end up winning if I actually followed Wyatt out of the building. Because that's one of the rules. The winner has to be present.

But here I am outside.

Here I am, walking away from what I'm guesstimating is at least a grand, probably a little more.

And for what? I don't even know if he's going to hire me. Or if he's going to apologize for smacking down that drunk and embarrassing me, much less ordering me outside like I'm a recalcitrant teenager.

I pick up my pace, my speed increasing along with my irritation. As I approach, he stands up straight. His mouth moves, as if he's going to speak, but I don't let him. Instead, I poke him in the chest with my index finger. "You owe me a grand," I say. "Probably more, but I'll settle for a thousand. In cash. Tonight."

I expect him to laugh. Or at least to ask me what the hell I'm talking about. Instead, he reaches up and folds his hand around mine. His palm is warm, and though this isn't an intimate touch, my stupid, traitorous hormones are reacting as if it were. As if we were the old Kelsey and Wyatt, holding hands on the far side of the golf course where no one could see us, least of all my father.

Roughly, I wrench my hand from his. "A grand," I repeat.

"Get in the car," he says.

I tilt my head, then cross my arms over my chest. His eyes follow my movements, and as I watch, the corner of his mouth lifts, and that tiny movement softens his expression. I feel my skin heat, because I wasn't expecting him to so overtly check out my breasts.

Then my blush deepens, as I realize he's not checking me out at all. Instead, he's reading my T-shirt.

"Dance like nobody's watching," he reads, then looks at my face with the kind of intensity I remember only too well. The kind that sends shivers through me. "Is that what you were doing in there?" he asks. "Dancing for yourself?"

I force my feet to stay planted on the asphalt. I want to run from the heat I see in his eyes. Because it's dangerous, I know it is. And yet I need him, and if I run, I'll only be hurting my brother.

I draw a breath, fix my eyes on an illuminated gas station sign shining somewhere behind him, and say very softly, "No."

"Look at me, Kelsey."

I do, my jaw set as I force myself to maintain eye contact.

"Tell me," he says.

"You know the answer." I'm proud that I've managed to disguise the tremor in my voice. "This was an audition, wasn't it? Who do you think I was dancing for?"

His throat moves as he swallows. "Get in the car."

"Pay me."

"I haven't hired you yet."

"A grand," I say, circling back to my original demand. "We both know I would have won. And we both know that you messed that up for me."

I cross my arms again, and this time I'm determined not to be waylaid by whatever he says next. He surprises me, though, by not saying anything at all. Instead, he reaches into his back pocket, pulls out his wallet, and peels off ten hundred dollar bills.

"Right," I say, because I'd actually forgotten how casual money must be in his family. "Chump change to you."

I expect a sarcastic reply, but he simply extends the bills. I reach for them, and as I pull the cash away, his hand closes over mine, the money held tight between our two palms. "I pay my debts, Kelsey," he says. "Always."

I'm unnerved, but I'm not sure if it's because of his touch, his words, or the tone of his voice. Whatever it is, I tug my hand free, and this time he lets the bills come with me. I quickly shove them into my purse, the clatter of an adding machine filling my head.

Only fourteen thousand more to go.

The thought hits me like a surgical strike, pulling me back to reality. And the reality is that I need a lot of money. A *lot* of money.

That thousand he shafted me out of isn't the prize I care about, and I shove the bills back at him. "Actually, forget the grand. I want the job." I nod toward the club. "I think I proved myself."

"Is that what you think?"

I stiffen, unnerved by the sharpness of his voice, a steely blade cutting right through any past—any connection—we may still have. "You saw me dance," I say defensively. "You know I can strike a pose. You know I can look alluring." I swallow, my cheeks burning. "And you know I can strip down and not turn away from the camera—or from the eyes behind it."

His expression hardens. "And if I was looking for a woman willing to flaunt her tits so some poor slob can fantasize that she'll take him home and fuck him like a porn star, then you'd totally land the job."

Without even thinking about it, I reach out and slap his face.

Then that same hand flies to my mouth to cover my own gasp of surprise. I cringe and step back, certain there will be retribution. That he's going to grab my shoulders. That he's going to slam me against the side of the car and demand I apologize.

He does none of that.

Instead, the stiffness leaves his body, and he draws in air as he drags the fingers of both hands through his hair. "Oh, hell, Kelsey. I'm sorry. That was a shitty thing to say."

I'm so surprised by the admission that I take a step toward him, and the irony is that I want to make *him* feel better.

"It's okay, really. And I don't think your work is sleazy or anything like that. That's not why I wanted you to see me dance here." I don't have to work to make my words convincing. Whatever else is going on between us, I would never lie about the impact of those spectacular, provocative photos. "Your work—Wyatt, those pictures are incredible. They're honest and real, and the women you've photographed are . . ."

I trail off with a shrug, because how can I say that I want to be like them. "Maybe I shouldn't have done this. But you made me so angry. All I really wanted was for you to see that I can handle the job."

"And you thought this would convince me?"

"Well, um, yeah."

"Hmm." He starts to circle me, and I instinctively step away, protecting my blindside by putting his gigantic SUV behind me.

"You can dance, but I'm not hiring a dancer." His words are low, almost as if he's talking to himself. But his eyes are on me with every word. "Still, you have the look I want. The persona, too. And you damn sure have the attitude."

"Like I said, I can do this."

"You definitely proved that you can push past your comfort zone. I'll even go so far as to say that not only are you absolutely fucking perfect for my show, but that no other model has come close."

There's a sharpness to his words. An anger. One that I'm certain has roots going back twelve years.

"But here's the thing." He stops circling me and instead comes straight toward me. I inch backward until my rear bumps the cool metal of the door. "So what if all those things are true? So what if you're perfect? Because even with all that going for you, how can I trust that you'll see it through? I only have a few weeks to wrap this up, and I can't be wrong. So you tell me, Kelsey. How can I trust you? How can I be certain that you won't bolt midway into the shoot? That you won't leave me hanging?"

That you won't break my heart?

He doesn't say that last out loud, but I hear the words clearly in my head. I swallow the knot in my throat and blink rapidly, trying to stave off a flood of tears. I messed so much up. So many people, so many lives, and all because I reached for more than I should have.

And maybe I should stop pushing and just walk away. I'll get the money somehow. If I have to, I can sell my Mustang, although it would kill me to do that. After all, Griffin painstakingly rebuilt it for me, and it would just hurt him all over again if I parted with it. Even if I was selling it to help him.

But walking away isn't an option. Not anymore. Now it's not just about me. It's about Wyatt, too. About everything he's been saying.

He needs me.

Maybe I can never make up for the way I hurt him twelve years ago. But I can help him now. And while that may not be everything, at least it's something.

"I won't run," I promise. "I don't know how to make you trust me. All I can do is tell you I mean it and hope that you believe me."

His eyes bore into me, as if he's trying to read the truth on my soul. Then he rolls his neck and starts pacing in front of me, his body as tense as a wild cat about to spring.

But even though that's the impression I have, I still gasp when he does exactly that, lunging toward me and caging me against the side of the Navigator, his arms on either side of mine. His body dangerously close.

"Why?" he asks.

His mouth is so close that his breath warms me, and the scent of whisky is strong enough to be intoxicating. For the first time, I wonder how long he was in the club before I noticed him. Did he sit at a table and drink while the other girls danced? Did he enjoy them? Or was he there only for me?

"Answer me," he demands, the heat in his words pulling me from my thoughts.

"I told you. I need the money. Please, Wyatt. Let me go."

"Why?"

"You're making me feel claustrophobic." That's a lie. I feel uncomfortable, yes. But not like that. What bothers me is the way my body is reacting to him. The way that, despite everything, I want him to lean in just a little closer.

"I meant, why do you need the money?"

"Oh." Bitter mortification sweeps over me. "That's really none of your business." I lever myself away from the car, as if I'm going to shove past him. "You want to get out of my way?"

He uses his whole body to push me back, so that now I'm completely flat against the car, and he's pressed against me, body to body. I feel my pulse kick up, and I have to clench my fists in order to fight the unwelcome urge to lean my head forward and kiss him.

"You're making it my business," he says, lifting one hand off the car so that he can run a lock of my hair through his fingers. "Tell me, Kelsey. Why did you walk through my door? What kind of trouble are you in that you need money so fast?"

"I just do. What does it matter why? I need fifteen thousand, and I need it before the end of the month."

"So that's all this is about?" His fingertip traces the curve of my ear, and I can't hide the shiver that cuts through me.

"That tickles," I say, as if that's all I'm reacting to. As if his touch isn't really affecting me at all.

"It's just about the cash?" He shifts his touch from my ear to my collarbone, exposed by the V-neck tee I'm wearing. "You're not looking for publicity?"

"Publicity? For what? Why would I—"

"I could lend you the money," he continues, putting his hand back on the car so that I'm fully caged once again.

"You won't," I counter. "And I wouldn't take it if you did. I don't want to be in anyone's debt, much less yours."

"Why not mine?"

I meet his eyes dead on. "Because you hate me."

He flinches, and for a moment he's completely silent. Then he slowly takes his hands off the Navigator and steps back, freeing me.

"I don't hate you, Kelsey. It would probably be easier if I did."

"Oh." I glance down so he can't see the tears that prick my eyes. I blink, then draw a breath to steady myself. Only when I'm sure I've got it together do I look back up at him. "Does that mean you're giving me the job?"

He exhales. Loudly. "Fine. You want the job? It's yours." He takes another step back and looks me up and down. "We start tonight."

I push away from the car, then stand rigid. "Tonight!"

"You have somewhere else to be?"

"I—no. Tonight it is."

He nods, apparently pleased with my acquiescence. "I can't be wrong about this, Kelsey. So I have some conditions, and they're non-negotiable. You don't want to comply, you walk away now. Is that clear?"

I nod firmly, hoping I look more certain than I feel.

"You saw the prints at the studio. The nature of my photos. They're not porn, and they're not snapshots from a strip club," he adds, aiming his thumb toward X-tasy. "But there is an edge to them. A raw sensuality I'm trying to convey. Do you get that?"

Once again, I simply nod.

"And that means I need you to wear what I tell you and pose how I direct. Agreed?"

"Of course," I say, a little confused. Because how else would this go down?

"Good. You have to do what I say, Kelsey. Like I said, that's non-negotiable."

"Well, yeah. Isn't that pretty obvious? I mean—"

"In front of the camera," he interrupts. "And in my bed."

I gape at him. "You're joking."

"I assure you I'm not."

"But . . . why?" I don't know what else to ask. More than that, I don't know what to think, what to feel. I know I should slap his face and storm off, but somehow, I can't quite manage.

"Why?" he repeats. "You already know why." He takes a single step closer. "I'm punishing you, Kelsey. Exactly like you said in my studio earlier today.

"I'm punishing you," he repeats, as I stand there mute and confused. "But you can still walk away if you want to. I'm leaving this entirely in your hands. You know my conditions. Now ask yourself what you want. And then ask yourself how much you want it."

He walks to the driver's side, opens the door, then pauses before sliding in. "I'll be in the studio. You've got one hour to make up your mind."

Then he slams the door and starts the car, and I'm left standing like an idiot in the parking lot wondering what just happened—and what on earth I'm going to do next.

11

Twelve years ago

Wyatt watched her, his body tightening with a combination of excitement and nerves, as she continued to unbutton the dress. The style reminded him of one of his grandmother's old movies, with a fitted bodice, a narrow waist, and a skirt that flared.

It suited Kelsey perfectly. Sweetly feminine, but with a definite allure. But right then, what Wyatt liked most of all was how the buttons went all the way from cleavage to hem. Because, holy shit, watching her fingers move over each of the flower-shaped buttons was like watching his most anticipated Christmas present unwrap itself.

Her fingers were at her waist now, so that the bodice of the dress parted in a way that made his jeans feel too tight. She wore a plain white bra that was just about the sexiest thing he'd ever seen, and that included all the lacy bras—and Photoshopped models—in the Victoria's Secret catalog.

But what really made his mouth go dry was the moment when she reached the button at the hem. Because that's when she parted the dress, revealing her perfect dancer's body in that unassuming bra and matching cotton panties.

"You're amazing," he whispered, as she let the dress fall to the floor, then crossed her arms, as if trying to hide. He moved closer, and he could hear the way her breath stuttered as he gently took her wrists and drew her arms away from her body.

She made a little whimpering sound, and he leaned in, quieting her with a kiss. He was afraid she'd be too nervous, but the moment his lips touched hers, he could feel the fire in her. She opened her mouth to him, letting him explore and taste her. And when she tugged her arm free of his grip and slid her hand around to cup the back of his neck, he knew that he'd won her completely.

He kissed her, long and deep, his hands on her shoulders and back as he held her close to him, the pressure of her body against his driving him absolutely completely crazy. "Kelsey." Her name was so sweet. He never wanted to stop saying it. "Kelsey, please."

"I—" She cut herself off with a little swallowing sound, and for a moment he thought his heart had stopped. Then she nodded, and Wyatt knew that it wasn't just Christmas, but also his birthday and Valentine's Day and every other holiday all rolled up together.

"You're perfect," he whispered, as he reached around to unfasten her bra. He felt her stiffen, but then relax as he stroked her skin, sliding the strap down her arm and then pulling the bra free.

He let it drop from his fingers as he reached up to cup her breast, thrilled by the way she moaned and pressed herself into his palm. "Wyatt," she whispered. "I want to, really. But I'm not—"

He couldn't bear to hear the words, and so he closed his mouth against hers again, persuading her with his touch rather than words. He wanted her to melt into him, to let him touch her and explore her. To feel the power that came with making her crazy.

And, yeah, he wanted to be her first.

"Please," he said. "Kelsey, you know we both want to."

She clung to him, her sweet body soft and warm against his, and he stroked her skin, hardly believing that this absolutely perfect girl was in his arms. "Okay," she said, and he about ripped his shirt to pieces trying to get it off in a hurry.

He toed off his shoes and peeled off his jeans, then took her hand and led her to the bed. He kept his briefs on. He was so damn hard he was afraid if he took them off he'd come right then, and he really, really didn't want that.

He slid onto the bed, then held out a hand for her to join him. She did, her breath coming fast, her skin flushed. She was spread out beside him, propped up on her elbow as he ran a fingertip over her, wanting to explore every inch of her. Wanting to take his time.

But damned if he could manage. The moment she whispered, "Kiss me," he was lost. He closed his mouth over hers, and he cupped his hand on her breast, then slipped it lower and lower until he found the band of those panties. He slipped his fingers inside, then almost exploded when he felt how incredibly wet she was. And then almost lost it again when she moaned and spread her legs, her hips arching up as if in demand.

He broke the kiss, wanting to see her face, and she nodded at him. "Please," she said. "I want to."

He swallowed, suddenly nervous, then pushed his briefs down, freeing his cock. She glanced down, then bit her lip.

"I'll try not to let it hurt."

"It's okay. I know it will. Do you have a condom?"

"Yeah. Oh, yeah." He scrambled off the bed and got one, then put it on while she watched. Then he met her eyes, and she nodded. *Slow*, he reminded himself. And he tried. But she was so responsive. So soft. But when he couldn't hold back anymore, she cried out, begging for him to stop, and he felt like a complete jerk.

He started to pull out, but she put her hand on his back. "No.

Oh, please, no. Just give me a second." And so he stayed still until she told him to move, and this time, she moved with him, and then he went and blew his wad, and made it end all too soon.

"I'm sorry," he whispered. "I didn't—you're just—oh, hell. I just wanted you too much."

"It was wonderful," she assured him. "Can we do it again?"

He grinned, and told her they could. And since he needed a little time, he spent it kissing every inch of her, until he was hard as stone and she was so, so ready.

They did it once more after that, then she curled up in his arms and they talked for a while.

"Are you thirsty?" he asked after a few moments. "I can get us something."

"My hero," she said. "I could drink a gallon of soda."

"Anything you want." He hurried to pull on his jeans and shirt, then slipped out the door, looking back at her once before closing it behind him and heading downstairs.

Since he'd forgotten to ask what she wanted, he grabbed a Diet Coke and a Sprite Zero from the giant ice chest on the back porch. He was about to go back inside when Patrick waylaid him.

"Where've you been? Grace has been looking for you."

"Then it's good that you couldn't find me."

Patrick rolled his eyes. "You might as well ask her out again. She's still got it bad for you, and it's not like you're seeing anyone else."

"True," he said, because even though it seemed like he was with Kelsey constantly, they'd tried to be less than obvious so that her father wouldn't find out. "But I don't have it bad for her."

Patrick cocked his head, and Wyatt felt like a bug under a microscope. "Is this about the landscape guy's daughter?"

"What are you talking about?" Wyatt asked, but at the same time he was kicking himself because he sounded so damn guilty. Apparently, he'd make a lousy spy.

"Just a guess. Is she here? Is that why you've been hiding?"

"Don't be an ass."

"In other words, you're just really thirsty." Patrick grinned as he nodded toward the soda cans.

"I'd flip you off, but my hands are full."

"Whatever, dude. Have fun hanging out in your room by yourself."

Wyatt rolled his eyes. And then, because it was worth it, he tucked the second soda under his arm to free his hand, then thrust his middle finger in the air.

"Rude," Patrick said, then laughed.

Wyatt laughed, too, and he was still grinning as he climbed the stairs back to the guest room. He tapped on the door, and was surprised when it swung open a few inches. Well, damn, he'd probably forgotten to shut it all the way, which was a total dick move, since she was undressed and in bed.

Idiot.

"Hey, sorry it took so long," he said, as he slid inside, and this time closed the door firmly behind him. He glanced toward the bed, expecting that she'd still be under the covers. But the bed was empty. And, he noticed, her clothes were gone.

What the hell?

The room had an attached bath, and the door was cracked open. The light was on, though, so he hurried that way, a ball of chiseled stone now rolling around in his stomach. "Kelsey?" He peeked his head in, then pushed the door the rest of the way open.

She wasn't there, either.

Seriously. What the hell?

Panic welled inside him, and he hurried from the room, almost running over one of the guys he recognized from the club. "Did you see a girl? She was in here earlier. Do you know where she went?"

"Dark hair? Pretty? She hauled ass out of here about five

minutes ago." He whistled. "Her dress was still half unbuttoned. What? You two have a fight or something?"

"Or something," Wyatt murmured, his panic giving way to confusion. And, yeah, to an increasingly growing anger.

Had she really run out on him? Why the hell would she have run out on him?

But she had. Less than five minutes later he was certain of it. At least four people had seen her flee the house, and two of them said her eyes were red and swollen.

He'd left her alone, and she'd started crying, probably mortified by what they'd done. She was such an innocent, and maybe he'd pushed her. Pressured her when she wanted to say no.

He'd been an ass. A bastard. A complete loser.

And because he wasn't man enough to wait until he was certain that she was really and truly ready, he'd not only broken her, he'd lost her.

Fuck.

For days, he tried calling her, but she never answered or called back. He wanted to drive by her house, but he didn't know where it was, and by the time he got someone at the club to look at her father's records and give him the address, the place was vacant.

"Yeah, my dad was pretty pissed," Patrick told him. "I guess old man Draper was lining up another gig, and didn't bother to tell anyone. Just waited until the last minute and flew the coop."

"That doesn't make any sense. He already had a job lined up in LA after the summer. You told me so."

Patrick shrugged. "Maybe they needed him early. Or maybe that was bullshit. All I know is he split."

That sucked, but if it was the same job, at least he was in LA. And Kelsey would be with him. He could drive down and see her before he moved to Boston. He had to find her. Had to see her. Had to know what the hell had happened.

Had to apologize for pushing her.

Except try as he might, he couldn't reach her. And when he tried calling again a couple of days later, figuring that you could never grovel too much, the message said the phone number was unassigned. Which meant she'd turned it in and gotten a new number.

It really made no sense, and he wanted to talk it over with his dad. But he and Wyatt's mom had gone to LA for the premiere of his mom's latest film. Even though Wyatt usually blew that stuff off, this time he was lonely for his parents. So he sat in the media room and watched the coverage of the premiere on one of the entertainment channels.

His mom looked incredible in a form-fitting sequined dress, and his father looked dashing in a tux. At the same time, though, he couldn't help but feel sorry for his dad, who was practically getting shoved aside so they could talk to Lorelei and take pictures with her and the muscled up action star who'd just signed on to play the lead in his mom's next movie, a family drama that the actor surely hoped would make him look like an Oscar contender, and get him off the spy-and-car-chase hamster wheel.

One asshole reporter even went so far as to ask Carlton Royce to step out of the shot, because he was just the husband. And from the angle of the camera covering the channel Wyatt was watching, he could see both fury and hurt flash across his father's Ivy League features.

Wyatt grimaced, then clicked off the television as soon as his parents disappeared into the theater. He considered calling Jenna for advice, but his sister was eleven years older than him, busy twenty-seven hours per day, and would just tell him that if the girl wasn't answering his messages, then he needed to take the hint and leave her the fuck alone.

Since he really didn't need to hear that, he decided that he'd wait another day or two. After all, things could only get better.

At least, that's what he thought.

When he went to the club the next morning to get in a few laps and burn off some of his nervous energy, he learned just how wrong he'd been.

"I always knew she was a little slut, but I never thought she'd take me seriously." The voice belonged to Grace, and even though the last thing in the world he wanted was to get back on Grace's radar, he couldn't stop himself from eavesdropping.

She was perched on the edge of a chaise lounge, leaning forward as she talked animatedly with Marsha and another girl he didn't recognize. She glanced up as he settled into a chair to eat some pancakes and try to get his mind off Kelsey by reading a mystery. As he settled in, he thought Grace smiled at him. But when she didn't look his way again, he decided that she'd simply been looking his direction, but hadn't actually noticed him.

"So what did you say?" Marsha asked.

"I told her it was a hundred bucks and our undying respect and devotion for any girl to bang a celebrity or celebrity spawn. Extra points if she managed it first."

"You're serious?" Marsha asked. "This is like a real thing?"

"Oh, please. Sleeping with the stars is the *only* thing. You want status anywhere in SoCal, then you either need to *be* a celeb or be screwing one."

"Have you?"

Grace giggled as her hand flew to her chest, Southern Belle style. "A lady never kisses and tells. But it's so much more fun not to be a lady. Of course, I have. My point is that I didn't think she would."

"How'd she even know? I mean, she cleans tables." Marsha's nose wrinkled.

"She overheard me and Amy talking," Grace said, nodding to the blonde pixie.

Amy nodded. "She was wiping down a table, but I could tell she was listening to us."

"She came up to me later," Grace said. "She was all shy at first, just saying how nice it must be to be a member and how she hated being invisible because, you know, she was *staff*."

Wyatt's stomach clenched as he recalled his conversations with Kelsey about how she felt invisible, and how even though celebrity was a pain, at least people noticed him.

"She wanted to hang with me. Asked if I wanted to go to a movie after work or something." Grace raised a shoulder. "I told her I really couldn't, and she asked if there was anything she could do to change my mind."

"What did you say?" Marsha asked.

"Well, I said I couldn't think of a thing, but she kept pestering me, so I told her about the contest. I guess she thought it was a good idea. I mean, you heard about what happened at Patrick's party, right?"

"No!" Marsha leaned in closer. "What happened?"

"She fucked Wyatt Segel!"

Amy and Marsha's eyes went wide. "Seriously?"

"Mmm-hmm." Once again, Wyatt thought that she glanced his way, but he couldn't be sure. And he looked down at his pancakes before she clued in that he was listening. "I met her on the stairs as she was leaving. Came flying down. Said that she was in now, and wanted to know if she got a trophy. Honestly, I was too shocked to answer. I just watched her race out the front door. I guess little Miss Young and Innocent was too embarrassed to stay with him after she banged him."

"He's sitting right there." Amy's low whisper was barely audible.

"Oh, shit," Grace said, though she didn't sound too perturbed. "Do you think he heard me?"

"He's not looking," Marsha said. "And there's a book by his plate. I don't think he heard a thing."

"Oh." Grace paused. "Well, that's good, then. We should go. I reserved a court for nine."

They stood up *en masse* and headed through the gate, their continuing chatter like so much noise in his head.

What the fuck?

What the horrible, awful, wretched, humiliating fuck?

He waited until he was sure they were gone, then he stood up, intending to leave. But he was too messed up to leave, so he sat back down again. Patrick saw him and started to walk toward him, but Wyatt waved him off, afraid that he'd fly into a rage if anyone came near. Or, worse, that he'd start crying like a baby.

She'd played him. She was just like all those girls his dad warned him about. The girls who only saw celebrity, but never saw him.

But no. Was she? Not Kelsey. Not really.

He couldn't believe it. He *wouldn't* believe it.

And yet all the evidence pointed that way. She'd disappeared on him. And she damn sure wasn't going out of her way to let him know where she was.

He closed his eyes and exhaled through his nose. He was seventeen years old and he was leaving for Boston in just over a week. He was practically an adult. And yet instead of handling this like a grown-up, all he wanted to do was have his mom hold him and his father tell him it was going to be okay.

Well, fuck it, then. He was just going to have to go to LA.

"I'm so glad," his mother said when he called to tell her he was driving down that morning. "We're stuck down here for at least three more days, and I was afraid we wouldn't have enough time together before you had to pack and head for Massachusetts."

"I'm just going to grab my backpack. I'll be there in time for a late lunch. Can we maybe go to Gladstones?" The Malibu restaurant was touristy, but he was in the mood to sit by the ocean.

"Why don't you go with your father, and we'll all three go somewhere tonight. I'm going to be stuck on the lot until tonight. The producers have notes." She sounded less than thrilled, and he supposed he understood that. She loved writing, but hated revising to please the corporate know-it-alls.

"Sure," he said, trying to sound like he didn't care. "Dad and I will just gossip about you."

"You do that. It'll be good for him. He's been in such a funk lately, and I hate that I've been so busy with work."

"He knows, Mom. But I'll entertain him. I'll drag him out for a walk or something."

"You're a good kid, Wyatt. Love you, baby."

"You, too, Mom."

He called his dad next, but there was no answer. He left a message, knowing his dad never answered the phone if he was reading or working on a client's spreadsheet. Then he went home, told his grandmother he was heading to LA for a couple of days, and hit the road.

He spent the drive trying not to think, and mostly managed that task by shoving a constant stream of CDs into the player. And whenever one of the songs touched on relationships or breaking up or broken hearts, he just pressed the button to pop to the next song.

By the time he reached their house in Beverly Hills, his mood had actually improved.

He left his car in the drive just past the gate, then walked to the front door. As far as Hollywood families went, the house was relatively small, but that was because his mom preferred cozy. Probably because she'd grown up in a mansion that required a map and a compass. They also didn't have live-in staff, though his mother kept a chef on call, and a housekeeper came in every morning when the house was occupied.

He entered through the kitchen, and saw the note from Tilda on the island outlining what she'd done and when she would be in the next day. "Hey, Dad! It's me," he called, as he punched in the code to deactivate the now-beeping alarm. "You busy?"

No answer, but sometimes his dad wore headphones while

he worked, and so Wyatt headed out of the kitchen and through the living area to the dark-paneled office that his father had claimed when his parents bought the house six years ago.

The door was shut, which was unusual, as Carlton usually kept it open when he was alone. Wyatt knocked twice, got no answer, and pushed the door open.

Or tried to. It moved about a half an inch, then stuck.

Annoyed, he shoved harder. The door gave, and he lost his footing and tumbled into the room, hitting his head on something in the process.

He broke his fall with his hands before twisting around to see what the hell had assaulted him.

His father's feet.

Immediately, he leapt up, the sound of his own scream ringing though the room.

He'd hit his head on his father's feet.

Carlton Royce had hanged himself.

Wyatt's father was dead. He was really dead.

And behind him, a white note was taped to the door, the words printed large with black marker.

I'm sorry. I couldn't take it anymore.

12

Wyatt looks up at me from where he's adjusting his camera on a tripod. It's aimed at a corner that's draped in white cloth and illuminated by lights of differing intensities.

The middle drape is long and flows out onto the ground, forming a silky floor upon which sits a four-poster bed, perfectly made with deep red linens and at least a half-dozen decorative pillows. A matching side table is next to the bed with two half-full wine glasses and a bottle beside it.

It looks like something from a high-end hotel suite. Actually, it looks like a honeymoon suite. It's a space made for romance, and my heart skips a beat as I look from it to the man behind the camera.

"You came."

I swallow. "Did you think I wouldn't?"

"Honestly, Kelsey, I didn't have a clue what you would do. I don't know you that well."

He says the words blandly, but I hear the anger buried inside, and I force myself to stand up straighter. It doesn't matter what he thinks. I'm only here for the job, after all. The more distance there is between us, the easier it will be to walk away once it's over and he pays me.

"Well, you didn't give me much of a choice. I need the money. So that means I put up with your demands." I try to mimic his tone, keeping my voice emotionless. But I can't help the way my eyes dart to the bed, or the small trill of excitement that shoots through me as I wonder what it is that he intends to have me do there.

Stop it, Kels, I order. *Don't even go there.*

I slide my hands into my pockets, wiping the sweat off my palms in the process. "So is that where you want me?" I tilt my head toward the bed, my voice as casual as I can make it.

I draw two breaths before he answers, and when he does he looks right at me, his gaze never wavering as he answers, "Yes," that simple word about as loaded and dangerous as a word can be.

For a moment, I'm lost in the past, remembering a time when there was nothing harsh between us. When it was just longing and sweetness, conversation and desire. When it was all new and full of possibility. When we hadn't hurt each other.

Before I hurt anyone at all.

I take a deep breath for courage and start to walk to the bed, but I stop when he holds up his hand. "Not yet." He steps back from the tripod and heads toward the far side of the room, indicating that I should follow him.

He's all business now. Any heat that might have been in his voice earlier has either vanished, or I was imagining it all along. "You need to understand what I'm doing. These images aren't for shock value any more than they're meant for some prurient purpose." As he speaks, he begins pulling the drapes off the covered images that line the walls. "I want to tell a story as much as I want to make a statement."

"What kind of statement?"

"About the strength of women. About beauty and sensuality. About how women are seen and how they see themselves. And," he adds, as he pulls off the last drape and looks directly at me, "about the freedom and power of acknowledging that sexual allure."

I bite my lower lip as I look back at the images. I'm not entirely sure I understand what he means by all that, but I know that I like the pictures. There's no shame on these walls. No fear inside these girls that they're being naughty. That they're breaking the rules.

Not one of them is hiding the secret fear that the universe will punish them because they've been so bold as to flaunt their sexuality. And looking at them, I can even believe it myself.

I want to believe it. And most of the time, I really do believe. But then my old fears seep into my mind. My father's voice telling me that bad girls get what they deserve. That being bad ruins everything. That it's like a curse. On me. On my family. On everyone I love.

I turn away, blinking rapidly to stop the tears that have begun to prick my eyes.

"Kelsey?"

I turn back, forcing a smile, hoping he can't see what I've been thinking. "It's wonderful. Truly. These images—I already told you how incredible the three I saw earlier are. Now that I've seen more, I'm even more impressed." I want to kick myself. I sound so formal. But I can't do what I want, which is to go to him and hold his hands and let him feel the truth inside me.

"I've grown up around some incredible women. And I've known women who melted my heart with a combination of sweetness and sensuality," he adds, turning away from the canvases to look at me. "I want to celebrate that. But the show's got an edge, too. I want to take the audience full circle. Because there are women who use sex as a weapon. And I want to show that, as well. Ultimately, it's all about the power of allure and seduction." His mouth tilts up into a smile. "I want to seduce the audience, Kelsey. And to do that right, I need you."

I nod. "That's what you keep saying. But, well—"

I lick my lips and try again. "How?" I ask, then cringe, realizing as the word passes my lips that I'm afraid he's going to answer in detailed, intimate fashion.

Wyatt, however, is in pure business mode as he indicates the photos on the walls. "All of these images are the prologue. A way for someone viewing the exhibit to become familiar with the theme. But you're the star attraction. One woman, one series of eight photos designed to explore the core theme while still playing to the overarching concept of the show. Innocence. Sensuality. Seduction. Eroticism. Debauchery. Confidence. All that and more."

I listen, entranced by the passion in his voice. The certainty of his vision. I can hear him in Santa Barbara all those years ago telling me that he intends to be a photographer, famous in his own right, and not because of his family. And from what I've seen of both the paintings and the man, I am certain this is the project that will launch him.

"It's why you're W. Royce," I murmur, speaking more to myself than to him.

"What?"

I shake my head. "Nothing. Except that I think it's going to be spectacular."

"So you understand?"

I glance around the room, taking in the photos and imagining how they will look in an actual gallery, the prints placed just so, with my images alongside them. "I think I get it," I say. "The idea at least. I'm not really sure what you have in mind for my pictures."

His mischievous smile reminds me of the old Wyatt, and when his dimple flashes my stomach flip-flops. "Don't worry," he says. "You will."

I nod, trying hard not to look nervous.

"There's more than just photos, though," he says casually. "For you, anyway."

I cross my arms and cock my head. "Yeah, I got that. Me in

your bed. Not exactly an acceptable hiring practice, but I made my decision and here I am, at your mercy."

He takes a step toward me, then another, his gaze raking over me as he walks, and making my body react in ways that I find both enticing and terrifying, all at the same time.

"I like the way that sounds," he says, the low timbre of his voice giving me chills. "And I fully intend to play our arrangement out to its full extent."

I swallow as perspiration beads on the back of my neck. I want to step back and give myself some distance, but I know he's trying to unnerve me, and I don't want to give him the satisfaction.

"Fine," I say. "Whatever. Right now just tell me what you meant when you said it wasn't only pictures for me."

He hesitates, as if trying to gauge my mood. Then he thrusts his hands out in illustration as he says, "Imagine a long hallway. Four pictures on either side, each of them you."

"Okay," I say. "But where are the others? These, I mean," indicating the photos that already surround us.

"In the antechamber. Visitors wander the chamber before entering the hall. The prologue, remember? That primes them. Then they enter the hall and see you."

"Photos of me. But you said it wasn't just photos."

"They walk down the corridor," he continues, doing exactly that. "And when they reach the end there's a curtain. Semi-transparent. Intricately lit. There's a stage behind it. And that's where you'll be. The woman from the photos, come alive. Posed and provocative, confident and calm."

"I—what? But I thought the show would be permanent at the gallery. How am I supposed to—"

"Just for the opening. In fact, just for part of the opening. Then you can leave the stage and we'll use a video projection."

He turns to face me, and I can see that his mind is whirring, visions of how to bring this show off racing through his head. "What do you think?"

"I—" I shake my head, trying to take all this in. "I think I'm a little overwhelmed."

He laughs, then nods. "Right. Sorry. I've been living this project for almost two years now. I get a little carried away."

"That's okay. I like it." The words escape before I can think about them, surprising both of us. He meets my eyes, his own narrowed with thought.

"I call the show *A Woman In Mind*."

I consider that, then smile. "I like that, too." I lift my hands and make air quotes. "W. Royce presents, *A Woman In Mind*. Did the idea start with a particular woman?"

"It did," he says slowly, sounding a little surprised that I asked.

"I thought maybe. You'd mentioned strong women earlier, and I know you're close to your grandmother. And goodness knows her story is amazing. I can't really imagine a more confident woman."

"I didn't think you knew that much about her. You told me back then you'd seen her movies, but—"

He cuts himself off, and I realize that we haven't really talked about "back then" at all.

"I've been reading about the Golden Age of Hollywood," I say to fill the awkward silence. "Because, you know. I live here, and I love classic movies." Mentally I kick myself. I had no intention of revealing that I'd gone on a spree twelve years ago, reading all about his grandmother and her movies. As if somehow that could bring Wyatt back to me, even if only in my fantasies. "What's the big deal?"

"Nothing. Not a big deal at all. And no. She's an inspiration, of course. But she's not the woman I imagined."

I wait for him to say more, but he doesn't continue. And for some reason, I don't want to ask. I think maybe I'm afraid of the answer.

"Right," he says after a moment. He rubs his hands together. "I guess we should get started."

"It's almost two in the morning," I protest. "You were really serious about starting tonight?"

He indicates the bed. "I see you there, spread out and sleepy. Consider it method acting."

"Sleepy?" I lift a brow. "Doesn't sound very sexy."

"Trust me," he says. "And take off your clothes."

13

Wyatt almost laughed at the deer-in-the-headlights expression on Kelsey's face.

"Erotic photos, remember? Did you think they were all going to be lingerie and lace?"

She wrinkled her nose in a way that looked just a little too adorable. "Um, kinda."

He was torn between laughing at her naiveté and pulling her into his arms to reassure her.

He chose a middle ground, and kept his arms clamped firmly at his sides. Ever since she'd walked through his door, he'd been fighting the desire to touch her, to reassure her. Hell, to just fall back into old patterns and talk to her.

The bottom line? He missed her.

But what he missed was a fantasy. A Kelsey that she'd once projected as part of a teenage game. A sexual long con.

And even if there had been a tiny bit of the Kelsey he thought he knew hiding beneath the surface, he was certain that the years had hardened her. Any girl who could play the kind of games she'd played back then couldn't hang on to any thread of innocent sweetness.

He'd loved a girl who'd been smart and sweet and sensual and exciting. But that girl had never really existed. She was an illusion.

An illusion that had haunted him for years, and that he was now trying to recreate with his camera.

There. He'd said it.

Kelsey wasn't just a girl, she was The Girl. The one he'd always had in the back of his mind. The one he didn't even realize had been his inspiration until she'd walked through his door. All along, she'd been his muse, and he hadn't even known.

And now that she was here, beautiful and tempting and all grown up, he couldn't help but think that it had been a mistake to conjure her at all. Because she was too damn tempting, and it was taking all of his strength to harden his heart.

"You're serious?" she pressed. "That's how we're going to start this. I just drop my jeans and panties, rip off my shirt and bra, and then stand here on display for you? No easing into it? No letting me even get the feel of being in front of a camera?"

He considered saying yes, but she looked so damned perturbed that he took pity on her. He hooked his thumb toward a door on the far side of the room. "There should be a robe on the back of the door. Undress in there, put it on, come back out here." He glanced at his watch. "We really need to get started."

He could practically see the battle raging across her face. Argue or change. And he was almost disappointed when she tossed her head and marched silently to the bathroom.

He waited impatiently, then tried to look professionally bland when she emerged from the room in the fluffy, white robe that she'd cinched so tight it was a wonder she could breathe.

She lifted a brow in what was an obvious question, and he pointed to the bed in reply. She headed there, then climbed on. The four-poster was tall, and she sat on the edge, her feet swinging like a child, her discomfort obvious.

With any other model, he'd talk to her. Make her feel comfortable. Try to soothe her into the role.

He knew he should do that with Kelsey. After all, she was the model he wanted. And yet he couldn't quite make himself do it. Maybe tomorrow. Right now, he wanted to see her squirm. Petty, yes. But he'd meant it when he said he wanted to punish her. Hell, he'd wanted that for years. The desire to punish was almost as intense as the basic, unflinching desire to simply have her in his arms again.

But that was him thinking with his cock, not his head. Because Kelsey Draper was bad news. He'd learned that the hard way, and Wyatt wasn't the kind of guy who made the same mistake twice.

He had no intention of using the tripod to take these shots, and yet he bent over and fiddled with the height and angle anyway, just so he'd have something to do while he got his head together. Because as much as he hated to admit it, she was making him more than a little crazy. Even something as simple as seeing her sitting so perfectly straight with the oddest mixture of trepidation and anticipation coloring her expression. He looked at her, and he wasn't sure if he wanted to kiss her or spank her or both.

All he really knew was that he wanted answers.

But at the same time, he didn't want to open wounds that had healed long ago.

Except, of course, she'd opened them again simply by walking through his door.

Shit.

He changed his lens, then changed it back, then realized he couldn't procrastinate any longer. He took the camera off the tripod and went to kneel in front of the bed, taking a series of shots as he moved.

"Probably won't make it in the show," he said, feeling centered again now that he was seeing her through a lens, "but I like it. You look fresh. Innocent." He stood. "It's a study in contrasts," he added, then tilted his head down so he was speaking more to the camera than to her. "We both know that looks can be deceiving."

Even with his head down, he could see the way her hands tensed, clutching the mattress on either side of her. *Good.* They needed to acknowledge the elephant in the room. The way she'd deceived him. The brutal game she'd been playing. That bullshit Hollywood game. That goddamned fascination with celebrity.

That was the mindset that had killed his father. And she was a living, breathing reminder.

Not that he needed a reminder. Hell, his life was a reminder. Wasn't that the whole point? Why he was Wyatt Royce now, and not Wyatt Segel? Because he had to prove to his family what his father never could? That he was one of them, even without the name?

"Wyatt?

"Lay back," he ordered, gratified when she complied. But it wasn't quite right, and so he slung the camera over his shoulder, then crossed to the bed, his head tilted as he looked her up and down.

As he watched, she drew a breath, which turned into a yawn. "Is this boring you?"

"I'm tired," she snapped. "It's well past my bedtime."

"Good. Stretch out. Pretend you're about to sleep."

Her brow furrowed, as if she wasn't certain he was serious. Then she did as he commanded, scooting up and pulling the covers down.

He almost stopped her, but a sudden vision of her naked body entangled in a sheet stopped him. "That's good," he said, leaning over so he could toss the bedspread off. "But I need you to take the robe off."

She did, staying under the sheet the entire time she squirmed out of it, then dropped it on the floor beside the bed.

"You're still just a little too covered."

The thin, red sheet was all the way up to her chin, and she bit her lower lip, her body going perfectly rigid as he drew the sheet down, exposing her neck, then her shoulder, then her breasts. He let his fingers graze her skin as he did, telling himself he was only doing that so that he would drive her a little crazy. After all, this was about sensuality, and he wanted the image to show her arousal.

All of that was true, of course, but the bigger truth was that he wanted to touch her. He wanted to feel her heat, the way she shivered under his touch. Wanted to know that she was responding to him. That she wanted him.

"Good," he said, when she bit her lip so hard that it turned white, then turned her face away from his. Her cheeks were pink, and her nipples tight. Slowly, he reached down and cupped her breast, then felt himself grow hard when she gasped audibly.

He ran his thumb around her nipple, amused when she squeezed her eyes shut. But that amusement faded to something much more dangerous when she opened her eyes and met his full on, because the expression of longing he saw there just about slayed him.

"Is this punishment?" she asked, and he almost melted on the spot.

"I guess that's for you to say."

She licked her lips, and he felt the quickening of his pulse. "I thought you were going to take my picture."

"That's definitely on the agenda. But I need to set the stage first." He whispered the words in her ear even as he reached down with his other hand and slid the sheet back over her leg, his palm stroking her smooth skin until only a sliver of material covered her.

Then he stepped back and examined what he'd created—and he had to admit she was perfect.

She was on her side, her head resting on her bent arm. Her other arm was draped over the curve of her waist, just above the swell of her hip. A bit of rumpled sheet rested on her hip, a small section of which hung down to keep her modestly covered. But just barely. Her thigh was exposed, as was her calf, and he liked the fact that though she was essentially naked and facing him straight on, he couldn't tell if she was waxed. But only that one intimate area was covered, and that added a punch of allure to the overall composition.

"Just like that," he said, raising his camera, then moving slowly as he took a variety of shots from different angles and with different exposures. "Now slide the sheet all the way off and cover yourself with your hand. Actually," he amended. "Don't just cover yourself. Spread your legs and press your hands on your cunt. And close your eyes, Kelsey. I want to see you get off. I want to capture it."

He wasn't even trying to yank her chain—not anymore. She was so damned beautiful. So ripe and strong and alluring, and he wanted that shot. Knew it would be perfect. A woman alone, exploring her body. He had to capture it. Had to pull it into the show.

He was so sure of the perfection of the image that it took him a moment to realize that she'd frozen. He bit back a sigh of frustration, knowing damn well that he'd moved too fast. Whatever he'd told her about punishment, he didn't mean it. Not really. Not if it meant losing the shot.

"Sorry," he said, and watched as her eyes fluttered to his. "That was wrong of me."

"I don't have to pose like that?"

"Not now. I get that it's too much. We can work up to it. Tomorrow. Or even the next day."

"But you want it."

"Hell, yes. It'll be stunning. I mean, come look at what we got right now, and it's only the first day." He turned to the monitor he kept set up on the far side of the room, then looked back to make sure she was following.

His breath hitched as he watched her slip back into the robe and then hurry toward him, her cheeks beet red. "You see?" he said when she arrived.

He stepped aside so that she could see the monitor and the incredible, sensual images of her he'd managed to capture.

She drew in a breath, then whispered, ever so softly, "I'm sorry."

"Are you kidding? These pictures are amazing. And we can get more tomorrow. You're right. It is late." He shoved a hand into his pocket, feeling almost like a teenager again. "I'm sorry if I've been an ass." He wasn't entirely sorry, and he still didn't trust her. But he was absolutely certain that with her in front of the camera, he'd be able to blow this show out of the water.

"Wyatt," she began.

"It'll get easier as we go on."

"*Wyatt,*" she repeated. "I'm really sorry."

He froze. He just froze. "What exactly are you talking about?"

"I thought I could. But I was wrong. I—I'm so sorry. I didn't realize it would be like this."

"Like what?" he asked, but she just shook her head.

"I'm sorry," she repeated. "I just can't do it."

14

I'm a block away before the tears start, and I pull over, my hands tight around the steering wheel as my body shakes with the violent onslaught of my sobs.

I was a fool to think I could do this—that I could display myself like that. That I could be so free, so open, with any man, much less Wyatt. A man who has always broken through my defenses.

A man who used to treasure me, but now cares nothing for me.

Less than nothing, actually. He reviles me, and why shouldn't he? I'm the one who left, after all. I'm the one who walked away and never looked back. And even though I may have fantasized that he would find me and call me and rescue me, I've always known that was a wish that could never come true.

For one thing, why would he try after what I did?

For another, how would he have managed to find me?

I know that we were kids back then, but that doesn't change the fact that I hurt him anymore than it changes the fact that I loved him. I did.

But love didn't make a difference. I screwed up, and I destroyed everything.

I'd thought I could handle tonight. That the fact that I needed the money would give me the strength to make it okay. But it's not okay. Because when he touched me, everything rushed back to me. Infatuation. Desire. *Need*.

I wanted him.

But more than that, I wanted him to want me. Maybe I was shy. Maybe I was awkward. But I wasn't scared. I was turned on.

He barely touched me, and yet I craved so much more. His hands on me. His lips hot against my skin.

With each infinitesimal change in the position of that sheet, I fantasized about his hands moving intimately over my body, not simply to set up the shot, but for his pleasure. And for mine.

He was a man I couldn't have—a man who rightfully despised me—and yet I would have willingly slept with him tonight, then slinked away in the morning hating myself.

He'd tempted me on purpose, of course. But not because he felt anything for me. He'd already told me as much, hadn't he? This was my punishment, and he was an expert at inflicting it.

Or maybe he wasn't.

Because instead of being something to endure, the night was something to treasure. Yes, I was scared. But I was excited, too. Not just because of how he touched me, but because I was pushing myself. I was breaking out of that shell. Going a little wild in ways I hadn't let myself go in years. Or ever, really, except for that one time twelve years ago.

That felt good. Bold. Like I was a butterfly pushing out of my cocoon.

But then he took me to the monitor, and when I peered down at the digital image, the reality of what I was doing struck me. This was just like twelve years ago. A bad choice. A dangerous choice.

And as I gazed at the monitor and the stunning, vibrant image of a confident, sexual woman who had my face and body, all I could do was stand there as my father's voice rang through my head. *Everything I've done for you, and you still turn out to be a whore. Just like your mother. And you'll get the same as she did, too. You keep acting like this, and you just see what you get.*

I couldn't do it.

I hate myself for letting him down—for letting myself and Griffin down, too—but I just couldn't do it.

And I know—*I know*—that my father is wrong. That it doesn't really work that way. That the bad things that I do don't punish other people. That my mother's affair wasn't the reason that she and her boyfriend died in a car wreck.

I *know* that.

I even know that posing for Wyatt's pictures doesn't make me bad or wicked or any of the things my father would shout at me.

It doesn't, and I get that.

But knowing and believing aren't always the same thing. And maybe it's better sometimes to just avoid walking that line.

Besides, I've never had the best judgment where Wyatt is concerned. He's like a hurricane dropped in the middle of my neat, orderly life.

Too much stress. Too much mess.

I'm better off without him. And I can still figure out some way to get the money.

The money.

I wince as I think of Griffin. I need to see him. At the very least, I should tell him that I'm going to have to sell the Mustang. Except he'll try to talk me out of it, so maybe it's better to just stay quiet. If I tell him after the fact, at least it will be a done deal.

I wipe my tears, then start the car back up. Now that Griff's in my head, I want him near, and so instead of going home, I head for his apartment in Silver Lake. I know I'm being silly, but the truth is, I don't want to be alone.

Since he's surely asleep by now, I let myself in, then drop my purse on the coffee table. Like my place, it's small. Just your basic layout, with a living area that flows into the dining area that flows into a hall with a closet-sized bathroom at the end. Griffin's bedroom's on one side of the hall, an almost perfectly square room with minimal closet space, and there's an identical, mirror-image bedroom across from it that Griffin uses as a sound studio.

The kitchen is across from the little dining area, and I go there next, then grab one of the cans of cold brew coffee that my brother is addicted to. I'm about to pop the top when I realize how stupid that will be. With Wyatt on my mind, I'm going to have a hard enough time sleeping. Add caffeine to the mix, and I'll be staring at the walls all night.

Fine.

Alcohol it is.

I'm not a big drinker. The one time in my life I drank bourbon was the one time in my life I messed up royally. Which is why I swore off hard liquor when I was fifteen, even before I was legally allowed to drink the stuff.

Now my drink of choice is white wine, and I'm certain there's a bottle in the fridge, because Griff always keeps a bottle chilled for me.

I open the fridge, then blink at the bright light in contrast to the darkened room. I squint as I peer in, then find not only a lovely Chardonnay, but also a box of cupcakes from Love Bites, which is my absolute favorite bakery. It's also inconvenient, since it's all the way in Beverly Hills. Griff must have had a meeting. Usually, he avoids Beverly Hills like the plague, and when he does go, he treats himself. And me, by default.

I debate, decide Griffin won't care, and grab one with yellow frosting and decorative fondant flowers.

"Cupcake thief."

I yelp as the kitchen light snaps on, then turn to face my brother. He's wearing grey sweatpants that hang loose around his hips and a jersey Tee with a mock turtleneck. He's worn his midnight black hair long for years, and now it's hanging loose around his face in what I like to call his sexy, rocker style, with most of it combed to one side so that it forms a curtain over most of the right half of his face, accenting the vivid green of his uncovered, right eye.

Looking at him, I can almost imagine that I never ruined anything for him.

"Up, Kels?"

I shake my head, realizing I've been standing in front of the open fridge, just staring at him like an idiot.

"Sorry. It's late. I was spacing out." I grimace. "I didn't mean to wake you."

"You didn't," he assures me, even though he's yawning. "I've been editing. Lost track of time."

He yawns again, as if to accentuate the point, then rubs his palms over his face before raking his fingers through his hair. For just a moment, the thick strands are pulled back, revealing what had been partially hidden before. But of course it's never truly hidden, not even when his hair hangs down. Because how could something as simple as a fall of hair hide the massive scarring that mars the right side of his face and his decimated outer ear?

It's been twelve years, and the guilt still plagues me. And even though I'm used to the scars now, I don't think there's ever been a time when he's taken off his shirt or pulled his hair back when I don't silently beg the universe to make it all have been a very bad dream.

"I thought you were coming tomorrow after your Zumba class."

I shake myself, literally shaking off this damn melancholy mood as he studies my face.

"Yo. Sis. You going to tell me why you're here? Or do I have to start guessing?"

I hold up the evidence. "Cupcakes and wine. Why else?"

"You didn't get the job?"

I frown. I'd forgotten that I'd told him I was at an audition.

Our conversation before I danced at X-tasy seems a million years ago.

"Oh, hell," he says. He comes to me, and though I expect a hug, instead he reaches for the cupcake box. "Grab your wine," he orders. "I think we're going to need more than just cupcakes."

I laugh and do as he orders. Then we sit at the wobbly Formica table we found one Saturday at the Rose Bowl Flea Market. I get paper towels to use instead of plates, but I pull out a real wine glass for me and a highball glass for him. Nothing fancy—we both live in homes furnished and stocked by Ikea—but I draw the line at drinking wine from a paper cup.

"I'm really sorry," he says, once we're settled and he's scooped up a chunk of frosting with his finger. "I know you were the best dancer in that room."

"I was," I agree. I'm modest about a lot of things, but not about dancing.

"Then why didn't you get the job?"

I shrug. "Technically, I did. And then I lost it again."

He leans back in his chair, a clump of chocolate frosting in the corner of his mouth. "You wanna explain how that works?"

"Sometimes, it's not really about the dancing."

"So, what? The producers have some sort of agenda?"

"You could say that."

He licks off the chocolate, then leans forward. "Okay, spill. What aren't you telling me?"

"Probably a lot," I admit. "I haven't told you about the rash I got last week—it's all cleared up now, by the way. And I never told you that Mr. Kingman had an affair with that woman who's always volunteering in the library."

"The assistant principal at your school?"

"Yup." It's summer now, so this gossip really is old. I have over two months before I have to think about being a kinder-garten teacher again.

"That's all nice and juicy, but not really what I meant."

"I know." I smile brightly. "Do you want to record that part you called me about, or is it too late?"

"You're not going to tell me any more about the job, are you?"

"Nope."

"Don't you teach a dance class at eight? Can you leap around a room on less than five hours of sleep?"

"One, I don't need to leap around the room. It was a class of three-year-olds. And two, they cancelled the class. So my Friday mornings are now free and clear."

"They canceled it? Just like that?"

I grimace. "Welcome to my exciting, yet unstable world. Yeah, just like that. But it's okay. I've applied at a few other dance studios. There are plenty of kids out there. And even more moms who want them to dance."

"You need to audition for a show."

I sigh and push back from the table. We've had this talk a billion times, and I'm tired of it. "The scene. Come on. Let's go."

"Fine." He pushes back his chair, too, and stands. "But you know I'm right. You should be spending your summers dancing professionally, not teaching kids. For that matter, you should be dancing professionally all the time."

"I know, Griff. And when the nice talent scout plucks me out of obscurity, I'll do that. In the meantime, I figure steady work is a good thing. So let's go do this, okay? Because I still have lunch with Nia and then my second and third grade tap class after lunch, and then the Zumba class after that. I thought it might be fun to sleep a little, too."

"You'll sleep here," he says. "I'll take the couch."

"I'll sleep here," I agree. "But I'm not kicking you out of your bed."

"Okay."

"Really?" He never gives in that easily.

"We'll argue about it after we fix the scene. Come on."

The spare bedroom is packed to the gills with a variety of computers and sound equipment. There is, however, no bed. I sit at the makeshift table, an old door placed over two triangular frames. It works, though, providing enough room for us to sit close enough to play off each other, and yet far enough apart that our microphones can be adjusted so as to not get interference from the other person's dialogue.

Griff does all the adjustments and a sound check, and I fight the familiar swarm of butterflies that have suddenly taken up residence in my belly.

It's weird that I get so nervous. I'm never shy about dancing—not unless my dad is watching. But he and Tessa, my stepmother, have lived in the Atlanta area for almost ten years now, so I don't have to worry about that too much anymore.

But recording these podcasts? It gets me every time.

"You look green," Griffin says, passing me a bottle of water. "But not as green as last time. Another decade or so, and you'll be as comfortable in the studio as you are on stage."

"Jerk," I say affectionately. "There's something about acting with my voice that ties me up in knots. Honestly, I don't know how you do it."

As soon as I've said those words, I cringe inside. He does it because he feels like he has to. It's hard to be out in the world with his scars, especially the ones on his face. Of course, he swears he loves the work, but sometimes I wonder if he wouldn't love something else better. If he got herded into this career because of my bad choices.

"When are you going to launch?" I ask, rushing to change the subject.

"I'm hoping for sometime in the next two months."

"That long? You already have at least a dozen episodes recorded."

"I want to do this right. That means I need to have the whole first season recorded, edited and ready to air. If it's a flop, I don't want to leave my four fans floundering just because I've lost enthusiasm for a show that only four people listen to."

I roll my eyes. "It won't be a flop. It's going to a runaway success."

"Thank you, Nostradamus. And thank you again, because if you're right and it's a hit, then I owe you part of the credit."

"Yeah, well, that's me. A walking, talking inspiration for artists the world over." I smile, but the truth is that I'm thinking of Wyatt. Of that one sunset long ago when he took my picture under the canopy of a massive oak, and he swore that I was his muse.

"At least you have the easy part," Griffin deadpans. "Being the inspiration is a hell of a lot easier than doing the work."

"Hey!" I protest for form, but the truth is he's right. Years ago, I started giving him bedtime story prompts. I came up with a scarred boy who lived in the shadows of an imaginary town, and who grew into a detective who worked in the shadows, fighting for the innocent.

Not very original, I grant you, but I was only a kid trying to entertain her brother in the hospital. I'd set the stage, and he'd spin out most of it, with me taking over when his meds made him groggy.

Soon, we were telling the stories all day, letting the detective's adventures entertain us when another afternoon of bad television was too much to bear.

Now, of course, Griff's taken the original kernel of my story and run with it. His scripts are amazing, and Edmond—the hero, in a nod to *The Count of Monte Cristo*—is brilliant, scrappy, tortured, and honorable.

Griff's written at least five new episodes since the last time I recorded, and I flip through his story bible to see what's happened.

"Ha! I knew Detective Wilson was going to be suspicious."

"Yeah, you're very smart. You ready?"

I take a sip of white wine, then nod, and he switches the microphone on.

I don't notice it when we're not performing, but my brother has an amazing voice. Deep and melodic and sexy. And that's just another reason I think the podcast has a real chance of becoming something.

"You still need a name for the show," I tell him when we finish recording the first scene, and he's doing something with the soundboard.

"It's on the list, believe me. But it's a very long list."

"You need to be more organized." I spend my life making sure everything I do is set up eons in advance, with all the t's crossed and the i's dotted. But Griffin just goes with the flow. Sometimes that makes me jealous. Most of the time just thinking about it makes me crazy.

"Ready for the last bit?" he asks, then starts the recording and cues me when I nod. I dive into the words, giving it my all, which really isn't hard because the story's so good. And this is a particularly fun episode because I'm a detective who's giving Edmond grief, and even though I love my brother, that's a role I know how to play.

When we finally wrap and he shuts off the microphone, I actually applaud. "I don't know how you do it. I think each episode gets better."

"I guess I'm just swimming in talent," he says, and I roll my eyes. Not because he's exaggerating, but because it's true. And every time I think about that, it makes me a little sad. Because in Hollywood everything is about appearances, and I'm so very afraid that talent alone isn't enough.

"Any new gigs?" I ask.

"I'm recording an audiobook, which is fun. And I get to work from here, which is a plus. And we're going to start recording the tracks for the movie next week. That's going to be a blast. Not lucrative, but you can't have everything."

He's just been cast in an independent film as the adult voice for the kid who stars in the movie. It's not much money, but the exposure should be amazing.

"I did get my signing check," he adds. "That was handy. Paid off my last two therapy bills."

"I hate that you're always working toward a bill," I say. What I don't say is that I wish I could afford to pay for his physical therapy.

He shrugs. "It's the American way."

I scowl. I don't like talking about his scars and the nerve damage and all the medical mess that goes along with it. I wish I could wave a magic wand and make it all go away, but the only wand I have is the clinical protocol, and I just walked away from the money to pay for it.

"By the way, they called me about the first appointment for the Devinger Protocol," he says, referring to the protocol I was just thinking about. "You know you're the best sister ever, right?"

My insides tighten up, just like they always do when we talk about his treatments. "Don't say that."

"It's true." He crouches in front of where I'm still sitting, then takes my chin in his hand. He forces me to look him in the eye. "And you're amazing for getting me enrolled in that program."

I lift a shoulder and twist my head, freeing myself. I've already paid the first five thousand, which pretty much cleaned out my bank account. That was to hold his spot and cover the initial testing and evaluation. The fifteen I'm still trying to gather covers his full enrollment into phase one of the protocol. And, if the results are in line with expectations, he'll be invited into phase two for free, where we could expect even more dramatic improvement.

"I still can't believe you can afford it," he says.

"It's not that expensive," I lie. "The hard part was getting all the paperwork in." That wasn't a lie. It had been a nightmare getting all the signatures I needed so that I could get the records in order to submit the files. "Besides, I told you. I started a savings account for you back when you were twelve." That also isn't a lie. But what he doesn't know is that since I'd been a minor, my dad was on the account. And he cleaned it out without telling me the year I started college.

"Well, I think you're a goddess. A responsible, overly organized—but in a good way—goddess."

"OC Draper," I say, reciting Nia's name for me.

"Give her a hug for me tomorrow."

"Will do." For about five minutes when I was in college, I thought my brother and best friend might actually date. But they defied me by just becoming friends. Which is probably better, as I don't run the risk of weirdness if they were to break up.

Still, it bothers me. Mostly because Griffin never dates. But when I point that out to him, he always points right back at me.

"Different reasons," I always counter.

"Bullshit," he says. "I don't like the way women look at me. You just don't want to be seen. Same issue, different sides. At least you can blame Dad and his fucked up version of morality and Karma or whatever the hell ridiculous philosophy he used to keep you and Mom in line. All I can blame is my mirror and my ego."

And me, I think. *You can blame me.*

Except he never does.

But I blame myself enough for the both of us.

15

Twelve years ago

Kelsey tapped the eraser of her pencil on the pad of paper by the kitchen phone. She'd scribbled the address down because Wyatt had told her to, but she knew she couldn't go to the party. How could she when her parents had told her she had to watch Griffin?

Which was ridiculous, really, because she'd been watching him since she was eleven and he was nine. Now he was twelve—practically thirteen!—and old enough to watch himself. But she *still* had to watch him?

It was unfair.

But then again, she was starting to realize how many things about her life were unfair.

"We're going to watch a movie later, right?" Griff shouted as he bounded down the stairs.

"I guess."

He skidded to a stop in front of her. The house had hardwood floors and his favorite thing when their parents were out was to skate on the floor in his socks. "What's wrong?"

"Nothing." She forced a smile. Then she ripped off the paper with the address and tucked it in the pocket of her jeans. "I was just trying to remember if we have any popcorn in the house."

He rolled his eyes. "Seriously?"

"Oh, come on, Griff."

His eyes went wide. "What's wrong with you?"

"Nothing. I'm just—nothing." She forced a smile. "If we're not having popcorn with the movie, then what are we having?"

"Well, not with the movie, but the last time Mom and Dad went out, we talked about doing marshmallows over the fire pit and making s'mores."

"Yeah, but not tonight." All she wanted was to watch one of his stupid action movies so that she could either stare mindlessly at the screen or fall asleep. Either way it would take her mind off the fact that she was trapped in this house, away from Wyatt, and that she was never in her whole life going to get to do anything she really wanted to do.

"What's wrong with tonight?" Griffin demanded.

"Oh, come *on*," she snapped. "I said no. Give it a rest. Now, do you want popcorn or not?"

"Jeez. What bug crawled up your butt?"

She aimed her most fierce scowl at him, and he held up his hands in surrender.

"Sorry! But I mean, honestly, Kels. You never want to do anything fun."

And that, she thought, was the absolute last straw. She *always* wanted to do something fun. She was just never allowed to.

"You know what? You watch whatever you want, okay? I'm gonna go out for a little bit."

"You're leaving me alone?"

"For crying out loud, Griffin. You don't need a babysitter. You're just a few months away from thirteen. But Mom and Dad think you're a baby, and they don't want me to go out."

"I'm not a baby."

"That's what I'm saying. And I'm going out. You won't tell?"

"What about the movie? And the s'mores?"

"You can watch a movie without me. And we'll do the marshmallow and fire pit thing some other time. We don't have any chocolate or graham crackers anyway, so s'mores weren't really on the agenda."

"When?"

"When what?"

"When is some other time?"

"Some. Other. Time."

He stared her down. "I'm going to tell Mom and Dad."

"You are not."

He deflated, all his bluster sliding out of him. "I'm not. You know I'd never tattle. But I really wanted to do the marshmallow thing."

"How about I buy some chocolate and graham crackers tomorrow? We'll keep them in the pantry for the next time Mom and Dad go out."

"Who knows when that will be," he said grumpily.

"Come on, Griff. Please?"

"Okay. Fine. Where are you going, anyway?"

"There's a party. And I got invited."

"Oooh." He made kissing noises. "What's his name?"

"Wyatt, and shut up."

"Wyatt kissy-face. Smooch, smooch."

Her cheeks positively burned. "You are such a turd."

He smiled, showing off his newly straightened teeth, just two weeks out of braces. "Sorry. Couldn't resist. Go on. I'll be good."

She hesitated, because now that everything seemed to be working out and she was really facing the prospect of going out, she was having second thoughts.

"What?" her brother demanded, going to the fridge, opening it, and then staring inside while all the cold air escaped.

She walked over and shut the door. "Maybe I shouldn't go."

"Oh, please. I'm not a baby. You said so yourself. And you'll be home before Mom and Dad, right?"

"Well, duh. Otherwise they'll know I went out."

"Then what's the big deal?"

"You're right." *That* wasn't something she said often. She loved her brother, but he could be a real pain in the butt. "Okay, but here." She scribbled another number on the pad, ripped the page off, and handed it to him.

"Should I memorize it and then eat it?"

She rolled her eyes. "I don't know the number at the party. So that's Wyatt's cell phone." She wished she had a cell, but her parents thought they were too expensive to get for the kids.

"Is he picking you up?"

"I'm walking. It's only a few blocks away." Just a few more months and she could get her driver's license, but tonight she was hoofing it.

She hurried upstairs to change into a sundress and sandals, then rushed back downstairs, told Griff goodbye, and headed out the door. She realized after a block that she'd forgotten to pull the address out of her jeans, but it didn't matter. She knew where Patrick lived. She'd gone with her dad once when he'd met with Patrick's dad to talk about doing some residential landscaping work.

As she walked, she let her mind wander. Or, more accurately, she let fantasies fill her head. That Wyatt would kiss her again. That they'd find a quiet corner where she could curl up next to him and get lost in those wonderful kisses—and maybe even more.

Except she didn't really want more.

Or maybe she did. He'd kissed her in the back of the car when they'd returned from the concert, and she'd definitely wanted more then. And, honestly, *kissing* didn't really describe it. It was more like making out.

Actually, it *was* making out. She bit the tip of her thumb as she remembered, glad that she still had a few more blocks to walk so that hopefully she'd stop blushing by the time she got to the party.

She'd been embarrassed at first, but then Wyatt had pressed a button, and an opaque glass barrier suddenly appeared, blocking their view of the driver. And, she assumed, vice-versa.

She'd almost asked Wyatt about that, just to be sure, but then he was kissing her and she realized she didn't care anymore, especially when he'd pulled her onto his lap and his arms had gone around her. That was when she'd stopped caring about anything except the way his body felt against hers and the wonderful things his hands were doing, and the way his mouth felt against hers.

Her blood had pounded through her that night. In her ears. In her chest. Between her legs.

She'd felt lost. Needy. And at the same time, she hadn't felt lost at all, because Wyatt was there. And the only thing she'd needed was him.

Now, all she knew was that she wanted more.

She quickened her step, anxious to get to the party—and to him.

Of course, when she did arrive, she was a total nervous wreck. Which was why when someone handed her a glass in the kitchen with an inch of golden liquid, she drank it down without hesitation, even though her mouth tingled from both the taste and the burn.

But she liked the way it made her feel. A little buzzed. A little more confident. And so when the guy asked her if she wanted another, she said yes. It made her head spin, but it also gave her courage. And, thus armed, she went out into the house to find the boy she was looking for.

It didn't take her long. She was standing by a giant flat screen TV when something inside her seemed to shift and she knew that he must be watching her. She looked around and realized she was right. And after a sip for courage—then the rest of the glass for good luck—she marched across the room, said hi, and kissed him. Long and hard and deep.

It was a blur, but he led her to a room with a bed. And even though she was terrified, she knew the moment she sat on that mattress that she wanted everything. Whatever he was willing to give, she would take like a beggar.

She hadn't thought he would start with a gift, but when she opened the box and saw the stunning silver bracelet in the shape of infinity, she thought her heart would burst. That she couldn't cram any more feelings inside her.

But then she was in his arms, and she knew how wrong she was. There was room for more. So much room.

And when he said he loved her, she believed him completely. More than that, she knew that she loved him too.

He wanted more than just kisses—that much she also knew. But the truth was, so did she.

Except she *shouldn't* want it. She knew that. She needed to say no and walk away. Heck, she needed to run. And all the way home, too, before she did something stupid.

She needed to rescue herself because her dad wasn't there and she was on the verge of doing something she shouldn't.

Something forbidden.

Something she wanted so very, very much.

She stood, and for a moment she was torn between staying and bolting. Then she looked at Wyatt, and all her fears fizzled away. *Wyatt.* How could she run from him?

She had no idea how she worked up the courage, but she stood. And once she was on her feet, and she was looking at where he still sat on the bed, there was no question anymore. Of course she was staying. How could she not when she was his?

With trembling hands, she unbuttoned her dress, becoming bolder when she saw the way he was looking at her.

And then he touched her, and it was all a sweet blur. His

hands on her. Touching her. Murmuring sweet words to her. She wanted it to last forever ... and at the same time, she wanted more, too.

She was scared, yeah. But she wanted it, too. And the want increased the more he touched her, until she knew for sure that this was it, and Wyatt was the one.

It hurt, but she'd expected it to. But he was sweet and gentle and the hurt faded soon enough. And then it was nice. Really, really nice. She didn't have an orgasm, but she'd read enough in books to know that was normal. And she also realized that it didn't much matter. Because she felt amazing without one. Just being beside him was incredible.

So incredible, actually, that they did it again.

She hugged the pillow close, sighing deeply as Wyatt stroked her hair. He'd made her feel so special. Like she was a princess. Like she was the most wonderful thing he'd ever seen.

For a while, they just looked at each other. So long, in fact, that she finally started to laugh. Which made him laugh, too.

"We should probably get up and go back to the party."

"Do we have to?" She didn't care about the party. All she wanted was to stay curled up next to him.

His lips curved down as he considered. "Actually, no. This is my room for the night. We can stay as long as you want."

"Really?" According to the clock on the bedside table, it was just past nine. Her parents had gone all the way into Los Angeles, and weren't due back until after midnight. "That sounds like heaven."

"Yeah?" He grinned. "But what on earth are we going to do?"

He kissed her again, and she was pretty sure that her toes caught on fire. When he broke the kiss, she rolled over, looked up at the ceiling, and sighed. "Wow."

"The only bad thing about staying in here is that there's nothing to drink except water." He nodded toward the bathroom. "Are you thirsty? I can get us something."

"My hero." She sat up, holding the sheet up over her chest. "I could drink a gallon of soda."

"Anything you want." He slid off the bed and pulled his clothes back on. It was probably rude to watch, but he was just so perfect. And he really liked her. *Her.* Honestly, it was more than perfect.

"Back in a few," he said, then winked at her before he slipped out the door. She fell back against the pillows, then pulled one over her face so that she could scream with joy and no one could hear.

She heard the door open and she tossed the pillow aside, surprised he'd made it back so quickly.

Except it wasn't Wyatt. It was her father.

She sat up, the sheet held tight against her as she scurried back until she hit the wall and couldn't go any further.

He stood in the doorway, the paper on which she'd written the address clutched tight in his hand. His eyes wide. His face red with anger.

"You little whore." He didn't shout. Didn't raise his voice at all. And somehow, that made it all the worse. "Get your clothes on and get outside. *Now.*"

"Daddy, I—"

"Shut your filthy mouth. And get to the car. Your brother's in the hospital. And it's all your fault."

All her fault.

He only said it once, but she heard it over and over as she threw on her clothes. As she raced out of the house to the front door, tears streaming down her face. As she sat curled up on the back of the car as they raced to the LA area burn center where her brother had been admitted after being airlifted all the way from Santa Barbara.

She stood there, her hands pressed against the glass as she looked at him, deep in a drugged sleep, his body mangled, his skin raw or completely burned off. She couldn't even go in the room. Couldn't tell him she was sorry. No visitors were allowed behind the glass. Not with the fourth-degree burns on his back and the side of his face. Not with the risk of infection.

Hour after hour, day after day, she watched him, wishing that she'd never left the house. That she'd never taken Wyatt's call.

Because her father was right. She'd done something very bad, and her baby brother was being punished for it.

She knew that. Deep down in her gut, she knew it was true.

Most of all, she knew that she'd never forgive herself.

16

"She walked out?" Lyle asked. "Right in the middle of the shoot?" He glanced sideways at Wyatt, breathing hard.

"Pretty much." They'd been jogging along the beach for almost half an hour, and at first the morning air had been invigorating. Now, though, Wyatt was starting to drag. He'd been up all night, and his lack of sleep was slowing him down.

That and the fact that he was worried about the project. Siobhan had called that morning to tell him that Roger Jensen, an arts and leisure columnist with the *Pacific Shore Examiner*, a glossy magazine that mixed legitimate news with tabloid gossip, was hounding her for an advance image from the show. "I told him no, but you might want to consider it. His column in the *Examiner* blog goes viral all the time. And the extra publicity would be nice."

"Forget it," he'd said. "No advance images. You know my rules."

"I do. But it's my job to run these things by you. It's also my job to check on you," she added, then asked for an update on his hunt for the perfect girl. Wyatt considered dodging the question, but Siobhan was a friend, and she was in this show as deep as he was.

"Found her," he admitted. "And then I lost her."

"Well, that's not good," Siobhan said. And when Wyatt agreed with that insightful assessment, she'd suggested that Cass could be the It Girl.

"Cass is stunning," Wyatt agreed. "But she's not the girl."

"Like I said, this close to the show, you can't be picky about *the* girl. You just need *a* girl. Pretty. Sexy. Photogenic. And one who doesn't bolt."

"Maybe," he'd said, knowing that he was running out of options. But also knowing that Cass was his last option. And Kelsey was his first.

And there weren't any other options in between.

Lyle had been jogging a few feet ahead, but now he slowed until they were pacing each other. "I thought you said this girl needed the money. Why'd she up and leave?"

"There's a slight possibility it had something to do with me being a complete and total prick."

"You?" He turned and jogged backwards so he was facing Wyatt. "I'm shocked."

"Fuck you. And if you trip and fall on your ass, I'm going to take a picture and send that shit to Instagram."

Lyle flipped him the bird, but turned back around. "If I ask how you were a prick are you going to kick sand in my face?"

"Let's just say I gave her a rough time. I convinced myself she had an agenda. Or that she was playing some kind of head game with me. Or that she figured the job would earn her some sort of golden key to open the door to Hollywood."

"Seriously? You thought she was messing with you because of who you are?"

"Don't act surprised. I know you get that shit, too," he added. "More than me, I'd think. The non-Hollywood grandson isn't nearly as interesting as an actual movie star."

Lyle grimaced. "Yeah, lately I've got a wide range of options for female companionship. More than I want, that's for damn sure."

"You don't say." Wyatt's voice dripped with irony. After several years on a hit sitcom, Lyle Tarpin's star had gone supernova when he starred in two movies that turned out to be box office sensations. That's one of the reasons they were out for a jog—because Lyle had just signed onto an established action franchise, and the director wanted him in prime shape.

"I'm living on kale and hard boiled eggs," Lyle had complained the other day. "And people think Hollywood is all about the glamour."

"Anybody special among those options?" Wyatt asked now.

"Not a chance. Besides, we've known each other for what? Two years now? You know I don't date."

"Not even Rip?" Wyatt asked, referring to Lyle's former TV co-star.

"Seriously? Come on, man. You of all people should know better than to listen to rumors," Lyle said. "Besides, I'm not gay. And even if I was, that asshole would be the last guy I'd fuck."

"Fair enough." Wyatt remembered the buzz back when the show was hot and the costars were feuding. "Just be careful. All that female attention you've been getting? It's just going to get more intense. You're on a fast trajectory, my friend."

Wyatt had no idea why he was advising Lyle. God knew Wyatt had no special insight into women. He wasn't in the habit of kicking women out of his bed, true, but neither had he dated anyone special in, well, ever. At least not since he'd been an adult. And the one woman who'd piqued his interest was a woman he not only didn't trust, but one he'd managed to scare off.

Not a stellar record, all things considered.

"I'm fine," Lyle assured him. "I'm just focusing on work right now."

That sounded perfectly reasonable, but Wyatt couldn't shake the feeling his friend was holding something back.

"You still haven't answered me," Lyle continued before Wyatt could press the point. "Why did you think this girl—Kelsey, right?—had an agenda?"

"Are you asking me about now, or about twelve years ago? Actually, hang on," he added, coming to a halt and bending over with his hands on his knees. Lyle didn't exactly stop, but at least he stayed by Wyatt, jogging in place.

Wyatt had to admire his stamina.

"Let's start with twelve years ago," Lyle said, and Wyatt relayed what he'd overheard from Grace. A conversation he could recite in perfect, morbid detail.

"Okay, I get that you were pissed. I would be, too. But she was a kid. Did you seriously think she was doing the same thing now? Not fucking you for points, obviously. But for a job or access or some such bullshit? I mean, how would being in with you or your family even help her? You said she's, what? A kindergarten teacher?"

"And a dancer," Wyatt said.

"Even so. You do remember that your family is in the movies, right? It's not like they own a dance troupe."

"Funny. But my mom's working on that film adaptation. You know, the musical that won the Tony last year. Maybe she thought that working with me could get her an in."

"Sounds dubious to me."

"Maybe, but struggling actors and dancers will try anything. It's a fact of this business. My dad sure as hell saw it." He glanced at Lyle. "You'll see it, too."

"I will," Lyle said. "But that doesn't mean everybody's got an angle. And listen, buddy, about your dad—"

"What?" The word came out harder than Wyatt had intended. He'd never told anyone about his father's death, or the things his dad had said before. No one, that is, until Lyle.

They'd been out drinking one night, and Lyle had told him a few things about his life back in Iowa, before he'd moved to

LA at sixteen. Not much, but enough for Wyatt to realize that Lyle'd had a shitty time of it, too. And when he complained that night about how ninety percent of the people he was meeting in town only cared about what his fame could do for them, Wyatt had shared his own sob story.

He'd thought he'd regret it afterwards, but he hadn't. He had only a handful of close friends, and he was glad to count Lyle among them.

That didn't, however, mean he wanted to talk about it now. A fact that Lyle obviously realized, since his shoulders drooped a bit.

"It's just that I know it's hard. Losing someone, I mean." His voice cracked with genuine emotion. "And you want to honor who they were, especially if you loved them. But that doesn't mean death made them right about things."

"You want to try talking in English? Because right now, this is gibberish."

"I only mean that just because your dad said that your family didn't value him, and that no one gave a flip about him except through your family, doesn't mean it was really true. And even if it was, that doesn't mean it's true for you." Lyle wiped the back of his neck with his towel as he stopped jogging. Then he dropped it on the beach and sat on it. "Or for Kelsey."

Wyatt took a second, then sat, too. He didn't answer; he just looked out over the ocean as he thought of Kelsey, a woman he really shouldn't want, but couldn't get out of his head.

The truth was, he'd never wanted to believe that she was only interested in his connection to Hollywood. He sure as hell hadn't believed it that summer, not during all the time they'd been secretly dating. But that didn't mean that his father's words weren't fresh in his head. And when he'd found his dad's body on the very day that he'd overheard Grace spewing her venom—

Well, he'd been angry.

Angry and, maybe, a little stupid.

He tilted his head back, looking up at clear blue California sky as he remembered Kelsey's words from just the other day. *"When I left, you didn't even try to come after me."*

She'd surprised him with that accusation. Because if she'd really been playing him, then how could he possibly have hurt her?

And the fact is, her claim wasn't entirely true, anyway. A few weeks later, after he was settled in Boston and had cooled down and his father's funeral was behind him, he *had* tried to find her. Tried, but failed.

First, he'd tried contacting her school. But she'd transferred, and the administration office either didn't know where she'd gone or wasn't willing to tell.

He'd had no luck by following her dad, either. Patrick managed to find out where Leonard Draper had gone to work after the club, but when Wyatt tried to reach him there, he learned that the man had never shown up.

All of which had made him think that maybe there was something bigger going on. A family thing. An emergency. Something.

But then Grace's words returned to haunt him. Because even if there had been an emergency, wouldn't Kelsey have at least called him? But she didn't. She'd run out of the party, and she'd never looked back.

At first he'd been afraid that he'd pressured her. But then, once he heard Grace, he'd believed that Kelsey had played him. And that painful conclusion had settled deep into his gut, then rotted there for twelve long years.

He'd been an ass.

He'd believed Grace over his heart. Because he'd *seen* Kelsey. He knew her, inside and out.

And he knew damn well that the only time she wanted a spotlight was when she was dancing.

So why had he listened to rumors instead of his own heart? His own head?

Because he'd been an insecure teenager.

So what did that make him now? An insecure man?

He sighed, then turned back to Lyle. "She messes with my head. She always has. And when she walked into my studio, part of me wanted to kick her out even while another part wanted to kiss her senseless."

He picked up a handful of sand, then let it spill out through his fingers. "She got under my skin twelve years ago, and she's stayed there."

"Because she pissed you off? Or because she hurt you?"

Wyatt cocked his head. "Why does it matter?"

"Pissed off is anger, and you can be angry at anyone. You don't have to care about the guy who cuts you off when you're trying to make a left turn, right?" He opened his water bottle and took a long swallow. "But hurt—well, if you don't care about someone, they can't hurt you."

"Then it was both," he said. And maybe that was the problem. He'd been angry at her for so long. But she'd hurt him, too. So deeply it had scarred his heart.

And ever since she'd come back into his life, he'd been walking a line. Wanting to punish her for the past. And for the present, too. For the way she was messing with his head.

But at the same time, he needed her for the show.

And damned if all of that mixed together didn't scare her right out of his studio.

"I need her back," he said flatly, then turned and looked at his friend. "I don't trust her—not completely—but I need her."

"So get her back. She still needs the money, right?"

"As far as I know."

Lyle nodded. "That's one thing in your favor. Have you called her?"

"Three times. She hasn't called me back."

"What about going by where she works? She left a resume, right?"

"Actually, no. Just a headshot and her phone number. But I know she teaches kindergarten and dance."

Lyle cocked his head. "How do you know that?"

"I saw her in the Beverly Center a few years ago, and so I did some digging. My friend Ryan's good at finding information. He tracked her down to an elementary school. It was summer, though, so only the administration office was open. They wouldn't give me her address, but they told me she taught dance during the summer to little kids and gave me the name of the studio."

"And?"

"And I went, but she didn't work there anymore. They didn't know where she'd gone."

"So you went back to Ryan," Lyle guessed.

"Actually, I gave up. She's the one who moved back to LA. She knew how to find me. But she didn't. So I decided I just needed to let it go."

"Right," Lyle said. "And how's that working out for you?"

Wyatt scowled, and Lyle laughed.

"Well, don't worry. It's a small town. And Evelyn will be at the party tonight," he added, referring to his agent. "Between her and your grandmother, they know everyone in the business. Don't worry. Someone will convince her not to dodge you."

Wyatt laughed bitterly. "Yeah, but that's only half the trick. Once we do, I have to convince her to come back."

Too bad he didn't have a clue how to do that.

17

"I get why you walked out on him," Nia says as she stabs a fork into her Cobb salad with no avocado, no cheese, no egg, no bacon, and no dressing. "But you do realize that you were also walking out on fifteen large?"

"Sixteen," I say, then grimace. "Wyatt offered to pay what would have been my winnings from the strip club, but I told him to keep his money."

She flashes one of her superior looks, the kind that only a woman as perfectly sculpted as Nia can pull off. "Did you lose your common sense in your sofa cushions? What is wrong with you?"

"He makes me frazzled," I admit, because there really is no other explanation. "He always has."

She reaches across the table and stabs three of my French fries with her fork.

"Hey!" I protest. "If you're hungry, try eating a salad with actual food in it."

"I have a bikini shoot coming up. I'm dieting."

I stare pointedly at the fries.

"That's not a cheat. It's my carb load for the day."

I consider suggesting we check *her* sofa cushions, but decide it really isn't worth it. Instead, I shove four fries in my mouth, just to make sure I get a few before she decides to load up a bit more.

"I still can't believe that W. Royce is your Wyatt."

"He's not *my* Wyatt," I say, making air quotes. "And I couldn't believe it, either."

"I don't get why you bolted. I mean, come on, Kels. You killed it at a strip club. *A strip club.* So I think you're ready for prime time."

I jab another fry into some ketchup. "Maybe. But I'm not sure I'm ready for Wyatt. He—"

"What?"

How do I explain it? That certainty that once I open the Wyatt door, I'll push through it at full force. I know that Nia will say that's a good thing, but it's not. That's a scary thing. And I liked the feel of his hands on me a little too much.

He's dangerous, that man. My heart already broke once over him. I'm not sure I could survive a second time.

"Kelsey?"

"He just scares me," I say, then wait for her lecture. Except it doesn't come. Instead, she just looks at me a little sadly and takes another bite of her pathetic, naked salad.

"And that's not the only reason," I rush to add, because suddenly it seems as if protecting my heart is a stupid reason that I have to justify. "It may be summer break, but I have a job. As a kindergarten teacher, you might recall. I can't pose like that. Once the school gets wind of it, I'll be out of work in a heartbeat."

I teach at a public school, and the district is pretty conservative. Even if it weren't, though, erotic kindergarten teacher photos just wouldn't fly. If the school didn't fire me, the parents would make my life miserable.

I can tell from Nia's face that this point resonates with her. "The photos were really that racy?"

"Even you couldn't imagine these photos," I say dryly, to which she raises her eyebrows with interest.

"That seals it, then. Whether you're in it or not, we're going to the premiere."

"Nia!"

"I'm just trying to lighten the mood." She pushes her half-eaten salad away and leans back. "Maybe you ought to do it anyway. I still say it would be good for you."

"No," I say firmly. "It wouldn't." I don't tell her that I thought that very thing last night, as I tossed and turned on Griff's bed, where he insisted I sleep despite my protests. I'd tell myself I could never pose like that, and especially not around Wyatt. Then I'd tell myself that the only thing in the world that I really wanted was to do exactly that. To feel for longer than a few short minutes the way I'd felt when he'd touched me last night.

In other words, I'm a mental mess, and I'm not even around the guy.

"Have you considered that you can see him but not pose for him?"

"You mean date him?" The idea makes my body warm in a positively lovely way. "I couldn't possibly."

Her gaze dips to my wrist. "Cool bracelet," she says, glancing at my silver cuff in the shape of infinity. "I don't think I've seen it before."

"Oh." I feel my cheeks burn, and I'm absolutely certain that Nia knows everything. "I've had it for a while."

"Uh-huh."

I slide my arm back under the table, then use my other hand to sip my iced tea. I'd gone home to change after I woke up at Griffin's. But I don't know what possessed me to pull the bracelet out of the box of keepsakes I store on the top shelf of my closet, much less why I decided to wear it today.

Then again, maybe I do know. Because the bracelet is a reminder of something I want—but also something I can't have.

Nia's eyes go from the bracelet to mine. "You want to tell me again why you can't possibly date the guy?"

"Dammit, Nia," I snap, and she laughs.

"*Tsk-tsk*. Language, Kelsey."

I sink back in the booth. "You're pushing my buttons."

"Too bad you want them pushed by someone else."

I glare, but otherwise ignore her smug expression and sing-song voice.

"I'm just saying."

"Fine," I snap. "You win. I'm not going to date him for a lot of reasons. Not the least of which is because he's not interested in me. He's still holding a grudge. All he wants to do is punish me. He said so himself."

"Oh, please. He said he wanted to punish you, and then he got you all hot and bothered? No. Trust me. He wants you. He's pissed at you, I'll buy that. But he wants you."

"Well, he can't have me, because there's still reason number two—he's not good for me."

"I'm not so sure about that, either," Nia says. "You're a mess today, I'll grant you that. But you're also kind of glowing."

"I am not." But I don't protest too much, because part of me knows she's right. Yes, I bolted. But the reason I did has a lot to do with the way he made me feel. Lit from the inside. *Alive.*

And, yeah, there might be a bit of a lingering afterglow.

But that really isn't the issue.

"Being with him isn't good for me," I repeat more firmly. "And it definitely isn't good for other people."

Her shoulders fall as she exhales, then reaches for my hand. "Sweetie, what happened to Griffin wasn't your fault."

"Yeah," I say, tugging my hand away. "It was."

"Fine. Whatever. I'm not going to argue about it anymore. You think it was your fault, then fine. Avoid Wyatt. But don't avoid life. You're wound up too tight, girlfriend. And you know your father's an ass—I know you know, because we've talked about it. You need to let go a little. Because if you don't, you're going to suffocate and die inside. You'll be walking and talking, but you'll just be a shell of Kelsey. You know I'm right, even if you won't admit it out loud."

I blink back a sudden rush of tears. Because she *is* right, but I'm not sure that matters.

"I'm scared," I whisper, and she deflates a little as she looks at me with compassion.

"I know," she says, and this time when she takes my hand I let her hold it. "But I promise I've got your back. Always."

Nia's words linger like some horrible prophecy as I arrive at the dance studio and greet my pint-sized dancers.

I look at them in their little pink leotards with the pretty pink bows in their hair, and I can't help but hope that their parents cherish them. That no one will ever warn them that they're hiding from life, and if they aren't careful they're going to suffocate.

I want these girls to know that they can grow up to dance and date and do whatever they want, and not have the voice of a wounded parent whispering in their ear, making them think they have to be someone other than they are.

The hard part is that I get it. I really and truly understand that my dad's to blame for the shell that Nia sees around me. And, heck, I see it, too. But shells are hard by definition, and I've been trying without success to break out of this one for years.

I shake off my melancholy and clap my hands. "Okay, girls. Everyone to the mirror for warm-up."

They scurry away, some graceful, some clunky. I don't think I have anybody in this class who'll grow up to take the stage, but what I want for them is to not only develop a love for dance, but to also be comfortable with their bodies. To realize that it really is only a shell, though hopefully not as stifling as the one Nia described. And that they need to take care of it even while they use dance to escape from it. Because no dancer ever stays inside herself. That's the point. To rise up with the music. To chase your soul. With your body only coming along for the ride.

"Can we jump, Miss Draper?" Amanda asks after the warm-up, and all the other girls bounce and shout, "Please, please!"

And even though I have another class planned out, I agree. Then line them up across the room, remind them of what to do, and then stand by as each races toward me, gathers her courage, and then leaps up, trusting me to catch her the way Johnny catches Baby in *Dirty Dancing*, one of my all-time favorite movies.

We do three rounds of jumps, then rehearse for the parent recital coming in four weeks. And then that's it. The time has literally flown by.

I accept all the hugs and promise I'll see them at the next class. Then I lock the door behind them, and for the first time in days I can completely relax. Because I don't have another class until Zumba, and nobody else is using this room until then.

I go to the jam box, turn on the music, and simply dance. Sometimes I rehearse a routine or try to choreograph something new. But not today. Today, I just want to get lost. And as the music takes me, I let go, relishing the freedom of the melody. The power that fills me. And not just the strength in my limbs, but the wellspring of emotion that rises inside me.

It's as if I'm soaring. As if gravity means nothing. It's wonderful and thrilling and exciting.

I'm letting go completely, and that's something I never do in the real world. But in here, with the music, I'm always me.

It's the only place I've ever truly felt like me.

But as I fall to the ground in time with the final strains of music, breathless and alive, I realize that's not entirely true.

I felt this way twelve years ago in Wyatt's arms.

I felt it again last night.

And I'm not sure that I have the strength to stay away from the one man who can truly bring me to life.

18

"Griff!" I yelp, as I clutch the door with one hand and the dashboard with the other. "If we die before we get to the party, I am totally going to kill you. And if you scratch Blue, I'm going to disown you."

"Chill," he orders. "I'm just doing what you never do."

"If you mean driving like a complete idiot down a twisty canyon road, then yeah. I never do that."

We're still well above the city in the hills that separate the Valley from the West Side, but he's slowed down a bit. Whether because the road's now reasonably straight or because of my griping, I'm not really sure.

"I should never have let you drive," I mutter.

"Nonsense. Blue loves it, don't you, girl." He pats the Mustang's dashboard, and I have to grin.

I also realize in that moment that I can't sell Blue. She's an easy route to a decent amount of cash, but there's no way I can part with her. I love her too much.

More important, so does Griff.

Which means that I have to do the shoot, figure out another way to earn fifteen grand really fast, or tell Griffin I don't have the money.

I already know I can't do the shoot. I'd be trading fifteen grand for unemployment once the show opened.

But I also don't have another way to earn the money really fast. It's not like I have the money in investments. After all, I'm the girl whose checking account is feeling warm and full and happy if it tops four hundred after I've paid the mortgage, utilities, and all the other necessary bills.

I've got some savings, sure, but it's mostly retirement accounts through my school that aren't vested yet, so I can't get to the money. I already pulled out five thousand from savings for the initial cost of getting him into the program, and now I have just enough in my account to cover a month of living expenses if I lose my job. Which I won't since I'm not posing for Wyatt.

And I can't take out an equity loan against the condo I bought at the height of the real estate market because that bubble burst, and I'm upside down.

A bad financial decision on my part, maybe, but I do love my little place in Valencia.

I could borrow from Nia, but I don't know when I could repay her, and I firmly agree with the adage of not mixing money with friendship.

Working more can't save me either. I did the math, and even though I've rearranged my summer so that I can offer two extra children's dance classes and one adult Zumba class, that won't earn me anywhere close to the money I need.

Which means I'm out of luck.

Or, rather, Griffin is.

I just don't quite know how to tell him.

"Hey," he says. "Where'd you go? I just took that curve at lightning speed, and you didn't even yell at me."

I smile. "Maybe I'm becoming a daredevil."

"Yeah, that'll be the day." He glances up at the cloth roof. "We really should have the top down."

"I love this car, and I love that it's a convertible. But I spent an hour on my hair, and you're crazy if you think I'm going into some big producer's mansion looking windblown."

"You look great," he says, because as brothers go, he's the best. "As a navigator, though, you're crap. Are we even close?"

"Oh, sorry." I'd been navigating until his Speed Racer tactics had thrown me off task. I open the app on my phone and figure out where we are and where we're going. "There," I say, pointing to an upcoming stop sign. "Turn right, and then it looks like we're going all the way to the end of the road."

The map doesn't lie. We end up at a gorgeous multi-level mansion perched at the end of a street that dead-ends over a canyon. Which means that the entire back side of the house more or less hangs off into space. Mildly terrifying, but I can't wait to get inside.

I turn to Griff. "This is your producer's house, right?"

"His name's Tim Falcon, but everyone calls him Bird. I know, it's stupid, but he's brilliant, so he gets away with it."

"And the movie's called *Warhol, Women, and the Great White Whale*?"

Griffin nods, and I give myself a pat on the back. I pay attention to movies once they're out, not when they're still in production. But now that Griffin's in the biz, I've been trying to get educated. Apparently this is a coming of age film set in the sixties with a protagonist who's fascinated with *Moby Dick* and pop art. Griffin is his adult voice of reason looking back on the teenage wackiness and angst.

"Ready?" he asks as he gives the valet his keys.

I nod, and one of the uniformed men opens the car door for me. I walk the short path to the house, step inside the already open front door, then gasp at the view.

I'd expected stunning, but this blows me away. There are no walls. Or, rather, there are, but they're entirely glass. So it really does seem as though we're floating in space.

I'm dying to get over to the far wall—I'm curious to know if the illusion is shattered the closer you get—but we get waylaid by a tall, skinny man with wiry, ginger hair and purple-tinted John Lennon glasses.

"Griffin! The man behind the curtain! The voice of the future! I am *so* glad you could make it." He grabs Griff's shoulders, then leans forward to deposit air kisses on either side of my brother's face while Griff endures this absurdity with an expression that resembles polite civility. But I know him well enough that he's wishing he could bolt.

"And who is this lovely creature?" The man turns to me, then glances back at Griff. "Your wife? Girlfriend? Mistress?" he adds with a wink, as I force a smile and tell myself that I can suffer through this party because I'm here for Griffin.

"Sister," Griff says. "Kelsey, meet Bird. My director."

"Oh!" I reach out to shake his hand, grateful I hadn't made some snarky comment earlier. Instead of shaking, he pulls me close for my own air kisses, followed by a rib-crushing hug.

"Darling, your brother is the best. The absolute best. The nuances he's bringing to Lorelei's script." He lifts himself up on the balls of his feet, making him look even more like a scarecrow, and peers around the room.

"I know she's here somewhere," he mutters. "And she simply must meet you. And say hello to you, too, Griffin. But damn that woman, where is—ah! Well, he'll do. Come here, come here. There's someone I want you to meet."

I practically go *en pointe*, but I can't see who he's waving over. At least not until a cluster of women to the left of Griffin parts—and there he is. Just standing there looking sexy as hell in tailored gray slacks, a white Henley, and a collarless gray jacket.

Wyatt.

I feel him as much as I see him. That sizzle on my skin. That squeeze around my heart. The warmth that infuses my blood, teasing me in all the right places.

He's looking at me, too, and though I know he must be furious at me for backing out of the project, his expression is entirely unreadable. Even so, I have to force myself to stand tall under the weight of his gaze. And it takes all of my strength not to reach out and clutch Griff's hand for support.

If Bird notices the tension between us, he doesn't comment on it. Instead, he hooks his arm around Wyatt's shoulder and pulls him closer. "Wyatt, buddy, you have got to meet this man. Griffin, this is Wyatt."

"Nice to meet you," he says, extending his right hand. Griffin takes it, and I hold my breath as I watch Wyatt's face, wondering if he's going to react to the feel of the burn scars or the fact that Griff's missing his right pinkie.

But he doesn't react at all, even though there's no way he can't have noticed, and in that moment I want to kiss the man. That's the hardest thing for Griffin—getting out and socializing, especially in Hollywood where everyone puts such a premium on physical beauty. So anytime someone overlooks his scars, I pretty much want to nominate them for sainthood.

"Wyatt is Lorelei's son," Bird says. "And Griffin here is Arnold's adult voice."

"Oh, right," Wyatt says. He'd turned his attention to me, as if expecting another introduction, but he shifts back to Griffin. "My mom met you at the audition. She said you knocked it out of the park."

"Good to hear. It's a great role. I'm thrilled to be part of it."

"With any luck, our little film is going to make a huge splash," Bird says. From what Griff has told me, he's a respected director, but he tends to do art films. This is a more mainstream project, but the budget is small. They're all hoping, of course, that it explodes once it's released.

But then again, I assume that's what everyone in Hollywood is always hoping. Personally, I'm just glad my brother has work.

Thinking about work, I glance back at Wyatt, only to find that his attention is already on me. "Hi," I say, because the silence is hanging awkwardly around the four of us, and I can't exactly pretend he doesn't exist.

"Sorry about that," Griffin says. "Wyatt, this is my sister. Kelsey."

"We've met," Wyatt says, before I can conjure words. "A long time ago, actually. In Santa Barbara." He extends his hand, and I take it without thinking. Then draw in a sharp breath when I see his gaze land on the infinity bracelet.

Griff looks between the two of us. "Well, that's a coincidence." Griff looks at me, the corner of his mouth hitched up just a little. "Why don't Bird and I go talk shop, and we'll let you two catch up?"

I want to kick him, but he just grins that annoying Griffin grin and slides away. He's never met Wyatt, but he knows the name, and when this party is over, I'm probably going to have to kill my brother.

"Looks like you're stuck with me," Wyatt says, as I tug my hand free. "I like your bracelet."

My heart twists. "Wyatt—"

"Walk with me," he says, and I do, falling in step beside him as easily as I used to all those years ago.

He leads us to the window, and we stand side by side, looking out over the hills, now tinted pink from the setting sun. The ground beneath us seemingly drops away, adding to the illusion that we're floating, which I suppose is appropriate since that's how I always feel around Wyatt.

"Listen," I say when I can no longer take the lingering silence. "I'm really sorry about last night. I know that I begged you to hire me, and then I totally bailed, and I really don't blame you for being upset, because—"

"You think I'm mad at you?"

I frown, turning slightly so that I can face him. "Aren't you?"

"I was—well, more irritated than angry. Mostly I've been mad at myself. That crap about punishing you. I had no right, Kelsey. I was just—"

He shakes his head. "It doesn't matter. The bottom line is that I was a prick, and I'm sorry, and I get why you'd be mad."

"I'm not," I say truthfully. Because the only one I'm mad at is me.

"Then why are you dodging my calls?"

"What are you talking about?" I swing my purse around so that I can get my phone out and show him there've been no missed calls. But my phone isn't there. "Ah," I say. "I think I see the problem."

I hold out my open purse for his inspection. "No phone. And it barely had any charge when I got to your studio. It probably fell out at Griffin's last night."

He laughs. "You're a strange woman, Kelsey."

I bristle a little. "Excuse me?"

"I'm not sure I've ever met a woman who wasn't surgically attached to her phone, and you've gone almost twenty-four hours without it."

"I'm a wonder among women," I deadpan.

"Yeah," he says, looking at me intently. "You are."

I swallow, feeling suddenly uncomfortable. "Why were you calling?"

"To apologize," he says. "And to ask you to come back."

"Oh."

"This show is pivotal for me. And I need you." He speaks with such intensity and honesty that it almost seems as though we're back in Santa Barbara, sitting under a tree holding hands. "And I know you need the money. It's good for both of us," he adds. "Kelsey, please."

A lump forms in my throat, because I have to say no. I have to disappoint this man once again. I'd hurt him when I ran out of the party, and now I'm doing the same thing all over again.

"I should never have even tried out," I say. "I should have just stayed far away."

For a moment, he simply looks at me, his expression hard. My stomach twists, because I'm sure he's agreeing. After all, I destroyed so many things.

The silence grows heavy, and as I scramble for something to say, *the* Lyle Tarpin comes over and hooks his arm around Wyatt's shoulder. I sit there like an idiot staring, because he's my first up-close-and-personal movie star.

"Any luck on your quest to find that girl? Evelyn's over by the bar if you want to enlist her help."

Wyatt clears his throat, then nods toward me. "Lyle, meet Kelsey."

"Kelsey," Lyle says. "Oh. Right." He points across the room. "Lovely to meet you, but I need to go over there now. I need privacy to extract my foot from my mouth."

I laugh, my star-induced nervousness dissolving. "It's okay," I assure him, but he's already heading off. I shift my attention to Wyatt. "Friend of yours?"

"My confessor," he says. "I told him I'd been an ass and needed to lure you back. I also told him I didn't know how to find you."

"And yet here I am."

"Yeah," he says softly. "Here you are. Have I managed to lure you?"

"I—I just can't. I need the money, you're right. But last night, when you . . ." I clear my throat. "Well, when I saw the photos of me, I realized I was crazy to think it would work. I'd get the money I need, but I'd be fired in a heartbeat."

"I'm not creating porn, Kelsey."

"No! Wyatt, please. I already told you. There's beauty and strength and . . . well, your work is amazing."

"Then what?"

I sigh, because I shouldn't have to explain this. "We both

know there are people who won't see it that way. And as much as I need fifteen grand right now, I need a career for the rest of my life."

He nods thoughtfully, then turns away from the window. He glances over the guests in the room, and I see when his gaze lands on Griffin. "What's the money for, Kelsey?"

I have to swallow the lump in my throat. "I told you it's none of your business."

"I'm making it my business."

"Wyatt . . ."

"A treatment? Plastic surgery? What?"

"Fine. Whatever." I'm too tired and flustered to argue. "It's for a new protocol. His burns—" My voice cracks and I blink furiously, because I am *not* crying at this party.

"His burns go all the way to the bones, and he doesn't have much range of motion on his right side. The protocol is supposed to help ease some of that by repairing some of the skin and nerve damage. I don't know how. I just know that there's been success in lesser burns and now they're trying to adapt the protocol for fourth-degree survivors."

I shrug. "He needs it, Wyatt. You can't see how bad it is when he's dressed, but he really needs this. And I really need to help him."

"I saw his hand," Wyatt says. "His arm, too. And even though he keeps it well-hidden, I have a sense of how extensive the scarring is under his hair."

I glance at him curiously.

"It's what I'm trained to do, Kelsey. I look at people. Really look at them."

I nod. "Right. Well, anyway, I've already paid the initial fee, and he's been accepted into phase one. That's what I need the money for. Another few weeks is all I have. All he has."

He nods thoughtfully, then turns back to face the window

and the rolling hills below. The sun sets quickly in Los Angeles, and the hills that had been tinted red in the sunset are now a series of contrasting grays, illuminated by the scattered lights of Hollywood's expensive homes.

Soon it will be completely dark, and all we'll see is the party reflected in the glass.

I glance between the lingering view and his face, wondering what he's thinking. But I don't expect it when he says, very softly, "I had no idea he was your brother."

"He uses a stage name. Griffin Blaize. It's his idea of a joke."

"How did it happen?"

I hug myself, suddenly cold. "It doesn't matter. It was a long time ago."

"About twelve years ago. That's what my mother said. She told me about this incredible voice talent. A really good-looking guy, she added. He'd be a great character actor, she said. But never a leading man. Not in this town. Not unless it was in an animated movie."

I see my face reflected in the glass now, and I see that his eyes are intent on me.

"She said that he told her it happened when he was almost thirteen. When he was living one summer in Santa Barbara."

I press a hand to my stomach, suddenly nauseous.

"It doesn't matter," I repeat.

He nods slowly, as if considering something, then faces the glass again, where the party now fills the view, and not the hills below. "I'll lend you the money."

"Wyatt." His name is a whisper.

"It would be my privilege."

"I—thank you, but no. I can't accept it. I can't take a loan from a friend when I know I probably won't ever be able to pay it back."

He studies me for so long I start to get uncomfortable.

"What?" I finally demand.

"So we're friends?"

I actually laugh. "Yeah," I say. "At least, I'd like to be."

But I bite my lip against the urge to say what I'm really thinking—that I'd really like to be so much more.

19

Wyatt watched her walk away, a slow burn of loss and longing rising in his gut.

With a frown, he turned back to the window, disgusted with himself. But even that didn't help. She was right there in the reflection, her back to him, her hips swaying as she crossed the room.

Right there, walking away from him again.

Well, that seemed to be their story, didn't it? But right then, he damn sure wanted a different plot line.

Wanted, yeah. But that didn't mean she was good for him. She'd hurt him once. And considering how quickly she'd snuck under his skin, it was only too obvious that she could easily hurt him again.

He needed to be careful. Focused.

Right now, the only thing he needed to think about in all the world was his work.

Strictly business all the way.

The only problem was that the vision he had for his business centered around her.

And as her receding reflection reminded him, she'd very firmly said no.

As he watched, she joined Lyle and his agent, Evelyn Dodge. He couldn't see Kelsey's face, but if he knew Evelyn, she was fully interrogating Griffin's big sister.

Evelyn was one of the coolest women he'd ever met. Bold and brassy. She reminded him of a younger version of his grandmother, actually, and it hadn't surprised him at all when he learned that both Anika and Lorelei had worked with her on several projects.

"All right, I'll bite." The voice came from behind him, and he turned to face Cassidy Cunningham. "What are you grinning about?"

She stood next to Siobhan, a turquoise streak running through her long dark hair. She wore a sleeveless silk tank, and the color in her hair perfectly matched some of the plumes on the intricately detailed tattoo of a bird that covered her shoulder and trailed down her arm.

Beside her, Siobhan could have seemed plain by comparison, but the pretty Irish redhead had such a strong presence that it was easy to see that the two were well-matched.

"That," Wyatt confessed, pointing across the room. "If Kelsey didn't know much about Hollywood before, after ten minutes with Evelyn she'll be better versed than a staffer with TMZ."

"Who's Kelsey?" Siobhan asked.

"The sister to the voice of Arnold," Wyatt said. "Griffin Blaize."

"Oh, I met him earlier," Cass said. "Really nice guy. He heard I do ink and wanted to ask me what I thought about covering up some of his scars with tats. Said he was thinking of doing it next year as a birthday present to himself."

"Can you do that?" Wyatt asked.

"Probably. It depends on the scar. And if I can't, we can always work the scar into a larger design. One guy wanted this really intense scar on his leg left alone—it looked like exposed muscle—but wanted me to ink a zipper around it. I have to admit, it looked pretty cool when it was done."

Siobhan made a face. "If you like horror movies. Unzipping your skin? Not for me."

"Hey," Cass said. "It was a stellar job."

Wyatt only laughed, but silently he agreed with Siobhan.

"Well, hopefully he doesn't want zippers," Siobhan said. "But we've gotten totally off topic. Because what I want to know is why Wyatt's been staring at Griffin's sister."

"Oh, is she the one you found?" Cass leaned sideways, as if to get a better look. "She's definitely got an allure."

"Wait, wait, wait." Siobhan raised a hand. "I thought you didn't have the girl. Or you did, but you lost her."

Wyatt raked his fingers through his hair. He really didn't want to have this conversation, but it looked like he was having it anyway. He moved between the women, hooking his arms through theirs, and steered them to a far corner.

"She was all set," he admitted. "But then she—I guess you could say she got cold feet."

"Is she a model?" Cass asked.

"No."

"Well, maybe that's why. It's hard to put yourself on display like that."

Wyatt laughed. "Siobhan offered you up if I don't get someone else. And unless I've been seriously misinformed, you're not a model."

Cass waved her hand with a dismissive, "Oh, please. I don't need that shit. I put myself on display all the time."

"True," Wyatt said, then looked between the two of them. "Which is why it can't be you."

"But—" Siobhan began.

"It's nothing personal," he said to Cass. "You're just too, I don't know, *strong*."

"Strong?" Siobhan repeated. "Wyatt, we're down to the wire, here."

"I know, but Cass just isn't the model I need. Sorry," he added to the woman in question.

Cass shrugged. "No, I get it. Kelsey has a look. Sex mixed with sweetness. I'm not sweet."

"No, you're really not," Siobhan agreed.

Cass glared at her. "Love you, too, babe."

"But it's true," Wyatt said, his voice turning wistful as he imagined Kelsey in his bedroom. "Kelsey would be as likely to wear a fluffy flowered robe as a slinky red dress. And you can imagine her in a virginal white nightgown with the covers up to her neck as easily as an Agent Provocateur thong with her wrists and ankles tied to the bedposts."

Cass stepped around the two of them and stared blatantly in Kelsey's direction. "I see what you mean," she said, earning a smack from Siobhan.

Cass laughed and held her hands up in defense. "Just looking."

"That's what I want," Wyatt continued as he turned to look at Kelsey. "Her everywoman quality."

"So find another everywoman," Siobhan said. "Just do it fast."

"There isn't one," he mused, his gaze glued on Kelsey.

"Then it's not really every girl, is it?" Siobhan said.

Wyatt had been silently cursing the fact that his show had hit a wall. But when Siobhan's words got through the noise in his head, he slowly turned. "Wait. Say that again?"

"Uh, I don't know exactly what I said. I just mean that you don't really want every girl. You want *that* girl. You just want every woman to think they could be her."

"Siobhan, sweetheart, you're a genius." He pulled her close and kissed her hard on the mouth while Cass broke into delighted laughter, followed soon by Siobhan once she got over the shock.

"I hope that means you have a plan," she quipped.

"I do indeed," he said, then started across the room.

"Wait," Siobhan called. "There's one thing I need to tell you. Jensen reached out again."

"No advance images," Wyatt said. "We've covered that."

"Yeah, well, this time he went through my intern. Told her he'd really like to focus on the show. I guess he's intrigued."

"Good for him. The feeling isn't mutual." At the same time, Wyatt wasn't stupid. And he knew that both the *Examiner* and Jensen had a reputation for both making—and destroying—careers.

He sighed. "Go on."

"He's looking for an exclusive advance peek. In exchange, he's offering a guaranteed series of articles on you and the exhibit."

No way No fucking way. "In other words, he's poked into my family life and wants to get closer than he can just by trolling public records."

"The upside is publicity," Siobhan said. "And my boss thinks he's making a solid offer. I think—"

But she didn't get the words out, because Wyatt threw up his hand with a very firm, "No. It's not solid, it's bullshit. He's interested in my family, not my art. Give him a sneak peek and we get all those perks? More like we give him an early look and that gives him time to aim the knives. Start to criticize. Leak bogus statements that the work is flawed. Unoriginal. That it's all just hype, and the grandson of a Hollywood legend is a no-talent hack who changed his damn name because he doesn't deserve it."

"Or they could rave," Siobhan said flatly.

"The answer is no."

"Good," she said, then shrugged when Wyatt looked at her with genuine surprise. "I told Keisha and Jensen I'd present the offer. I didn't say I agreed with it."

Wyatt actually laughed. "There's a reason we're friends," he said. "And now I need to go see about another woman." He gave them each a quick hug, then started across the room for a second time.

Only this time, Kelsey wasn't there.

"I think she and Griffin went home," Evelyn said. "Too bad, too. I like that girl, and I hate to drink alone. Join me?" she asked, holding up an empty glass.

"What the hell," he agreed. "Let's go see where we can fill that for you and find a fresh one for me. And while we're chatting, maybe you can write down Griff's phone number for me."

When she did, he offered to trade a favor for a favor, but just the suggestion insulted her. "I play a lot of Hollywood games, but I don't trade like that. Not with friends. What do you need with my client? You planning his photo shoot?"

"His sister's," Wyatt admitted.

"Ah. Looks like I'm getting a tiny peek into the Wyatt Royce secret sanctuary. I know about Cass, of course. But I don't think you've formally announced any of the models, have you?"

"And I won't be announcing Kelsey, either. I really do want it kept secret, Evelyn."

"I know, and I will. Trust me, I've been working in this town for decades." She tapped her head. "There's a lifetime of secrets locked up here. I can hold on to one more."

"Hey," Griffin said the next morning when Wyatt called from his studio. "If you're looking for my sister, she's not here."

"I am, actually. I know she's teaching a dance class today, but I don't know where. I was hoping you could help me out with an address." He was pacing the studio, ignoring the curious looks from JP, who was seated at a worktable across the room. Beside him sat Mike, the contractor who was overseeing the creation of the stand-alone hall and stage that Kelsey would ultimately dance on.

Assuming Wyatt could find her and convince her.

"Griffin?" he pressed, when the man at the other end of the line stayed silent.

"Listen, it's none of my business, but—actually, you know what? It *is* my business."

"What are you talking about?"

"I don't know all the details of what happened between you two in Santa Barbara, but what I do know is that it took forever for her to get over it. Hell, I'm not even sure she did get over it, because it's all twisted up in her head with what happened to—shit. *Fuck*. Never mind. All I'm saying is that if you hurt my sister, I'll hunt you down and kill you. Okay?"

Wyatt frowned, trying to parse out the undercurrent of what Griff was saying. But he definitely caught the major theme. "I'm not going to hurt her. I'm trying to hire her. Well, I'm trying to hire her again."

"Hire—wait. *You're* the job? The one she got and then lost?"

"I've got a show coming up. I want her to model for me."

"It's not a dance thing?"

"No, not really."

"Huh."

Wyatt could picture the other man's confusion, but he wasn't about to explain that he wanted his sister to pose for erotic photos.

"I thought you fired her," Griffin finally said.

"Did she tell you that?"

"Actually, no." Griff paused, and Wyatt could hear him take a sip of something, probably water. "She said she lost it. You wanna tell me what happened?"

"No," Wyatt said. "I just want to know where she is."

The silence on the line lingered so long that Wyatt started to fear Griffin had hung up.

When he finally did speak, his melodic voice was low, even menacing. "All right," he said. "But remember what I said. You hurt her, and you and I are going to have a problem."

"Fair enough," Wyatt said, and scribbled down the name and address of a dance studio in Valencia. Then he stood up, grabbed his keys off his desk, and headed for the door.

"Hey, hang on," JP called, trotting across the room toward Wyatt. "You're out of here?"

"I have an errand." He nodded toward Mike. "How's it going?"

"He knows his stuff. He has an idea for the hallway that should keep it secure but also easy to transport. Because when this show's a hit, you'll be traveling all over the country, right?" His grin was wide, and Wyatt laughed.

"That's the plan. And that sounds good. I do need you to make one change to the stage, though. Tell Mike we need a pole."

"A pole," JP repeated. "Can do. But you do remember that we have a stage but no girl, right?"

"I know," Wyatt said, his voice hard and determined as he met his assistant's eyes. "But there will be."

According to Griffin, Kelsey taught a ten o'clock class with toddlers, then had a thirty-minute break before she taught Zumba. Since he'd arrived at ten-forty, he fully intended to use her break to convince her.

He'd found the place easily enough. *Dance Heaven*, located in the corner space of a strip shopping center. All of the windows were tinted, but it was the cheap kind and had peeled off around the edges. He stood at the end of the sidewalk and peered in through the crack.

The studio was nothing more than one giant room with two doors in the back, one that said *office* and the other *restroom*. Mirrors covered all the walls, and on the wall opposite to him, a barre had been permanently attached as well.

Now, a group of little girls stood at the barre, doing some sort of up and down ballet move. They held on with one hand, while the other rose and fell with the bending of their knees.

As far as he could tell, none of the kids were in sync with the others, but Kelsey didn't seem frustrated at all. She walked the line, adjusting one girl's arm, another's leg. Then she walked to the front of the line, put one hand on the barre, and demonstrated how the move should look.

He was in awe.

It was just a boring bend of the knees as far as he could tell. But she had such grace and beauty that the simple act of watching her filled him up.

He could have stayed there forever, but she glanced at the clock, stepped away from the barre, and clapped her hands. Soon the little girls were scurrying to gather their things, then running to get a big hug from Kelsey before racing outside where, Wyatt now saw, a cadre of mothers were waiting in cars for their emerging kids.

He waited a moment to make sure all the girls were out, and was about to go in to talk, when he took one more quick glance through the crack in the window tinting. And then he froze. He just absolutely froze.

She must have turned on some music, because she was moving across the floor in obvious time to something. Or maybe the music was in her head. He didn't know. All he knew was that she moved like liquid magic, as if the world was a perfect place, and always would be if only she could dance.

It was beautiful. Hell, it was transcendent.

And if he'd had the chance, he would have watched her forever.

Unfortunately, forever was cut short when a group of women in workout clothes crossed the parking lot *en masse*, chattering about cardio rates and calories and low-carb lunches.

Wyatt checked his watch, cursed, and realized he'd spent Kelsey's entire break entranced by her. Damn.

One of the women glanced his way with a frown, then nudged the woman next to her. Soon, they were all staring at him, and not in a friendly way. "Go," one of them whispered to another. "Just go on inside."

What the hell was that about?

He knew the answer quickly enough, because a moment later, Kelsey stepped outside, her brow furrowed as she looked up and down the sidewalk. But when she saw him, her expression cleared, and she laughed. "It's you," she said.

"It's me. Why is that funny?"

"The ladies in my Zumba class thought you were a Peeping Tom. Or possibly a deadbeat dad out to kidnap one of my students and whisk her off to the South Pole or something." She nodded toward the windows. "Lots of drama in there right now."

"Sorry to disappoint, but I'm drama free."

"I doubt that."

"Well, I'll make an effort, anyway."

She nodded, and they stood awkwardly until she finally cleared her throat. "So, I need to go teach . . ."

"Right. Sorry. I just needed to see you. Can we talk?"

"How'd you find me?"

"Your brother."

"Mmmm." She drew a breath. "Listen, I don't think this is a good idea."

"Why not? I just want to talk. Really."

She glanced down at the sidewalk. "You're bad for me, Wyatt Segel," she told the ground. "You make me lose my self control."

"Is that so horrible?"

She lifted her eyes to meet his. "Have you met my brother?"

He cocked his head, trying to follow her train of thought. "I don't know exactly what happened to him, but I'm certain it wasn't my fault."

"Maybe not. But it was mine."

"Kelsey—"

"I have to go. Time for warm-up is over." She started to walk away.

"Wait!" He heard the desperation in his voice, and hated himself for it. But for fuck's sake, he *was* desperate, and now really wasn't the time for cool, distant pride. "There," he said, pointing to Java B's, a coffee shop on the far side of the parking lot. "Please. After your class. I'll be waiting."

She didn't answer.

"Please," he repeated. "Please, Kelsey. Don't walk out on me this time."

20

Wyatt finished two black coffees and a blueberry muffin as he waited for her. Although technically he didn't finish the muffin. He destroyed it by picking it apart as he thought about what he was going to say, about how he was going to convince her.

He had a plan, sure. One he'd been thinking about since the party last night. Revising and refining it in his mind.

It would work. Hell, it was practically perfect.

All he needed was Kelsey.

He froze, a third cup of coffee almost to his lips.

It.

All *it* needed. The plan. Not him.

This was about his show, not about him and Kelsey. There was no him and Kelsey, and there hadn't been for a long time. And even if he was inclined to start something up again, now wasn't the time to do it. Not when everything rested on her participation in the show. Not when a personal quarrel could unravel everything.

Not when he didn't even know if she still wanted him.

Fuck.

His mind was running in circles. One hour sitting there

staring out the window and his head was in the goddamn clouds.

He swept a mound of muffin debris into his palm, then walked to the trashcan by the door to toss it. As he did, he saw the door to the studio open, and he felt an unexpected chill of nerves, as potent as the first time he'd met with his advisor in Boston to show off the photos for his senior project.

And why not? Back then, his future had been riding on that project and his advisor's reaction. Now, his professional life was riding on this show and Kelsey's participation.

He grabbed a napkin and roughly wiped the muffin crumbs off his hands, along with the sweat on his palms. Then he stood there, barely breathing, as the women emerged, sweaty but invigorated after their workout.

They waved to each other, piled into Volvos and BMWs, then drove off.

But Kelsey was still inside.

Wyatt wished he had the coffee he'd left on the table. At least then maybe he could wash down the fear that she was simply going to blow him off.

He started to turn away, intending to do that very thing, when he saw the door to the studio move. He stood still, holding his breath, as Kelsey emerged wearing a flowing skirt in some sort of knit and a simple white T-shirt. A lime green duffel hung over her shoulder, and she scanned the parking lot before heading toward a blue Mustang. Then she opened the door, and, for a moment, just stood there.

His chest ached, and he realized he was still holding his breath. Slowly, he exhaled, his eyes on Kelsey as she looked toward the coffee shop and then back to the car.

"Come on," he muttered. "Just come on over."

An elderly man pouring cream into his coffee looked sideways at him, as if Wyatt might be the dangerous sort.

Well, if Kelsey made him wait any longer, he just might be.

As he watched, she tossed her duffel into the backseat. And then, after one more glance between the car and the coffee shop, she started walking his direction.

"*Yes.*" Wyatt did a fist pump, which was more than the elderly man could handle. He scurried away as Wyatt headed back to his table.

He was seated by the time Kelsey entered, pausing just inside the door as she looked around. He waved casually, as if he'd just been sitting there doing nothing more interesting than checking his emails.

She came over, flashed a tentative smile, and sat down. "Hey," she said, then tucked a strand of hair that had come loose from her ponytail behind her ear. Her face glowed from exertion, and beads of sweat dotted her hairline. She wore no make-up at all.

Wyatt thought she'd never been prettier.

"Thanks for coming," he said, forcing himself to keep a business tone when everything inside him wanted to reach across the table, grab her hands, and beg her to do the show.

"I—well, I guess I thought I owed you that much." She had a small purse with her, and when she pulled out a lip balm and rubbed it on her lips, Wyatt caught himself staring.

Get a grip. The order was swift and firm and accompanied by a mental kick to his own ass.

"I appreciate that," he said. "And I wanted to ask you a question."

"Okay." She made the word into two long syllables, as if she was apprehensive about what he was going to say next.

"If it wasn't for your job—teaching kids, I mean—would you do my show?"

He leaned forward, expecting her to say yes. Why wouldn't she? He'd seen the way she danced at X-tasy. Not to mention her ease in front of the camera once she got over the initial trepidation.

And he knew for certain she needed the money.

She'd say yes, and he'd launch into his idea. She'd agree, and they'd move forward from there.

It was a perfect plan.

Except for the fact that she foiled it by saying no.

"I'm sorry," he repeated. "*No?*"

"Or, well, I don't know. But I don't think so." Her brows had drawn together, and her straight posture had dissolved to a slouch. She looked like a little girl called in to confess to the principal.

"But . . ." He rubbed his temples. "Well, I know you need the money. So why not?"

Her throat moved as she swallowed, then her shoulders lifted as she drew a deep breath. Finally, she tilted her chin up so that she was looking straight at him. "Because of you."

"Me," he repeated.

She flashed a little half smile. "You make me do foolish things."

There wasn't a damn thing suggestive about her words, and yet that's how his body responded, as if they were in a bar drinking martinis instead of coffee, and she'd reached over and boldly stroked his cock.

He closed his hand around the cardboard cup and focused on the heat—and on not crushing the thing and sending the rest of the coffee flying. Mostly, he focused on not reacting at all, at least not in a way that she'd notice.

"Foolish things," he said, nodding thoughtfully. "Like what? Like posing for me? I have to disagree. That wouldn't be foolish at all."

She tilted her head to one side, looking at him like he was crazy. "How can you say that? I already did it, remember? I already know it was—"

She cut herself off suddenly, her lips pursing tight together.

"Oh, no," he said, and actually heard laughter in his voice. "You were about to agree with me."

"No, I wasn't."

"Then what were you going to say? Posing for me was . . ." He trailed off, making a circular motion with his hand as if drawing the words out of her.

"Hot," she finally said, her face taking on the tinge of a serious sunburn. "Okay? Satisfied? Posing like that was hot."

He stared at her for a moment, a little baffled, a lot relieved, and even more turned on. Then he leaned back in his chair and crossed his arms over his chest. "Yeah," he said. "It was."

"And hot equals foolish. Plus," she added, "that's not who I am."

He thought he had pretty solid evidence to argue that point, but he also knew he'd never convince her. Not now.

"Fair enough," he said. "But here's my problem, and bear with me, okay? I've got this show in just a few weeks. And because it's a whole big production with catalogs and publicity and on and on and on, I don't even really have that much time. So let's say ten days. All I need from you is ten days. Hell, we can do it in five, if we work long hours. Five days and opening night. That's it, Kelsey. Five days. That's three grand a day just to stand in front of a camera."

She started to speak, but he held out a hand to silence her. "Wait. Let me finish."

When she nodded, he counted that as a point in his favor and rushed on.

"You say that's not who you are, but you don't see what I see. You have the look I've been searching for. The image that's been in my mind for all these years, ever since the concept for this show was nothing more than the kernel of an idea. It's all those bits and pieces that make up you. Even the part of you that dances."

He thought that had grabbed her attention, so he rushed on. "I told you about the stage at the end of the hall? A sensual woman behind a gauzy screen. What if she's dancing? All of the passion and power captured in the still images coming out through music and motion."

"That's nice," she said softly. "It even sounds like fun. But I can't be the one who does it. I told you. My job. And it's—"

"Not you. Yeah. I know. But that's the beauty of it." He leaned forward and boldly took her hand, letting her warmth fuel his passion for this project. For having her be part of it. "Kelsey, it doesn't have to be you."

Slowly, she pulled her fingers away from his. "What are you talking about?"

"You could be anonymous."

"But—but all the pictures you have so far. Almost all their faces are lit. And they're looking at the camera, and they're bold and sensual and unashamed and it's wonderful."

"I'm glad you think so," he said sincerely.

"I told you I love the work, Wyatt. I just can't be part of it."

"Kelsey Draper can't. But maybe an anonymous woman can."

"But—"

"You're going to say that's not the point of my exhibit, but maybe it is. Maybe the idea of the show is all those specific women in the gallery leading up to one ideal of a woman. An anonymous woman who represents all those things you were just talking about."

"I don't think that's me."

"And I think that's for me to decide."

"Anonymous," she said, and Wyatt tried hard not to cling to the hope that one word fueled in him.

"Completely anonymous."

She bit her lip and nodded slowly as he held his breath and forced himself to stay silent. Finally, she spoke. "Will you let me think about it?"

Disappointment curdled in his gut. "Of course."

"Okay." She pushed back from the table and stood. "Well, um, I should go."

He leaned over, his hand landing on her purse. "Wait."

"Wyatt, please. I just need to think."

"I know. I get that. But I also think you owe me an explanation."

She eyed him warily. "For what?"

"Kelsey," he said gently. "What happened to Griffin?"

For a moment, she just stood there. Then she sat down again.

"Please," he pressed. "Don't you think it's time to tell me what happened the night of the party?"

21

I freeze a little at his words, and I want to disagree. *No*, I'd say. *No, it's not time. I don't want to talk about it. I don't even want to think about it.*

But I can't say that. Because even though I'd rather run out the coffee shop door, I know he's right. It is time. And he deserves to know what happened.

"How long have you known?" I ask. "About the night of the party, I mean."

"Technically, no time at all. I'm just making guesses here. But after I met him—after I learned how old he was when he got burned—I put it together. There was an accident that night, wasn't there?"

Frowning, I hug myself. "Accident," I say, the word bitter on my tongue. "That's just too clean a word for what happened."

"Hey, hey." His voice has dropped to the gentlest of whispers, and I don't realize why until he leans across the table with his napkin and gently brushes the soft skin under my eyes.

I manage a watery smile in thanks, and then try to clear my head enough so that I can tell the story. But I'm not having much luck.

"Let's walk," he says, rising and coming around the table to pull out my chair.

I grab my purse and stand, tilting my head up as I do. "Are you taking care of me, Mr. Segel? Or should I call you Mr. Royce?"

"Call me Wyatt, and yes." He takes my hand, and leads me out the door. I expect him to release me once we're outside, but he doesn't. I realize that I'm glad, and it's not because I crave his touch—though it's true that the memory of his fingers on me during the photo shoot keeps teasing me.

No, what I crave is his support. His strength. And even though I know I'm playing with fire, right now I will eagerly cling to him.

As we walk across the parking lot, I expect him to ask me again about what happened to Griffin. But he doesn't. He's silent, his hand firm in mine, as if he's giving me both strength and time.

In that moment, I remember the thing that I loved most about him. The way he'd take care of me and support me. He treated me like I was special. Like my wants and dreams mattered.

All these years, I've thought of him as dangerous. But maybe he wasn't the danger at all. Maybe the danger was all inside me.

We reach Blue, and as we walk beside her, I run my fingers over her waxed surface, then stop and lean against the hood. Wyatt releases my hand and stands in front of me, his hands sliding into his pockets.

"He gave her to me," I say without preamble.

"The car?"

"I call her Blue."

He eyes the Mustang and nods, his eyes bright with amusement. "Not the most original name, but it suits her."

"It does," I say defensively. "It's a perfectly good name."

He holds his hands up in surrender. "The best name. And Griff gave her to you? She's gorgeous."

"He found her in a junk yard, did the restoration work himself, then gave her to me for my twenty-fifth birthday. I—"

I break off because tears are threatening again, and I refuse to cry.

"I totally baby her," I continue when I'm sure I'm not going to start weeping again. "Griff says I baby her too much, actually. That I need to put her through her paces on the highway or in the desert or something. He thinks I need to cut loose."

"Maybe you should. Sounds fun."

"Maybe."

"Then why don't you?"

I lift a shoulder, but I don't answer. I don't really need to. Even though he says nothing, I'm certain Wyatt knows that I don't cut loose that often. As in, pretty much never.

I push away from the car and start walking again. "At any rate," I say as Wyatt falls in step beside me, "he's so good to me. Like the best brother in the history of brothers. And I know it's hard for him—just every day stuff, you know—but he hardly ever complains, and he'd do anything for me. I mean, he *does* do anything for me. And it's wonderful, but it's horrible, too, because—"

I stumble on the words, my throat clogged with unshed tears and my heart racing from the emotional weight of everything I'm saying.

I draw a breath and force myself to finish the sentence I'd just left hanging. "Because it's all my fault."

Wyatt doesn't look like he believes me, but to his credit he doesn't try to tell me that I'm wrong. Instead, he just listens as I tell him the whole story.

He already knows about the party, of course, and I explain about Griffin, and how he wanted to make s'mores and melt the marshmallows over the fire pit.

"I never thought he would without me," I say, my throat tight with the memory of that night. Of my father telling me so brutally about what Griffin had done. Telling me it was my fault because I'd left him. Because I'd gone off to whore myself out.

Telling me that my brother might die because I'd been bad.

And me believing it, because of course he was right.

I lick my lips as we reach the sidewalk in front of the studio. I want to keep walking, but there are shoppers out this morning, and I'm feeling raw and exposed.

"Is there a class?" Wyatt asks, nodding toward the studio and obviously reading my mind.

"Not for two more hours. But Anita—the next teacher—usually comes in an hour early."

"Then we have time." He reaches for my purse without asking and pulls out the studio key, then opens the door for me. He follows me in, locks the door, and looks around. A moment later, he's dragged out one of the tumbling mats used for the early morning Mommy-Baby classes. He spreads it out, gestures for me to sit, then joins me.

"I'm going to guess Griffin decided to make those s'mores."

"He still likes them," I say. "I can't look at one without feeling sick."

"What did he do?"

"After I left, he tried to light the fire pit, but he didn't know how. And he turned on the propane, but couldn't get the igniter to work. So he got gasoline from the garden shed. Which was bad enough by itself, but he also didn't turn off the propane."

Wyatt winces, and I press my lips together as I nod.

"He used a match," Wyatt says softly.

"The flame jumped. At least that's how he describes it. The firemen say the propane was concentrated around the fire pit because there was no wind. But he had some gas on his hand, and then it caught the sleeve of his shirt."

"Long sleeves for a chilly night," Wyatt says. "Even in the summer."

"That's all he remembers. The firemen say there was a cloud

of flame. He must have turned, because it got his right arm and back and shoulder, and also that side of his face. He doesn't have the outer part of his ear. Did you see?"

Wyatt shakes his head. His silence is solemn.

"It burned off a chunk of his face. He was lucky it missed most of his scalp, so he's still got his hair. But it burned him so much. And so deep. All the way down to the bone. He lost his pinkie—you saw that. They had to amputate it."

"That's not uncommon with fourth-degree burns," Wyatt says, and I must look surprised because he adds, "I did some volunteer photography work at a clinic years ago. I saw a lot."

"Then you get it. At least some of it. How horrible it is now. How terrifying and painful it was then. And it all happened because I wasn't there. I was—"

I cut myself off; he nods. "You were with me."

I wipe away an errant tear and nod miserably. "Losing my virginity while Griffin almost lost his life."

He moves beside me and puts his arm around me. I rest my head on his shoulder and close my eyes as he strokes my hair and my back. "I get it," he says softly. "I do. But it wasn't your fault."

"It wouldn't have happened if I'd stayed."

"Maybe. Maybe not. But that only makes it horrible. It doesn't mean you're to blame. Me either, for that matter."

I pull back, surprised.

He exhales. "You must have blamed me, too. At least a little bit."

"Did I? I don't think so." And the truth is, I didn't. I made the decision to go. I broke the rules. I was a bad girl, just like my dad said. Wyatt was just being Wyatt. He tempted me, sure. But I'm the one who left my baby brother alone.

I look at him. "If you're thinking that I didn't call you because I was mad at you, that wasn't it. At first, I was scared. And in trouble. I didn't have phone privileges for months."

I hug my knees to my chest, remembering those awful days, my head filling with the memory of the sickly sweet smell of the burn ward, a combination of infection, flesh, and sterilization chemicals.

"I pretty much lived in the hospital. And even when I could call—well, how could I hold onto something good in my life when I was the one who did such a horrible thing?"

He takes my hand and squeezes it. "I get that. I do."

"I'm sorry. Truly. I never thought that me not calling would hurt you. I was too wrapped up in me. And later, when I did think about you, I was too ashamed to call."

His thumb brushes the back of my hand, the gentle sensation soothing me. "You thought about me?" he asks, and though there is a teasing lilt to his voice, I think I hear a whisper of hope.

"Yes," I admit, my mouth going dry as I meet his eyes. "All the time."

I see a flare of heat in the pale gold of his eyes and wonder what I've ignited. But I'm proud of myself too. It's not exactly wild and crazy, but as far as cutting loose goes, that revelation might count as among my personal best.

"Me, too," he says, and I feel a nice little squeeze around my heart. "And you should know, I did try to find you. I even called your school, but you were gone."

"You did?"

He shrugs as if it was no big deal, when to me it's huge. "You said that first day that I didn't come after you. I guess I just wanted you to know that I tried."

"Thank you," I whisper.

For a moment, we just sit like that. Then he clears his throat and asks, "So how did you find out? About the fire, I mean."

"My dad. He found the address to the party. I'd left it in the pocket of my jeans. He walked in while you were getting me a soda. He called me a—a whore. He told me what happened."

"That lousy son-of-a-bitch." The anger in his voice is as sharp as a blade.

"And he said it was my fault. That I was bad, just like my mother had been, and because of that my brother almost died."

"Oh, baby." He takes my shoulders and turns me so that I'm facing him. "It wasn't your fault. You have to know that. And you weren't bad. You were a teenager. You went out. You disobeyed your parents, yeah. But Griffin was old enough to stay on his own. You coming to the party isn't the cause. And that's true even if we had a crystal ball and could prove he'd have been fine if you'd stayed with him."

I nod, sniffling. "I know all that. I do. Really. It's just—"

I shrug, then tell him what I so often tell myself. "Knowing it and believing it are two different things."

He makes a scoffing sound. "Your dad did one hell of a number on you."

I try to smile, but don't quite manage. "He had a lot of time to perfect the skill."

"I knew he was strict in Santa Barbara, but I didn't know—"

"It's because of my mom. My real mom, not Tessa. She had an affair. And I guess she and the guy were driving somewhere. And there was an accident when I was two. They both died, and the driver of the other car was also killed."

"And as you grew up, your dad told you that the accident happened and all those people died because your mom was bad. That she was a whore."

I conjure an ironic smile. "It's like you were sitting right next to me."

"All the more reason for you to come be my model."

I stretch my legs out in front of me and lean back, propped up by my arms. "How do you figure?"

"You say you get it. That you know your dad was full of it. You just don't believe it."

"So?"

"So let me help you believe it. You work for me and you'll be cutting loose by definition. I mean, it may be art, but you're still going to take your clothes off."

I laugh. "Gee. You're so convincing."

"And you get to dance. And you get the money. All that's good, right?"

I nod, then frown as something else occurs to me. "You really didn't know why we left town? You didn't hear about the fire?"

"Not a thing. I left for Boston soon after, but I'm not sure I would have heard even if I stayed. The house didn't burn, right?"

"No. Griffin bore it all."

"That's part of it, then. It probably made the news, but I didn't bother reading the papers. And that wasn't a neighborhood that would have been on my radar."

"Nobody mentioned it at the club?"

"Not that I heard, but I mostly kept to myself. And I only went back a couple of times after you dropped off the planet."

"I really am so sorry."

He stands, then reaches a hand down. I take it, then laugh when he pulls me up so quickly I end up pressed against him, his arm around my waist.

"How sorry are you?" he asks, his voice rumbling through me.

"Wyatt . . ." His name is a protest. It's also the only sound I can manage. Because I'm desperately fighting the urge to lean into him and let him close his arms around me and simply hold me tight.

"I'm just saying that if you think you owe me, you can always offer compensation by way of doing my show."

Immediately, I relax. And when I tilt my head up to look at him, I see him looking back with equal amusement.

"It's true that I tend to be highly motivated by guilt," I admit. "But I'm also working hard to fight that impulse."

"Don't fight it," he says as he takes a step back. "Listen to your brother. He seems like a smart guy. Go a little wild, Ms. Draper. Cut loose. Take a risk."

"Is that what you are? A risk?"

"Risk, reward. I'm pretty sure the two are tied together."

I grimace, but mostly because I don't have a snappy comeback.

"Seriously," he says. "You're just going to ignore your little brother's advice? Your poor brother Griffin?"

Now, I laugh. "You're terrible. You know that, right?"

"Terrible, but also brilliant. Give me your purse."

"What? No."

"Fine. Then just give me your keys."

"Wyatt . . ."

He holds his hand out, palm up. "Come on. Hand them over."

"Why?"

"I think you know why." He wiggles his fingers. "Come on, Kelsey. Snails move faster than this. Just give me the keys."

I do. I have no idea why, but I do.

"All right," he says, dangling them from his fingers as he grabs my hand with his free one. "Let's go."

22

It's about a forty-five minute drive from Valencia over the winding San Francisquito Canyon Road to the Antelope Valley, but I'm pretty sure that with Wyatt behind the wheel, we're going to make it there in under half an hour.

Blue's top is down, and the wind on my face is invigorating. We're on a two-lane road that winds like a ribbon through brown hills dotted green with scrubby native plants. We're heading into the western portion of the Mojave Desert, and the world outside the car has a raw, sparse beauty.

"Nobody but me and Griff has ever driven Blue," I point out as he takes a curve marked forty at over fifty-five.

"And yet here I am behind the wheel. I wonder why that is?"

Since that's not a question I want to examine too closely, I change the subject. "Where are we going?"

"Isn't the drive enough for you?"

He's teasing me, but I consider the question seriously. "You know what? It is." And I mean it. I haven't gotten in Blue and hit the road in a long time—actually, not ever. I'm a destination kind of girl. I like to know where I'm going and how I'm getting there, because otherwise I feel twitchy and out of sorts.

But today, with Wyatt, I feel free.

I lean back in my seat, then kick off my shoes and put my bare feet on Blue's dashboard. My hair is still in a ponytail and I reach back and pull off the elastic. I'll have to deal with the knots later, but I want to feel the wind in my hair.

After a moment, I turn on the stereo and plug in my phone. For the most part, Griff restored the car to its classic condition. Her blue paint was an exception for me—according to Griffin, the shade, called Tropical Turquoise, really belongs in 1965.

The radio is also pure Griff. He loves music, and the idea of a radio that was almost fifty years old just wasn't going to hack it. Which explains why my little Blue has an awesome sound system.

A moment later, I have a CD in and Tom Petty's "Free Fallin'" blasting out of the speakers. Somehow, as we're driving fast on this open road, it seems appropriate.

"Tell me something," I say, when the song ends and I turn the volume down. "When I first came to your studio, you asked what kind of game I was playing. And then you said it again." I put my feet on the floor so I can turn in my seat and see him better. "What did you mean?"

He doesn't look at me, but his hands tighten on the steering wheel, and the car slows until we're actually driving within the speed limit.

"Wyatt?"

His chest rises and falls twice before he speaks. "Do you remember what I told you about my dad?"

I think back, nodding a little as those days in the Santa Barbara sun come back to me. "I know he was a CPA. And I remember that he felt invisible, too. The way I sometimes did."

"Yeah. And he always felt like someone wanted a piece of him. Like he wasn't valued because he wasn't a big name in

Hollywood. But at the same time his only value was that he was close to big names in Hollywood."

"People wanted favors, you mean?"

"People wanted everything. Do you know why my grandmother has no mailbox? People kept stealing it. She finally had a drop slot installed in the fence with a box behind it. If they want her mailbox, think how much they want time or attention from her family."

"That must have been hard for him." I reach for his hand, gratified when he takes it off the steering wheel and twines his fingers with mine. "Hard for you, too."

I already know that he's using W. Royce for the show because he wants to make a splash in his own right. But hearing this makes me understand that decision even more. What I don't understand is what this has to do with him saying that I was playing a game.

"A Hollywood game," he explains when I ask him.

I shake my head, not following.

He releases my hand long enough to run his fingers through his hair. "When I came back with the sodas that night and found you gone, I thought I'd pressured you. That you were angry at yourself. At me. And that you bolted."

"Oh, Wyatt. No."

"I was kicking myself. I couldn't believe I'd been such an insensitive prick. I knew how inexperienced you were. How strict your family was. It should have occurred to me that you couldn't handle it. At the very least your first time shouldn't have been at a huge party with dozens of kids roaming around the same damn house."

"No," I whisper again. I want to tell him how wrong he is—how wonderful he made me feel—but he rushes on.

"I felt like the world's biggest ass. Or at least I did until I went back to the club and overheard that bitch Grace and her idiot friends."

"Why? What did they say?" I couldn't imagine what Grace could possibly say about me leaving. But when Wyatt tells me—about the game, about winning points for sleeping with a celebrity kid—I'm pretty sure I'm going to throw up.

"That bitch," I snap. "That goddamn *bitch*."

Beside me, Wyatt actually laughs.

"What?" I snap, irritated by pretty much the whole world right then.

"It's just that if I hadn't already realized that Grace was full of shit, hearing you curse would convince me."

"Oh." I lift a shoulder. "Yeah, I still don't do that very often. I'm kind of a freak that way."

"A refreshing freak," he says, erasing the rest of my foul mood.

Wyatt's grin fades, however, and he turns serious again. "My dad killed himself that day."

"What?" His shocking words chill me to the bone.

"I found him—I found him hanging in his office."

My chest clenches. "Wyatt, no." I swallow as tears prick my eyes. "I heard that he committed suicide, but only long after the fact—I didn't hear much about anything those first months when Griff was in the hospital. And I heard he died in LA. So I never thought—I mean, it never occurred to me it happened around the time Griff got burned. Oh, God, Wyatt. I'm so sorry."

"He just couldn't take it anymore," Wyatt continues." And I thought—" His voice breaks. "*Fuck*. Kelsey, I should have known better. I should have known *you* better. But all of that mess got into my head. I let myself believe Grace's nonsense."

He exhales loudly, and he's squeezing my hand so tight I have to fight the urge to pull it free.

"I think that, instead of being angry with my dad, I let myself be angry with you," he continues. "And I let myself believe all of it. That everything my dad thought—about the world not valuing him—was true. I'm sorry," he says. "I'm so sorry."

"It's okay," I say, my heart breaking as I clutch his hand tighter. "You had to believe it. It was the only way you could handle it."

He frowns thoughtfully as he looks at me, then turns his attention back to the road. "Yeah," he says softly. "That's pretty much it."

We drive in silence for a while. Me, trying to think of something to say to make it all better. Him, lost in whatever memories our conversation has dredged up.

About the time we hit the valley and the terrain levels out, he turns to me again. "Even when I was angry, I thought about you all the time. I didn't want to, but you were in my head. You got under my skin, Kelsey, in a way no one else ever has.

"I've dated," he continues. "And God knows I'm not a monk. But seeing you again . . ."

My breath hitches, and my heart flutters at his admission. "Me, too," I whisper.

For a moment, neither of us says anything, and as the silence hangs heavily, I reach for the radio to start the CD again. "Wait," he says. "Do you have any Aerosmith? Maybe 'Walk This Way'?"

I peer at him through narrowed eyes. "Why?"

"Because we're here." He slows the car and pulls onto the shoulder. We're on a sun-bleached road somewhere on the outskirts of Lancaster, and there's really nothing to see.

"Here? Where is here?"

"Pretty much nowhere." He points in front of us, toward the road that seems to go on forever. "This area was built up mostly on a grid. And it's not very populated."

"So?"

"So, I think it's your turn to drive." He kills the engine, then gets out of the car.

I remain, a little stunned, as he walks to the passenger side and opens the door for me. "And sweetheart," he adds, as I take his hand. "You're going to want to go fast. Like rollercoaster fast."

I hesitate. "You're kidding, right?"

"Griffin's right. This baby has some serious power." He tugs me up to my feet, one hand going around my waist as he bends down to whisper in my ear. "Trust me. You're going to enjoy the ride."

I shiver—then I blush, because I'm certain that he can feel my reaction. Not only to his touch, but to the flurry of wicked thoughts that the word *ride* has spurred.

His low chuckle reverberates through me, and I step back, needing some breathing room. "What if I get a ticket?"

"I'll pay it."

"What if my insurance goes up?"

"I'll pay that, too."

I frown. "What if I wreck the car?"

He takes my hand, gently lifts it, and kisses my palm. "You won't. Now go."

"Or?"

He steps back, then slowly looks me up and down, my body heating at his very thorough, very intimate gaze. "Or I'll suggest another way of cutting loose. Right here, right now, in the backseat of this car."

I swallow a sudden lump in my throat as sweat beads on the back of my neck. "Wyatt, I don't—"

"Then I suggest you drive, Kelsey." He slides into the passenger seat and shuts the door. "Now."

Oh. My. Gosh.

I suck in air, wishing I was bold enough to say no to the driving and see if he follows through on his backseat threat. But I know that he would—Wyatt's not the kind of guy to make idle threats.

More than that, I want it just a little too much. And between the lesser of two evils, blasting down a long, straight road seems the more prudent choice.

I slide behind the wheel and start the car, then glance over at him. "You better buckle up," I say, reaching into the glove box for my sunglasses. I slip them on, then use my finger to tip them down as I look at him over the rim. "I don't have any Aerosmith, but it's still going to be quite the ride."

He bursts out laughing, then swallows the sound as I work the clutch, slam the car into gear, then peel off the shoulder, skidding a bit on the gravel.

Twenty. Thirty. Fifty. She's up to seventy before I've barely taken a breath, then faster and faster until—

"Wyatt! Look! We're over a hundred." My hands are clenched around the steering wheel—but that's just for control. The rest of me is feeling loose and free and unconstricted. It's like jumping without a net, and I've never done that. Never.

And right then, as Blue eats up the ribbon of asphalt, I think for the first time that maybe that's a little sad.

"Wyatt," I say, letting up on the accelerator and gliding to a stop on the shoulder.

He looks confused, and I can't blame him, because I'm staring at him as if he's something lost that I've just found. Or, more accurately, as if he's a map to something I lost long ago.

"Hey," he says, his voice urgent. "Are you okay?"

I taste salt and realize I've started to cry. Suddenly, I laugh, the sound completely inappropriate, but oddly perfect. "No," I say. "I don't think I am."

I draw in a breath for courage. "Will you help me?"

The confusion on his face shifts to concern, and he reaches for my hand. "Anything. I already told you I'll lend you the money for Griffin's treatment."

I shake my head. "No. No, not that. It's—okay, here's the thing. There's this little girl in one of my classes. And the other day, she dropped a Cheeto, then ate it off the floor."

Wyatt's looking at me as if I've gone a little crazy.

"Her mom almost lost it," I explain. "I mean, seriously almost lost it over a Cheeto. Made the girl spit it out, then rinse her mouth out with water, then gave her this whole lecture on cleanliness. It was absurd. The kid's going to have a germ phobia for the rest of her life."

"Poor kid."

"I know, right? That's what I was thinking. But then I realized, that kid is me. I can drop a chip and eat it, but it's still the same. My dad's voice is in my ear all the time. *All. The. Time.* At least that little girl might actually dodge eating something nasty. All I'm dodging is my life."

"I hear you, but from where I'm sitting your life's not too bad. Decent job. Two jobs, actually, both of which you love. A brother who adores you. A really fabulous car. And an offer on the table to be the centerpiece model of what is shaping up to be a pinnacle project in the history of photography."

I laugh. "Well, you might have a point. But here's the thing about my good life. Is it really mine? Or is it the life-in-a-box that my dad built for me?"

He shifts, his attention fully on me. "Go on."

I take off my sunglasses, then tilt my face up toward the sun as I organize my thoughts. And, yeah, as I gather my courage. "It's not that I want to rush into a bar, grab a guy, and—you know—go at it in the bathroom."

"Fuck," he says. "You can say the word."

"Fuck," I say, feeling wildly decadent as the word slides off my tongue. "But that's not my point. I'm trying to say that even though I don't want to go pick up strangers, I'm still missing something. I want more. I want to audition, not just teach dance or practice. I want to cut loose, like you said. Like Griffin has said. I want to shake off this good girl naiveté.

"I want to go a little wild," I continue. "To flirt and fool around and I don't know. It's stupid. I just . . . I guess I just want to know that the world won't collapse on itself if I do those things."

I turn my head so that I can see him, expecting him to look amused. Instead, he looks as though he's been listening to every word I've said. Listening, and understanding.

"I want to do the show, Wyatt. Anonymous, like you said, because I can't risk my job. But I really want to do it."

I can see the relief wash over him. "Thank you," he says. "But that's helping me. You said you wanted me to help you."

I nod, now suddenly nervous. But I force myself to continue. "What you said before. About me doing whatever you say. In front of the camera, and . . ."

"In my bed?"

I nod. "I want that. I want . . ."

I trail off, not certain what I meant to say.

"You want to be like the women in my photos," he says. "Bold. Feminine. Strong. Women who go after what they want. Passionate women. Sensual women." The corner of his mouth lifts devilishly. "In other words, Kelsey, you don't want to be your daddy's girl at all. You want to be bad. Or, rather, you want to be the kind of woman who he'd call bad."

I take a deep breath as the truth of his words resonates through me. "Yeah," I finally say. "That's exactly what I want."

23

Bad.

The word kept going round and round in Wyatt's head. The word—and all of its wonderful, delicious, tantalizing possibilities.

Of course, that particular word could also be a portent that this was a very *bad* idea.

That, however, wasn't a possibility that Wyatt wanted to consider. Not now, when everything had suddenly turned his way. When the woman who had been his muse for all these years was not only back in his life, she was in his show.

More important, she was in his bed. Or, at least, she would be. And damn soon, too.

He knew it might not last. That she might be interested only in using him to push past her fears. That when the show ended, she might simply walk away, and once again he'd be left only with her memory.

He knew all that, but he didn't care. Because not only was he selfish enough to want her any way he could get her, he was also arrogant enough to believe that he could keep her.

And, frankly, he was sentimental enough to believe that the

bond that had developed between them that summer had never been severed. Frayed, maybe. But it was still there, and Wyatt intended to follow it back to her heart.

"Wyatt?" Her hands were so tight on the steering wheel that he feared she'd bend the thing. Nerves, he knew, but he was damn proud of her for pushing through. "What do you want me to do?"

He couldn't hide his smile, and when he met her eyes and her cheeks bloomed pink, they both laughed out loud.

"Maybe I should rephrase that," she said.

"Baby, I think you phrased it just fine."

Her blush deepened, and damned if the reaction didn't drive him absolutely crazy. Didn't make him want to drag her over the gearshift and kiss her senseless.

Bottom line? He wanted her. Plain and simple. More than that, though, he wanted to help her. To show her the power in pleasure. To help her break free from her father's bullshit chains and be like the women pictured on his walls.

And it wasn't just that sensual confidence he wanted for her. He also yearned to see her finally follow her dream. To dance, if not on a stage, then in life. Free and on fire, the way she was when he'd watched her through the studio window.

He wanted all of that, and more.

"What do I want?" he repeated. "Right now, I want you in my studio in front of my camera. I want you on that bed, your eyes wide. Your lips parted. Your skin flushed. I want to watch you. I want to take thousands of pictures of you. And then, Kelsey, I want to touch you."

He reached over and tucked her hair behind her ear, caressing her cheek as he did so. "What do you want?"

"Um, what you said is good. Yeah. I think that'll do just fine."

He chuckled. "I think you better let me drive."

"Right. Good plan."

She slid out of the car, and he did the same. Once he was

behind the wheel and they were back on the road, he glanced sideways at her, noting the way the knit skirt fell almost to her ankles.

She caught him looking and smiled.

He indicated the skirt. "So what are you wearing under that?"

To her credit, her blush didn't bloom too deep. "Well, duh. What do you think I have on?"

"I can think of a thousand things. And nothing," he said. "You tell me."

"Underwear."

"Show me." He recalled in intimate detail the panties she'd worn the night of the party, and he expected that she hadn't strayed far from those simple white briefs.

"Pardon me?"

"Take off your panties," he clarified, working very hard to keep his voice even. On the one hand, her reaction was adorable. On the other hand, his jeans had become uncomfortably snug.

"Umm."

He hit the brake at a four-way stop, then turned to look at her. "We had a deal. This will only work if you follow the rules and trust me."

"I do. But . . ."

"What?"

She swallowed, the only sign that she was nervous as she looked him in the eye and said, "It's just that I don't see a camera or a bed."

Damn.

"I always have a camera," he countered. "Even if it's only on my phone. But you make a fair point," he continued, before she could argue. "So I'll let you decide. You can wait until we get to the studio to do what I say, or you can take your panties off right now."

"I get to decide?"

He nodded casually, knowing he'd moved too fast. This was new territory for her, and while he was happy to play erotic games, he needed to remember exactly who he was playing with. "Absolutely. Totally up to you."

"Okay, then," she said. And when she reached under her skirt and managed to discreetly remove a pair of red lace panties, he just about drove the damn car off the road. Because not only had she just surprised the shit out of him by yanking them off, but because he knew what that really meant—that this was about them. About Kelsey and Wyatt. And not just about the job.

And that one factoid made him as hard as steel.

"Should I just leave them here?" she asked, smiling sweetly as she hooked them over the rear view mirror.

"You know you're not playing fair."

"Maybe not," she countered, her face lit with pleasure. "But I like the way it feels to finally be in the game."

24

In Antelope Valley, I'd felt bold and in control, the sensation of cutting loose and racing Blue down the open road fueling my confidence.

Driving back through the canyon, I'd felt sexy and clever, delighting in my ability to not only surprise Wyatt, but to light that fire of passion in his eyes.

But now, in Santa Monica, all of my strength and confidence is fading, replaced by a flutter of nerves that has me tapping my foot and twisting my skirt in my hand.

And the closer we get to Wyatt's studio, the more nervous I become. Because I'm not just going to be on display for Wyatt, but for the world. And even though I admire those women who already hang on his walls, I can't help but hear my father's voice like a low drone in my ear. An early warning system of some approaching doom that I could have prevented if only I'd been a good girl, the way I was supposed to be.

Wyatt's studio has access to a multi-level parking garage, and once he kills the engine, he turns to me, frowning slightly. "I lost you somewhere, didn't I?"

I shake my head and try to conjure a smile. "I'm right here.

Really. It's just nerves." That, at least, isn't a lie. "Just the thought of being in front of a camera like that."

He doesn't answer for a second, and I'm not sure if he believes me or not. But then he smiles gently and squeezes my hand. "You'll do great. You already did, remember?"

I laugh. "Yeah, but then I ran."

"A valid point," he concedes. "But you're not going to do that this time."

"No," I promise. "I won't."

I mean it, too. But that doesn't still the butterflies in my stomach.

The parking structure exits onto the street, and so instead of entering through the alley and the studio door, we go in through the gallery. It's a retail space from which Wyatt sells his work, and the walls are covered with stunning landscapes, vivid seascapes, and beautiful architectural shots.

"These are amazing," I say.

"They're not bad," he agrees. "And I've been making a decent living. But they're not my passion. Just like teaching kindergarten isn't yours."

I'd been looking at a photograph of a tide pool, but now I tilt my head up to look at him. "Are you lecturing me?"

"Just calling them as I see them. You should be dancing."

"I dance."

"Hmm," he says, which clearly isn't agreement, but since he's also not arguing, I move on, hoping to change the subject.

"When did you go to Paris and London?" I ask, pointing to some photos on a far wall. "And is this Moscow?" I turn back to him. "Are these yours?"

"What makes you ask?"

"I don't know. The style is different. The composition. The use of light. Is it a different technique?"

"You were right the first time. My friend Frank took them. I sublet him studio space on the second floor, and share this part of the gallery with him. He's in Bali now, I think. Possibly Alaska."

I laugh. "Well, I hope he packed well."

"I can't keep track. Come on," he says, taking my hand. "The studio's back here."

We go down a short hall, and then through a steel door to the familiar studio where I'd come to audition. "This place is bigger than it looks."

"I have the second floor, too. It has two apartments and a shared kitchen."

"Do you live here?" The thought amuses me. Like an old-time artist living in a garret.

"Not technically. Frank lives and works in his apartment, but I use the other as an office. It has a Murphy bed, though, and lately I've been sleeping here. It's easier than going home even though I'm just over in Venice Beach." He smiles at me. "Better now?"

The question surprises me, and I realize that my nerves have faded. "Yeah," I say. "Better take some pictures quick before the nerves come back."

"I would, but I think you'll appreciate me waiting just a little longer."

I don't know what he means until he pulls out his phone and sends a text. A second later I hear a door open above us, then I see two sets of legs descending the stairs on the far side of the room. A moment later, I see who the legs are attached to, a lanky guy with a mop of dark hair that he wears in a man-bun, and a petite blonde in very impractical heels.

"Kelsey, this is Jon Paul, my assistant."

"Just JP," the guy says.

Wyatt turns his attention to the girl. "And you are . . . ?" He trails off, and she thrusts out her hand toward him.

"Leah," she says. "I'm Siobhan's intern. She sent me over to drop off some mockups for the front of the catalog."

"They're on your desk," JP says. He looks at me. "Is she—I mean, are you—"

"She's just here for an audition," Wyatt says, then shoots me a warning look before I have the chance to ask him what the hell he means.

Leah looks at me. "I hope you get it. The show's so exciting. And the press is going to be all over it. Roger Jensen's already said he's going to cover it."

"Who's that?" I ask, and Leah looks at me as if I asked who Neil Armstrong was.

"He's an editor with the *Pacific Shore Art Examiner,* and he's brilliant. Plus, he has a syndicated column."

"Oh, well. Then that's great," I say, surprised that Wyatt doesn't look more pleased by news of the coverage.

"We were just about to head out," JP says. "I finished working on the plans with Mike, so he's good to go on the construction. But if you need me to help set up for Kelsey's audition, I can stay."

"You go on," Wyatt says. "I've got it."

"Great meeting you," Leah says, with a little wave to both of us.

JP says the same to me, and then they both head out. As soon as the door shuts behind them, I turn back to Wyatt. "Auditioning?"

"You're anonymous," he retorts, and I nod with sudden understanding.

"There's no way around JP, I'm afraid. But there's no need for an intern to know who you are. Hell, I'll keep it from Siobhan if I can. What?" he asks, peering at me.

I realize I'm smiling so broadly my cheeks hurt. "Nothing. It just feels nice to be taken care of."

"I like taking care of you," he says in a way that makes me feel all soft and gooey inside. "Speaking of. How are you doing? Butterflies still gone?"

"They're starting to come back," I admit.

He takes my hand and leads me over to the wall, then pulls the drape off one of the pictures. It's a woman standing in a steamy shower, her body dappled with soap bubbles. She's stroking herself, one hand on her breast, the other between her legs, and she's biting her lower lip in a way that makes it clear she isn't just washing.

But at the same time, she's staring straight through the water and the steam at the camera, at the audience. And she's bold and beautiful and unashamed.

"Remember what you told me in the parking lot?" he asks. "That you saw beauty and strength in my photos? Well, that's what I see in you. That's what the camera will see."

I gather his words and wrap them around my heart, wishing I could keep them with me always, because they calm me. More than that, they strengthen me.

"I'm sorry to be nervous," I say.

"Do you trust me?"

"Yes," I say without hesitation.

"Then we'll do just fine." He nods toward the bed, still set up as a set. "Are you ready?"

"Don't I need a mask or something?"

"No. I want to see you. But I'll make sure to block your face later. There's a lot I can do in the darkroom, okay?"

"Darkroom?"

"I mean that in the broad sense," he says. "The show is a combination of images I've captured both digitally and on film. Some prints are purely digital. Some are purely film. Some are a mix. So when I talk about the darkroom, I'm talking either the literal room, or a figurative digital darkroom."

"I know nothing about photography," I tell him. "But I'm impressed."

He laughs. "Very glad to hear it."

"Do I need makeup?"

"Not tonight. For one, I'll be masking your face. For another,

I'm shooting digital tonight, and we'll just do one or two poses to get you warmed up. I'm not even going to worry too much about the lighting. Just a little bit of reflected light and we'll be good to go." He smiles. "So, are you ready?"

I nod, though I'm not at all certain, and he sends me off to the bathroom to change into the fluffy robe again. "There's lingerie in a bureau in there," he tells me. "I have a slew of designers donating to me. Pick a thong you like and wear it under the robe."

He isn't kidding about the lingerie. The chest is crammed full of silk and satin in a variety of colors. I choose a thong in a deep purple. Then swallow hard when I realize he didn't tell me to choose a bra.

When I return to the studio, I have the robe cinched tight around my waist and feel a bit like a housewife. "I don't know what to do with my hair," I tell him. I haven't touched it since I took it out of the elastic, and it's wild and wind-tousled. "If you hand me my purse, I can brush it out."

"Not a chance. You look sex-rumpled and amazing. Which is pretty much the look I'm going for. Come on over here and climb onto the bed."

I do, then follow his instructions until I'm kneeling on the bed, my knees together and my rear on my heels. My back is straight, and pressed against the post. And my left arm is out of the robe, which hangs loose on that side.

"Good," he says.

"That's it?"

He chuckles. "No. That's a start."

He stands back, then rakes his eyes over me, his careful inspection firing my senses. And, oddly, settling my nerves.

After a moment, he turns around and moves a white screen that's a few yards away from the bed. I realize it's reflecting light, presumably for a softer effect.

He walks around me, then makes a few more adjustments, lost in his work. It's fascinating watching him, and the last wisps of nervousness fade away as I realize that I'm a part of this world that he loves, and essential to what he's trying to accomplish.

After a moment, he comes over to me sporting a wicked grin. "The lighting's set. Now it's time to work on you."

"Right," I say, expecting the nerves to return. But they don't. Because now I'm in Wyatt's hands, and I know he'll take care of me.

"We're going to do a lot of vignettes over the next few days, and I'll pick the eight best. Some in a kitchen. Some at a desk. Some out in the world. Each one is supposed to tell a mini-story. And they build to a sensual climax—that's the dance. You'll still be anonymous, but you will need a mask for that. We'll film it opening night, and use that film for the run of the show."

"Do you need me to choreograph it?" The idea excites me. I've done choreography, but never with such an intimate purpose.

"Can you?"

I nod enthusiastically, and he smiles. "Well, then I guess we make a good team," he says, and I swallow a happy sigh.

"This is the lovers' vignette," he says, indicating me and the post. "He's gone away, and he wants to be sure she waits for him. So he binds her to the post." He slides his hand up my left side, his skin grazing mine so softly I have to bite my lip to keep from trembling.

And then, when his hand brushes the curve of my breast, and then strokes higher, teasing my nipple, I bite my lip even harder.

My breasts ache, and my nipple tightens, and I fight a whimper because I want his touch. But he doesn't satisfy my craving. Instead, his hand continues upward until he reaches my arm. And then, very gently, he raises it. Then he uses the sash of the robe to tie my wrist to the pole.

"Once bound, her lover goes away," Wyatt continues. "But he's gone too long. She's lonely. Frustrated. And her thoughts turn to what will happen when he gets back. But she's impatient and doesn't want to wait. With her right hand, she emulates her lover's touch."

Now, he lifts my hand and places my palm over my breast. His eyes meet mine, and as he moves my hand so that my palm lightly strokes my nipple, I see the flare of heat, and feel a corresponding tug between my thighs.

His lips curve up, as if he's perfectly aware of my reaction, and as he watches my face, he gently removes my hand and slides it down my belly until my fingertips graze the elastic band of the thong.

"She imagines his touch," he says, as he slides his palms down my thighs, urging them apart until I'm kneeling with my knees spread so far I'm almost doing the splits. He takes my right hand again, then places it on my inner thigh, covered by his own hand. "She strokes herself," he says, sliding my hand up until my fingertips graze the thin strip of material that is the crotch of the panties. "Teases and plays with herself as she waits for him, getting wetter and wetter and more and more turned on."

He moves my hand so that my fingers slide under the thin material and I'm cupping myself. "She's wet," he whispers, and I am, and I want him.

"So very wet. And she waits, longing for him. She closes her eyes," he says, as I do exactly that. "And as she thinks of him, she strokes herself. Teasing and touching and desperately wanting."

He pulls his hand away, but as he does I feel his breath at my ear as he whispers. "You're so lovely. Don't stop. And don't open your eyes."

I make a little whimpering sound, but I do as he says, feeling the bed shift slightly. My fingers slide over my slick skin, and I gasp when I hear the distinctive click of a camera. My eyes flutter open, but Wyatt shakes his head. "No. Don't stop. I want to watch you."

He lowers the camera, and there's a wild heat in his eyes that fires through me. I don't know if he wants me, or if he just wants the shot, but I'm so aroused now I don't care. I close my eyes again and do as he asks, feeling my body firing as the camera clicks and whirrs again and again and again.

When I'm close—desperately close—he tells me to open my eyes. I do, and find him sitting at the other end of the bed. "You're amazing," he says. "That was incredible."

"Oh." I press my thighs together, suddenly shy.

He comes to me, and I anticipate his touch. Bold and hard and demanding. His hands on my breasts. His mouth on my skin.

I expect him to finish what I started. To quell this need he's fired inside me.

I expect all that . . . but all he does is untie my hand. "I think we may have a good one among all those shots."

I frown, confused by both his words and by the fact that he's backed away to sit on the far side of the bed again. "Only one good one? I thought—"

"What?"

I swallow, blushing. "Just that I thought you were probably getting a lot of good shots."

"Definitely," he says, and there's so much heat and desire in his voice that I'm even more confused. "You were exceptional. But I meant good for the show. And for those, I'm incredibly picky."

I frown and he laughs. "Photography's a numbers game sometimes."

"Oh."

"Why don't you go get dressed?"

Disappointment cuts through me. "Um, okay. I'll change and head home." I'm feeling overly exposed, and confused enough that getting out of there seems like a good idea. "What time do you want me back tomorrow?"

"How about eight. If we're cramming the shoot into five days, I'm afraid they should be long ones."

"Okay. Sure." I stand awkwardly. "I'll just go change."

He reaches out to touch my arm as I start to walk to the bathroom. "It's a long drive to Valencia. Maybe you should stay."

I look at the bed. "Here?"

"I was thinking you could stay in my office. You can have the bed. I'll sleep on the couch."

"Oh." A fresh shock of disappointment cuts through me. Considering he'd demanded I remove my panties in the car, I'd been expecting something much different here. Maybe he was just trying to keep me comfortable during the shoot. But that's done, and if we're going to his bedroom . . .

To say I'm confused would be an understatement. Especially since I flat out told him I wanted to—as he put it—be bad.

So where on earth is the badness?

"Kelsey?"

"I guess," I say. And then, because it really is a long drive, I say, "Yeah. Actually, that would be great."

He tells me to grab a nightgown out of the bureau, which I do, then I follow him up the stairs. He's a perfect gentleman. Pulling out the Murphy bed. Making sure I'm comfortable. Telling me he'll be right on the other side of the room if I need anything.

And then he goes off to the couch, and I slide under the covers, and I lie there, absolutely unable to sleep. Because, seriously, what is going on here?

Finally, I can't take it anymore. "Wyatt?" I whisper to the dark. "Are you awake?"

"Do you need something?"

"Answers," I say.

"Answers?"

"You told me I had to do what you said in front of the camera and in your bed."

"And you did. You were great today."

I frown. "Yeah, but I thought—" I cut myself off. What am I

supposed to say? That I thought he was going to touch me? That I thought he was going to take me to bed? I *did* think all that, but I'm not sure I want to admit it out loud.

Except I want to know.

"I guess I thought you were going to touch me . . . more."

"Did you?" His words are casual, but I think I hear a thread of heat under them.

I consider turning on a light since I can't see his face, and on the one hand, that bothers me. But on the other, it gives me courage.

"Yeah," I admit. "And don't tell me I had the wrong impression. That's what you said from the beginning. So why didn't you?"

"A few reasons," he says. "For one, it was a dick move for me to insist on that in the first place. I was pissed at you, and it was stupid and manipulative. For that matter, it was probably a lawsuit waiting to happen."

"I won't sue," I say dryly, earning a laugh.

"Well, the biggest reason is that you didn't want me to."

I sit up in bed. "Wait. *What?* I never said that."

"You did," he insists. "In the car. You talked about what the women on my walls would want, and how you wanted to be like them. Well, tell me, Kelsey, would those women wait? I mean, if there was a man they wanted, would they hesitate at all?"

I'm silent.

"But I guess that's the real question," he continues. "Is there a man you want?"

My heart jumps a little in my chest. And when I answer, it's a whisper. "Actually, there might be."

"In that case," he says, "I think you should go after him."

25

I draw a deep breath, trying to quell my rising panic.

Go after him? I've never gone after a man in my life. Going after men was definitely not on my father's approved activity list. And while I may have deviated far away from the ridiculous parameters he set for me, that doesn't change the very basic fact that I have absolutely no experience whatsoever.

At the same time, I'm ninety-nine percent sure that Wyatt's a sure thing, and that knowledge does a lot for my courage. Couple that with the fact that my body still aches for a touch that never came, and it's easy to find the moxie to get out of the bed and go to where he's stretched out on the couch.

It's dark, but I can make out the outline of his body under a thin blanket. His eyes are open, reflecting the tiny bit of light in the room. And I can see that he's amused.

Immediately, I resolve to change that amusement to something quite different.

"Hi," I say, then slowly pull back his blanket.

"Hi, yourself," he says.

I sit on the edge of the couch as I press a finger over his mouth, then trail it down over his chin, his neck, his collar bone. He's not wearing a shirt, and I trace my finger lower and lower, relishing the way the muscles in his abdomen tighten as I graze his skin. And then, just about the time I hit the band of his briefs, I pull my hand away.

He makes a small noise of protest, which fuels my courage, and this time, I get on the couch and straddle him, my knees just above his hips so that I'm rubbing his cock every time I move.

And moving is exactly what I intend to do.

I move my hips back and forth, back and forth. I'm not wearing underwear, and my bare sex is rubbing the cotton of his briefs, and the friction is doing quite a number on me.

But I'm getting myself off, and that's not what I want. So I shift again, this time leaning forward so that I can kiss my way up his body. And when I reach his ear, I whisper, "You said the women I admire go after what they want? That they demand it?"

"Mmm."

"Well, I know what I want, Wyatt."

He'd closed his eyes, but he opens them now and looks at me with interest. "Do you?"

"I want you to be in charge." He says nothing, so I rush on. "That's what excited me originally. When you said that I had to do what you said in front of the camera and in your bed. What *you* said. So that's what I want. That's what I'm going after. A man who takes charge."

I lick the edge of his ear, then whisper. "So tell me. Am I cheating?"

He chuckles. "No. I don't think it's a cheat at all. Or if it is, it's a cheat I like." He props himself up on his elbows. "Stand up," he orders. "And take off your nightgown."

I start to protest, then realize this is my doing, so I obey. I toss the gown over the arm of the couch and stand naked in front of him.

He sits up, then crooks a finger so that I approach him. Then he slips his fingers between my legs and teases my clit until I'm certain that my legs are going to collapse.

"Tell me what you want," he says.

"You. I just want you."

His dimple flashes as he smiles. "Good answer."

He stands and strips off his briefs, then sits back down. "I'm going to fuck you, Kelsey. Because I've been thinking about it since you walked into my studio. I want to bury myself inside you. I want to feel you come, your muscles tightening around me. And then I want to hold you close as you fall asleep in my arms."

I make a kind of whimpering noise, and he chuckles. "Do you want me to wear a condom? I'm clean—I've been tested—but it's up to you."

I shake my head. "No. I want to feel you. And I'm on the pill. For cramps," I add.

"Then straddle me."

I do, and though it's still almost pitch dark, I can see the heat on his face as I look in his eyes. His cock is as hard as steel, and I rub against it, moaning a bit because that's ultimately unsatisfying—I want him inside me.

He's teasing us both, I know, and I can tell when he can't take it anymore either. He reaches between us, puts the tip of his cock at my core, and tells me to lower myself.

I comply, moving slowly and gently. But then he takes my hips and pushes me down even as he thrusts his hips up, so that he's deep inside me and I cry out in surprise at the pleasure of being so thoroughly filled.

He cups my breasts, pulling me close so that he can tease my nipple with his tongue as he uses one hand on my hips to lift me up and down on his cock.

It's as if I'm on sensory overload, and a wild pressure builds inside of me, higher and harder and fuller, until the pressure has no way to escape and it finally bursts out of me in a wash of sparks and colors.

I collapse forward, clinging to him as he thrusts inside me again and again. Then I feel his body stiffen and hear his low, rough moan as he explodes inside me.

"Oh, baby," he says as he pulls me close, wrapping his arms around me.

We sit like that for a bit, merely breathing, then he picks me up and carries me to the Murphy bed. He uses a tissue to clean me up, then slides in next to me, the cool sheets heaven against my warm body.

He pulls me close and wraps his arms around me. Then he whispers, "I'm very glad you're doing the show, Kelsey Draper."

And the last thing I think before I drift off is, *Me, too.*

Wyatt may be happy with yesterday's shoot, but today is a billion percent better as far as I'm concerned. "You could have just told me," I complain while his hands ease slowly up my inner thighs, spreading my legs until I'm splayed across a straight back chair at exactly the angle he wants me.

Wyatt only smiles. We both know he's right. I had to go after what I wanted.

And what I wanted—what I *want*—is Wyatt.

"Arms behind the chair," he orders, and I comply, grabbing my wrists behind the chair as I tilt my chin up and look to one side as he told me to earlier. My legs are so wide it's almost painful, and I'm completely naked.

Completely. Freaking. Naked.

Well, except for the extra long string of pearls that is wrapped twice around my neck to form a collar, then dangles down between my legs to pool on the wooden chair seat. The pearls provide absolutely zero in the way of modesty, but the feel of them against my skin is undeniably erotic.

Wyatt circles me, examining me critically. "Perfect," he

finally says, then lifts the camera and starts to shoot. "That's it. Now tilt your head and bite your lip—fuck, Kelsey. That's it. That one's going to be magic."

His words caress me as intimately as a hand. And though somewhere in the back of my mind I hear my father telling me that I'm a nasty, dirty girl who's going to get what she deserves and bring doom down upon the planet, right now, all I feel is power and heat, passion and desire.

The Kelsey who would have run screaming from this situation is nowhere to be seen. Instead, I'm reveling. My body hot, tingling. There's something so delicious about being seen through the camera. About knowing this moment—*this passion*—is captured on film.

And, of course, about knowing that when Wyatt puts the camera down, he'll pull me into his arms.

I feel brave and bold. More than that, I feel like I've finally grown up. That I've shed the fears of my childhood. And there's no way that I ever could have managed that if it weren't for Wyatt and the intimacy we shared last night.

Wyatt.

How the heck had I survived the last twelve years without him? This man who'd uncovered a part of me I'd buried so very long ago.

"Beautiful," Wyatt murmurs, finally setting his camera on a nearby table.

"So I can move now?"

He flashes a wicked grin. "Not just yet," he says, then kneels in front of me.

"Wyatt . . ."

Now that he's no longer looking at me through a lens, I feel exposed and suddenly shy. Which, of course, is absolutely ridiculous.

"Shhh," he says, then goes silent as he rests his hands on my thighs and kisses my inner thigh, right above my right knee.

Then his lips travel higher and higher, and I'm holding my

breath as his mouth closes over my sex—and also over the pearls. I feel his tongue tease my clit, and I also feel the movement of those pearls. It's strangely erotic, and even more so when he takes one hand off my knee, and then very gently eases part of the strand of pearls inside me.

"Wyatt!" I gasp, but he only laughs, then lowers his mouth so that his tongue is teasing my clit as he slowly—torturously slowly—pulls out the string of pearls even as his finger slides inside me.

The sensation is insane. Incredible, and I writhe against his finger hoping for more. Deeper, harder, I don't know. I just want what he is giving . . . only so, so much more.

He's taken me right to the edge, and I can't wait to explode. I'm on the precipice, the verge—

And then suddenly I'm not.

I realize I've closed my eyes, and now they fly open again. "What—?"

"No more pearls," he says, then steps back and stands up.

"Wyatt," I protest. "I want more."

"Good. I like you wanting."

"Wyatt," I protest again, because he's made me completely crazy . . . and is tormenting me by not following through. "You are not a nice man."

But he only smiles, a wicked gleam in his eye as he unties me. "Go change," he says after a moment. "It's already past noon. JP will be here soon."

The problem with me being anonymous is, of course, keeping me anonymous. We decided that JP can be in the loop, because he really needs to be in the office so that he can work on prep for the show. Wyatt's promised that he'll set up the lighting himself, and that JP won't be in the room during a shoot—and for that matter, he won't see the images that show my face—but the secret is just too hard to keep.

We also decided not to bother with makeup. Wyatt said he

could add lip color in the lab or darkroom or whatever, and the rest of my face will be hidden. And the odds of finding a makeup artist on such short notice who'll sign a nondisclosure are slim.

"Are we done in the studio? Or are you going to meet with him and then kick him upstairs?"

"Actually, I was thinking that today we'd do some beach shots."

Since I never turn down a walk on the beach, I agree eagerly, even though I'm a little nervous about how he intends to do show-worthy images on a public beach in the middle of the day.

He has me put on a thin, white cotton sundress from his wardrobe closet, and then we walk the short distance to the Santa Monica Pier, where we grab ice cream cones, then stand at the rail looking north toward the Palisades. "I have a house there, you know."

I glance sideways at him. "In the Pacific Palisades?"

"Yup."

"I thought you lived in Venice Beach."

He nods. "I do. I rent the Palisades place to a family with kids. It's part of my trust, so I keep the income. But I prefer living by the beach."

"And paying for it with your photography business," I say, remembering what he'd told me back in Santa Barbara.

He meets my eyes. "You remembered."

"Sure," I say softly. "I remember everything."

He just looks at me. But the moment breaks when ice cream drips from my cone onto my hand, and I toss it into a nearby trashcan. I'm about to pull a tissue from my purse when Wyatt takes my hand, then slowly licks away the ice cream, sending wild shivers running all through my body. "Wyatt," I say, his name barely a breath.

His lips curve in a hint of a smile. "I like the way you taste."

My cheeks heat, and not from the beating sun. A moment

passes, and I clear my throat. "I thought we were walking on the beach."

"We are," he says, still holding my sticky hand. "Come on."

We backtrack, then follow the path down to the parking lot and then onto the beach. I'm wearing sandals, and I take them off to walk in the surf, laughing when the waves crash higher than expected and dampen the hem of the dress.

"Sorry about that," I say, even though I'm not really sorry. It feels wonderful to be walking in the waves.

Wyatt's a few feet away, making sure his camera doesn't become the target of an angry sea. "Don't worry about it," he says. But a moment later, he says, "Actually, come this way."

I'm not sure what he's thinking, but I follow him back towards the pier. The light is dappled under there, mostly shadows, with a few streaks of sunlight breaking through between the planks above.

He points to a barnacle-covered post. "Stand there," he orders, then uses his hand to direct me to exactly the angle he wants so that one of those sunbeams illuminates my chest.

"Nice," he says.

"Is this just for you? Because it's not exactly erotic."

"Are you kidding?" he says, as he comes over and unbuttons the top three buttons on the bodice. The dress has spaghetti straps, so I'm not wearing a bra, and the thin material rolls back, so that the curve of both breasts is exposed. "Remember, we're telling a story. And sensuality isn't always about sex. Besides," he adds with a devious grin. "I'm not finished staging you."

He takes a step back and starts looking around, obviously scanning the area for something, though I have no idea what. Finally, he crosses to the other side of the pier and gets something from behind me. But since I'm under strict orders not to move, I don't know what it is.

I expect it must be something amazing—a nautilus shell, perhaps—so I'm surprised when I see a battered toy pail.

"What on earth?" I ask as he takes off his shirt, lays it on the ground, then carefully sets his camera on it.

Then he walks to the surf and fills up the pail, all without answering me.

"Wyatt," I protest. "What are you doing?"

"This," he says, then empties the pail all over my front, drenching the dress completely.

I yelp and splutter—because the Pacific is freaking cold—and start to step away from the post.

"Pose," he orders, pointing sternly at me as I freeze—literally. He snatches up his camera and takes a zillion shots. And when he's done—when he shakes off the sand and hands me his shirt—I glance down and realize that the wet sundress is completely transparent, revealing my pink panties and my very tight nipples.

"That one just might be my favorite," he says, then takes my hand. "Come on. Let's head back."

I release his hand long enough to slip into his shirt, breathing in the scent of him as it slides over my face. We walk hand in hand, and the moment feels more intimate than everything we did last night.

"There's a party at my grandmother's estate on Monday," he says. "It's the seventieth anniversary of the release of her first movie. She was fifteen and it was a huge scandal because of course her father cast her, and the press was saying that she was going to crash and burn."

"*The Girl in the Moon*," I say. "I love that movie. And she was brilliant."

"Of course she was. My great-grandfather was nobody's fool. And he only hired people with talent. Family included. At any rate, all the usual suspects will be there. Hollywood elite. Los Angeles society. It's going to be a crush."

"I bet you'll have fun. Crowded, but they're all coming to honor your grandmother."

"It'll be more fun if you come with me."

I pause. "Really?"

"I want her to meet you."

"Oh." Those butterflies are back, and I feel all of fifteen again. "I'd love to come." I glance down at the drenched sundress. "I can do better than this. But I don't know if I have anything that really fits the occasion."

"No problem," he says, with the kind of gleam in his eye that should make me nervous but right now only makes laugh. "You can just leave that to me."

26

"I definitely should have brought my camera," Wyatt said, as Kelsey did a little twirl in the dress he'd picked out for her. It was classic black, with a form-fitting velvet top that reminded him of a dancer's leotard.

The skirt was equally on theme, made from three layers of gauzy black material that had enough transparency to make it racy but not indecent. The material hung in varying lengths, so that it not only flowed as she walked, but flared out when she twirled. And though the dress didn't reveal them, he liked knowing that underneath it all she wore the black La Perla panties he'd bought to complete the outfit.

She'd said it before about a dozen times, but she thanked him again as he opened the door of his Navigator and helped her in. "For the dress and for the experience," she added. "I've never been shopping quite like that."

"It was my pleasure," he said, meaning it. Usually, shopping bored him. And usually, he avoided calling on his Hollywood pedigree.

But for this, he'd decided to take the leap. He'd felt like Richard Gere in *Pretty Woman,* after she'd been snubbed by the snooty women on Rodeo Drive. Only in the movie—which he'd seen far too many times on far too many bland dates—they didn't play the scene right. At least not as far as he was concerned.

No, the point wasn't that Julia Roberts got her outfits. The point was what Gere could do for her. What Wyatt could do for Kelsey.

And he'd felt like Santa on Christmas morning as the sales team from one of Beverly Hills' most elite clothing stores brought rack after rack of cocktail dresses, shoes, and accessories to his studio for her to try on.

In the end, he'd picked out two, but when she said she'd only accept one, he insisted it be the black one with the look of a dancer. "It's you," he'd told her. And she'd slid into his arms and kissed him, right there with the store manager looking on.

It had been a sweet moment, but now, as he maneuvered the Navigator toward his grandmother's Holmby Hills mansion, he felt a growing heat. She looked wildly, deliciously sexy next to him, in the stunning dress and black heels and her hair piled high, so that loose tendrils curled at her neck.

But it was when he noticed the bracelet that he really felt that pang of desire. The infinity bracelet that he'd given to her in Santa Barbara. That was the second time he'd seen her wear it, and that simple connection between them tugged at his heart.

"You're staring," she said, smiling.

"You're beautiful."

Her smile widened. "I think it's the dress."

"I know it's the woman."

She sighed happily and leaned back in the seat. They'd worked all morning in the studio, and now, on their second full day of shooting, he already had an excellent collection to choose from. Three more days, and he truly believed he'd be able to curate the perfect show.

She'd left around three so that she could teach one dance class before heading home to change for the party. And when he'd picked her up, he'd been delighted by her tiny but tidy Valencia condo.

Still, they had a way to go until they reached his grandmother's. And beside him, Kelsey tilted her head back and took off her shoes. "Usually I'm the one making this horrible drive. It's nice to be able to relax."

"You could move closer in."

"Most of the classes I teach are around Valencia," she pointed out. "And so's the school once we're back in session. But more practically, I can't afford it."

He nodded. He understood, of course, but he hated that once their five days were over, she'd be so far away.

Beside him, she closed her eyes. "Can I put my foot on the dash?"

He chuckled, liking the image of a woman in such an elegant outfit sitting like that. "Go ahead," he said, then about drove off the road when he glanced over and saw how stunningly sensual she looked with her right foot up and that thin skirt draped over her uplifted leg, providing just a bit of modesty and hiding the La Perla panties from his view.

He knew they were there, though, and he clenched the steering wheel tighter and wished that they were heading to his studio and not a party.

Then again . . .

"Take off the panties," he said.

She turned to him, opening her eyes as an impudent smile played at her lips. "*Déjà vu*, Mr. Segel?"

"Something like that. But I believe you were very clear that you wanted me to be in charge. Panties," he repeated. "I want them in my pocket during the party. Not under that skirt."

"Oh." She licked her lips. "I kind of like that. But we can't do it."

"Do you want to tell me why?"

"Because we don't have time to backtrack to my condo. I left the panties on my bed."

She spoke casually, but her words cut a hot path through him, right down to his cock, and he had to fight the very real desire not to pull over and drag her into the back. It was a hell of a big vehicle, after all, and the seats did fold down.

That, however, was impractical. Better to suffer in delicious silence.

But he didn't intend to suffer alone.

He leaned over and turned the air conditioner on full blast.

"Hey!"

She started to pull her foot down.

"Oh, no," he said. "You don't get to move."

"But it's blowing right—*oh*."

He saw her stiffen and bite her lower lip.

"Chilly?"

"You, sir, have a devious streak."

"I don't disagree."

He glanced over and saw the outline of her now-tight nipples against the form-fitting top.

His fingers itched to tug the skirt down. To slide his hand over her thigh, then tease her pussy. He knew she'd be wet. Hot and wet despite the cool air. She was waxed, and his fingers would slide over her, teasing her senseless until she closed her eyes and fucked his hand.

He'd touched her so many times, felt her explode against him over and over.

And yet it was never enough. He wanted *this* touch. *This* moment.

But he couldn't have it. Because the reality was that they were in traffic, and he really had no interest in making the news by causing a twelve-car pile-up.

So he kept his hands to himself, silently urging the car to eat up the miles, and told her to touch herself.

She turned slowly to face him, her brow pulled down into a frown. "Do I have to?"

"I thought that was our deal."

"It is. And I will if that's really what you want. It's just that . . . well, it's just that I'd rather wait until we get to the party. And then have you touch me."

He made it to his grandmother's mansion fifteen minutes faster than the navigation system had estimated. He also bypassed the main gate, ignoring the hired valets, and headed around back to park at the service entrance. They'd get in faster. Would probably bump into fewer people. And he could get her upstairs to the room that he'd claimed as a child, lay her back, and fuck her senseless.

That was the plan. The execution was harder than he'd anticipated because it seemed that half the party was mingling in the garden area behind the house, and if they went that way, they'd be waylaid for sure.

Well, hell.

He took her hand. "We're taking another way in."

He thought she'd protest. Say something about how they were being silly, acting like horny teens. But all she did was nod and whisper, "Just hurry, okay?"

Hell yes, he was going to hurry.

They eased around the side of the garage, following the path used primarily by the landscape crew. It snaked around to the back of the house and the huge French doors that opened off of his grandmother's private study, which was never open during parties.

"This way," he said, leading her down the very route he used to take when he snuck out of the house as a teen. He'd never officially lived in the mansion, but he'd stayed so often with his grandmother that he'd been given his own room.

The French doors were locked, of course, but the key was hidden in a ridiculous statue of an elephant just to the left of the door. He retrieved it, opened the door, and then put the key back.

"Wow," Kelsey said, the moment they entered. The room itself wasn't lit, but it was lined with glass display cases that remained dimly illuminated at all times. The cases were filled with memorabilia from all of Anika's movies, as well as all the awards she and her father had ever won.

Anika had wanted to include Lorelei's and Jenna's awards, too, but they'd stubbornly refused, saying they'd keep their own awards at their own homes, thank you very much.

Wyatt, however, intended to put his in the case. Just as soon as he earned one.

For a moment, he stood beside Kelsey, taking it in as if for the first time. And he felt a swell of pride—and that familiar tug of insecurity. Because what if he never had a trophy for that case?

Beside him, Kelsey squeezed his hand. "You're going to be there, too, someday," she said, and the words cut straight to his heart. Not because she'd propped up his ego, but because she understood what he wanted.

When he didn't respond, she tilted her head a little to look at him, and that was when he realized he couldn't wait another second. He pulled her close, then slid his hand under that flimsy skirt as his mouth captured hers.

She tasted so damn good, and he had to have her. Hard and fast if they couldn't have slow and easy.

"Turn around," he ordered, and when she did, he cupped her breasts so that her rear nestled close against him.

He slid his hand down and found her pussy, as hot and wet as he'd imagined in the car. He stroked her, touching her like she'd asked, and growing harder and harder with each moan, with each millimeter she spread her legs. And when she begged him to "Please, please fuck me," he just about lost it, because that was not a Kelsey Draper kind of word, but it was damn sure a Kelsey kind of sentiment.

"Here," he ordered, pulling her over behind the desk where there was a section of wall with nothing on it. He'd considered the desk, but it was his grandmother's, and that just wasn't going to work for him.

Besides, he liked the idea of her legs wrapped around him, her back against the wall, and his cock deep inside her. Liked it so much that he unfastened his slacks and lowered his fly, then pulled out his cock. Her eyes met his, and she nodded just a little, her teeth grazing her lower lip.

He picked her up, ordering her to hook her legs around his waist, and when she did, he slipped his hand between them, sliding two fingers inside her pussy first just to make sure she was ready, and then gently maneuvering her until his cock was right at her slit and one quick thrust would pin her to the wall as he buried himself in her.

He did just that, his free hand covering her mouth as she cried out. Then she leaned forward and wrapped her arms around his neck as he claimed her, this woman who had always been his in mind, but was now his in body, too.

Deeper and deeper, harder and harder, until he felt her body start to shake with a coming orgasm. He slipped his hand between them and teased her clit, pushing her that final bit over the edge. Her pussy milked him, her muscles clenching and unclenching with such intensity that he came with unexpected speed, emptying his load inside her, and then stumbling back, Kelsey still in his arms, as they laid on the ground and recovered.

Maybe a minute passed, maybe an hour. But they finally managed to get up, get their clothes straightened, and slink out the door.

And the moment they did, they bumped into his grandmother.

27

I can't believe I've been caught having party sex by one of Hollywood's greatest legends. Me of all people.

Not that she technically caught us, but considering the smile tugging at her mouth and the twinkle dancing in those famous blue eyes, I'm pretty sure she knows.

Her smile widens, flashing brilliantly white teeth. She's eighty-five years old, and she still looks amazing, the classic bone structure of her face coupled with the wrinkles around her eyes and mouth making her look like a goddess of wisdom.

"You must be the young woman Wyatt's dating," she says in that wonderfully famous throaty voice. "Kelsey, isn't it?"

I'm already holding tight to Wyatt's hand, but now I squeeze it tighter in an effort not to hyperventilate. *Anika Segel is talking to me.*

I draw a breath and pretend like I'm calm. "Yeah. That's me. It's so wonderful to meet you. I've been a fan forever. *The Girl in the Moon* is one of my all time favorite films. You gave such an amazing performance it's hard to believe it was your first role." The words spill out on top of each other, and I'm certain I must sound like a starstruck fan. Especially since that's exactly what I am.

"Well, aren't you sweet. And I understand you're something of a performer yourself. A dancer, isn't it? Wyatt's said some lovely things about you. He's said you're quite talented, but then again he would, wouldn't he?"

"Grandmother . . ." he says with a warning tone.

"I'm just saying the only real judge is Kelsey herself. Assuming she's not one of those ninnies who refuses to be self-critical. The things you see on television these days . . ."

She waves her hand as if wiping away the lingering words, then peers at me. "So, my dear. Are you any good?"

"I—well, yeah." I draw a deep breath, awed that she's standing here chatting with me. "I am."

"I believe you." She steps back and looks me up and down. "You certainly have the look of a dancer. I've known many, you know. Gene and I spent a great deal of time together. At any rate," she continues, looking at me seriously, "you must speak to Lorelei. The project she's working on has several dance numbers."

My stomach tightens at the thought. "Oh, I don't know . . ."

"Nonsense. You must. You're far too pretty and Wyatt says you're far too talented not to be a success."

"Oh. Well, I'm flattered," I say.

"And I've embarrassed you. I'm so sorry, dear." She leans in confidentially. "Wyatt mentioned you blush." She turns her attention to Wyatt, who looks a little pink himself. "You're right. It's charming."

"I think it's time to see to the other guests, Grandmother."

"He's trying to get rid of me," she says to me. "But I can take a hint. Ta-ta, darlings," she adds, then turns and walks off, calling out, "Martin! You old devil, do come give me a hug."

"She's wonderful," I say, as Wyatt takes my hand. "And so normal."

"She is," he says with a laugh. "Wonderful and normal. And we're very close."

"I was surprised you told her about me."

"Do you mind?"

"No," I say, pulling him to a stop and putting my arms around his waist. "I like it."

I tilt my head up for a kiss, then sigh happily.

"She's right about the dancing," he says. "I don't understand why you're hesitating. I mean, surely you're not still hearing your father's voice in your head. Not if you're doing my show."

"He's still there a little bit," I admit. "But definitely not as loud."

"So why not go on auditions? Not for the small performances you do, but for the theater. For a company."

I shake my head. "I don't know," I say, then sigh. "Maybe after all this time, I'm afraid that if I start chasing my dream I'll never catch it."

I look at him as I say those words, and see a flicker of something in his eyes. "What?"

"I was going to say that it's not the result that matters, but the chase. But considering how much I have riding on this show coming off successfully, maybe I'm not the person to say that."

"No, you're not." I hip-butt him. "We're a lot alike, you know. Must be why we're dating." I grin. "You told your grandmother we're dating."

"Aren't we?" he asks.

My smile is painfully broad. "Absolutely, we are. But why didn't you tell her I'm doing your show?"

We enter the ballroom and are suddenly surrounded by celebrities. It's like standing in the middle of an entertainment magazine.

"So? Why didn't you tell her I'm the girl?" I press, as a waiter comes by with glasses of wine.

"She doesn't know about the project," he says, and I freeze, my wine not quite to my lips.

"Really?"

"She knows there *is* a show. But that's it."

I nod slowly. "You want to be a hit. To prove you're a Segel."

He meets my eyes, then nods.

"You're going to," I say sincerely. "This show. I have such a good feeling."

"I've had a good feeling ever since you joined," he replies, then leans in for another kiss.

I hear a catcall and pull away, confused.

Or, at least, confused until I see Griffin and Nia approaching from a few yards away.

"Hey, man," Griff says to Wyatt. "Good to see you again."

"Love the dress," Nia says, then smiles at Wyatt and extends her hand. "I'm Nia."

He arches a brow. "Nia Hancock?"

She glances at me. "Gorgeous and psychic. Quite the combination."

I roll my eyes. "Wyatt Royce, meet Nia Hancock."

"Best friend, protector, and sometimes job facilitator," she says. "The pleasure is mine."

"Why are you here?" I ask her, and she glances toward Griff.

"He's here because he's working on that movie with Lorelei. I'm here because his usual date—that means you—bailed on him."

"Excellent," I say. "Anyone else here I know?"

"Know?" Nia says. "I don't think so. Know *of*. Definitely."

"She's been playing the celebrity sighting game as we walk the house," Griffin says.

"I think that's cheating here. I'm pretty sure my grandmother invited all the celebrities. At the very least, she crossed the ninety-five percent mark."

"Oh, fuck me," Nia says. "You're Wyatt *Segel*."

"I thought you knew that," he says, but Nia's scowling at me. "You never told me he was one of *those* Segels."

I shrug. "Sorry. It never occurred to me."

She swoops her right hand under her left arm. "Water. Bridge. Moving on. The point is that everyone is here. And now I need to borrow my girl," she says to Wyatt. "Because we totally have to gossip. Fair enough?"

To his credit, he laughs, then kisses my cheek. "I'll find you."

"You better."

Nia and I head off, with her pointing out everyone I don't recognize. "That's Nikki and Damien Stark," she says gesturing towards a man I recognize as the tennis star turned billionaire entrepreneur.

"He paid a million for her nude portrait," I say, feeling a kinship with the woman. "It was supposed to be anonymous, and then someone found out."

I shiver, thinking how awful that would be if it happened to me with Wyatt's show.

"And that woman they're talking to is Jane Martin—she wrote that movie about the kidnapped kids. And the guy to her left—isn't he hot?—that's Dallas Sykes."

"Really?" One of my guilty pleasures is reading the tabloids, and he was all over it for a while. "They called him The King of Fuck. I guess he slept around."

"They're married now," Nia says. "But there was so much scandal, remember?"

I don't, and she's about to clue me in, when two stunning women walk over and introduce themselves as Wyatt's mother and sister. Like Anika, they're both down to earth, and before they continue to mingle, Lorelei stresses that I really should audition. "I can't get you the role, but I can get you access. And in this town that's important."

"Thank you," I say, and I really am grateful, even though I probably won't ever take her up on it.

We wander some more, and I realize after a while that Nia has been steering me to a quiet corner. "Okay," she says once we're sitting on a small divan, fortified with fresh glasses of wine. "Tell me what's up with Wyatt."

I consider dodging the question, but Nia's my best friend. And I don't really want to dodge. I want to talk.

So I tell her the one thing that I've been holding inside. The one thing that's been building in me for days. "I think I'm in love," I say, but instead of congratulating me or even arguing with me, Nia rolls her eyes.

"Girl," she says, "you fell in love twelve years ago. Love is not your issue."

I frown. "What are you talking about?"

"Everyone thinks that love is the end. Fall in love and live happily ever after. That's bullshit, sweetie. Love is work. Like serious fucking work." She lifts a shoulder. "And I worry for you."

"For me? You don't think Wyatt will work at it?"

She slouches back against the divan. "I don't know him. Not yet. Not really. I'm sorry, Kels, but if you want the cold, honest truth, you're the one I worry about. You've put yourself in a box for so long, sweetie. I'm not sure you can fit anyone else in there with you."

I start to say something, but she talks over me.

"Which means the only way it'll work is if you come out of the box. And I don't know if you can do that. Not if it gets hard and scary. Because Kels, you're the girl who's always playing it safe. And sweetie, love doesn't have a safety net."

I'm in a sour mood as we leave the party and head toward the car an hour later, Nia's words still ringing in my ears.

Wyatt glances at me, his brow furrowed. "You want to talk about it?"

I shake my head. "It's nothing. Just best friend stuff." Not exactly a lie, but also not the truth.

He looks like he's going to argue the point, but the chirp of my phone signaling an incoming text cuts him off.

Since it's probably her, I dig in my purse for my phone, only to frown when I see that it's not from Nia, but from one of the other teachers.

I applaud you, but what an exit strategy. Hope it works out for you.

"Nia?" Wyatt asks, and I shake my head and hand him the phone.

"Another kindergarten teacher. I have no idea what she's talking about."

"Maybe she sent it to the wrong person."

It makes sense, and I start to tap out a response to let her know her text went astray. But I'm distracted by the fact that both Damien Stark and Siobhan—who I met once at Wyatt's studio—are standing by Wyatt's Navigator.

I know Siobhan's connection to Wyatt through the show, of course, but it takes me a second to remember that Damien Stark is the patron of the Stark Center for the Visual Arts, where Wyatt's show is scheduled to open.

I slow my pace, cold dread building inside me.

"Should I even ask?" Wyatt says.

"It's not good." Stark pushes off the car and walks to Wyatt.

"Considering you don't exactly get involved with the day-to day-operations of the center, I assumed as much. Tell me fast," he says. "If it's bad, you might as well get it over with."

"Should I leave you alone?" I ask them.

"No." Wyatt takes my hand. "You're with me."

"She needs to stay anyway," Damien says. "I'm sorry, Kelsey."

The dread in my stomach forms into a hard knot. Because there's no reason for a man like Damien Stark to know my name. Not unless I somehow ended up on his radar. And I shouldn't. Because my photos are supposed to be anonymous. No one's supposed to know except me and Wyatt and JP.

But they do. I can see it in their eyes. Stark and Siobhan.

"What happened?" I demand.

"Leah," Siobhan says, exhaling slowly. She passes me a digital tablet displaying a collage of social media posts. I'm too shocked to really focus. But I see enough. One of Wyatt's images of me with my face blurred out. And it's side by side with photos of me teaching dance and playing Red Rover at a kindergarten picnic.

"What are these?" I whisper, as beside me I feel Wyatt getting stiffer and stiffer with rage.

"Rumors," Damien says. "She started a rumor campaign, apparently with the blessing of Roger Jensen. It seems he told her that she'd be getting you a ton of free publicity."

I clap my hand over my mouth, fighting a sudden urge to be sick.

"She told us everything," Siobhan said. "JP saw the post on Instagram and realized she must have taken it from the office one day when they were going to dinner. She got close to him on purpose. Presumably, she clued in that Kelsey is your primary girl."

"That little bitch," Wyatt says.

"She's been fired. I have Charles on damage control. My lawyer," he adds, looking at me.

"But it's out there already," I say, passing Stark my phone. "People know."

A combination of anger and frustration wash over his face. "Damn that girl." He passes the phone back to me. "I'm so sorry. But please know that if you do lose your job, the center will cover your salary until you find a new one."

"That's nice of you," I say, "but no." I hug myself in defense against the cold that has seeped into my bones. The icy chill from the cloud of doom that I've known was out there since the beginning.

"Kelsey," Siobhan begins, "you really should—"

"No," I repeat, my voice low. "I knew this would happen. It's my fault as much as Leah's." I turn to Wyatt. "I pushed the envelope. I did all the things my dad warned me about. And see?" I demand, my words bitter and hard. "See what happened?"

"It didn't," he says. "Leah's idiocy is all on her. It has nothing to do with you."

He holds my hands tight. "This will be okay."

"But it won't."

"We can still do the show. And if you are fired, you can audition for shows. You can teach older kids. You can choreograph music videos. This can be a beginning, not an end."

"I'm sorry," I say to all three of them as tears stream down my face. Then I meet Wyatt's eyes. "I'm so sorry."

"Kelsey, please. You make the show. Your beauty. Your sensuality. Baby, I need you. Griffin needs you. And if you've already lost the job there's no reason not to do the show."

But none of that matters. Not now. Not when the weight of every lecture my father ever gave me is crashing down on me. "I'm sorry," I say before I turn to walk away. "But I really just can't."

28

Wyatt was numb.

He'd been numb for almost twenty-four hours, and he was starting to fear it was going to be a permanent state.

For hours, he'd been sitting on his rooftop deck, staring out at the Pacific, and trying to make sense of it. So far, he hadn't managed.

On the contrary, he flat out couldn't believe it. None of it. Not that she'd walked. Not that he'd let her. Not that Leah-the-bitch had spread those damn photos all over the Internet.

He could sue, of course. She'd stolen the physical photo of Kelsey. And he might, just because the bitch deserved it. But honestly, he couldn't work up the energy. Because what good would it do?

It couldn't get Kelsey back.

Couldn't reshape the show back to the way he wanted it to be. For that he needed Kelsey. But she'd made it perfectly clear she was out.

Thank God, Cass was going to fill in. She'd agreed to come by for a short session tomorrow morning at eight, but it wouldn't be the same. Her energy was different. Her presence.

He was shooting images with a theme in mind, and she just didn't fit.

He'd make it work—hell, he had to make it work. But it was no longer the show he'd dreamed of. It would do okay. It would get decent press. But this show wasn't going to launch his career. Wouldn't prove to anyone—much less himself—that he deserved the Segel name.

It would make a tiny splash in a very big pool. And that would be that.

God, he'd been a fool. He'd feared she wouldn't see it through that night at X-tasy. And he damn sure should have listened to his gut.

She'd walked away once before and destroyed his life.

This time she was walking away and destroying his career.

He was a fool, all right. He'd gone with his heart instead of his head. And now he was paying the price.

With a deep sigh of regret, he leaned back, kicking his feet up onto the railing as he watched the sun sink low over the Pacific. He had a cooler full of beer next to him, and he'd already downed three. If he sat here all the way until sunrise, he might even work his way through all of them.

The bell over the rooftop door chimed to indicate that someone was at his front door, but he really didn't give a shit. Kelsey still hadn't been to his house, so it wouldn't be her. He wasn't expecting any deliveries. And his friends knew to text before coming over.

He reached down, grabbed another bottle, twisted off the cap, and took a long swallow. Then another and another, until the bottle was drained. Because what the hell. He was already sore from the knife she'd stuck in him. Might as well anesthetize the wound.

A moment later, the door behind him creaked open, and he sat bolt upright, the bottle held tight by its neck, as if that would do any good against an intruder.

Except this intruder was one he could probably take—Anika

Segel—and she was looking at him with such a mixture of concern and irritation that he almost laughed.

"Three stories," she said. "And no elevator. I'm eighty-five years old, young man. Answer your goddamn door."

He tossed the empty beer into a nearby bin and was on his feet in an instant, dragging a chair toward her. "I had no idea it was you. Sorry. Why didn't you call me? I would have come down."

She snorted. "I managed, didn't I? And we need to talk."

"You heard what happened."

"I made Damien tell me. Don't be upset with him. That boy may have more clout than God, but I'm an old woman with an agenda, and that trumps most everything. So," she continued, "our Kelsey was going to be in your show and got cold feet."

"That pretty much sums it up," he said.

"You know, I do miss Carlton."

It was such a non sequitur that he froze in the process of dragging his chair over by hers. "My dad?"

"He was always a breath of fresh air. Always had a perspective other than this ridiculous bubble we live in." She patted his arm. "Our Kelsey's a bit like that. Although I suppose if we keep encouraging her to audition for dance numbers, she may lose that."

"You think she shouldn't audition?" The moment the words were out of his mouth, he wanted to call them back. What did he care anymore whether she auditioned or not?

"I think it depends on what Kelsey wants," Anika said.

"She wants to dance. She wants the stage. She's scared of it." He held up his hands. "That's a big part of why she bolted."

"Mmm. And what are you scared of, baby boy?"

He hadn't heard the endearment from her in years, and it warmed him enough that he considered the question honestly. And then actually answered it. "That I'm never going to live up to Grandfather. Or Mom. Or you."

She waved his words away. "Listen to you. What a load of

nonsense. What have I done? Nothing except working a job I loved and raising a family I adore."

"And you had an incredible public life," he pointed out.

"True. But that's only the surface story. Pass me a beer, Wyatt. Where are your manners?"

He pressed his lips together so he wouldn't laugh, then complied. "Surface story?" he repeated as he twisted the top off. "What do you mean?"

"Just that, yes, I lived in the spotlight, but I like being the center of attention. It suits me. And so I went for it. And I did okay, if I do say so myself. But what if I'd never gotten my break? Been born into another family? I don't know, but I think I'd still be acting. Maybe not in movies. But on a small stage in Kansas. Maybe playing the nurse in *Romeo and Juliet*. Or perhaps I could be in *The Little Foxes*. I always adored that play."

"You're teasing me," he said, but she shook her head earnestly.

"I'm not." She sat up and reached for him, tapping lightly on his chest. "If it's inside of you—here—then go for it. Because you want to. But not because you think it matters to me or your mother or Jenna. Do you think Jenna cares about the cameras? She only cares because it gives her the clout to open more restaurants and try out more recipes. That girl would cook in a log cabin if that was her only option and you know it."

It was true. He did know it.

"But my dad—"

"Your dad had other problems. And maybe your mother should have told you some of it after he died, but I think she hoped you would all move past it."

"Dad thought she didn't respect him. That you didn't."

"Carlton was a good man. But he was a fool in a lot of ways. That was one. He was a good CPA. Goodness knows he got my financial house in order after that ridiculous shyster—well, never mind. I loved that boy. And if he felt less because the spotlight left him in the shadow, then I'm truly sorry. But that was only him. Your mother adored him. I adored him. Like I said, it was nice to have someone around who didn't read *Variety* before the actual news."

"I thought *Variety* was the news," he deadpanned.

"There? See? You are one of us." She smiled, and in that moment he wished he had his camera. "So you tell me, Wyatt. What is it you want? The spotlight? Fame? A family? Respect?"

The answer came fast, without him even having to think.

Kelsey.

When he cut through all the crap, all the ambition, all the garbage, she was the only thing he saw.

And it was time he told her so.

29

"You should have told me that's where the money was coming from," Griff says as he cracks two eggs into a skillet. "I thought it was from that savings account you started a zillion years ago."

I shake my head, but don't tell him that Daddy emptied that account out ages ago.

"I'm really sorry," I say for one more time. "I'll borrow the money from Nia—it's weird taking money from a friend, but she understands and—"

"You don't need to do that."

"—and I'll pay her back eventually with—" I look over at him from where I sit at the Formica table, something in his tone catching my attention. "Wait. Why don't I?"

"I have the money."

I sit back in my chair. "You have the money?"

"Well, technically no. But I'm officially in the protocol, and I don't owe a dime."

"Oh." I'm very confused. "How?"

"You, apparently."

Now I'm even more confused, and I tell him so. "So speak slowly and use small words."

"I guess Stark offered to cover your salary if you were fired, and you said no?"

"Yeah. So?"

"Well, I guess he doesn't do *no* well. He asked Wyatt what you were supposed to get paid, and Wyatt told him about the protocol."

"And?"

"And apparently he owns the company."

I blink. "Say again?"

"The company that's doing the trials is a division of Stark International. So he pulled strings. At any rate, I'm in. Because of you. Or because of that bitch Leah," he says with an evil grin. "But I'd rather thank my big sister."

"You're in," I say, more to myself than him. "That's—wow."

Part of me thinks I should call Stark and say that's really unacceptable. After all, I turned down the salary reimbursement.

But since that would be insane, I don't make that call. Instead, I hop off my chair and race over to hug my brother. "This is so amazing!"

"I know, but don't get excited yet. I'm only in. Who knows if it'll end up doing any good. I may not get any range of motion back."

But I refuse to be deterred. "It's fabulous," I say as I reach for my phone. My hand halts midway to my back pocket though.

I was about to call Wyatt.

Griff's watching me, and I can tell from his expression he knows exactly what I was doing. "Now you really don't have to be in the show. You don't need the money." He meets my eyes. "Unless there's something else you need."

There is, of course. I need to shake off the specter of my father. I *know* it. And with Wyatt, I'd been managing it.

But then all that progress had been ripped to shreds because of a few stupid pictures. And everything I'd believed I'd fixed in myself unraveled all over again. And in the unraveling, I'd hurt the man I love.

I sigh deeply.

I need to get back on track. I need to kick Karma to the curb. Most of all, I need Wyatt.

I need him desperately.

But after the way I walked out, why on earth would he want me, too?

I'm about to explain all of that to Griff when my phone rings. I snatch it up, hoping it's Wyatt—and then I'm absolutely shocked when it is.

"Hi," I say softly.

"Hi, yourself. You're not in Valencia."

I blink and stand up straighter. "You went to my condo?"

"I figured it was the logical place to find you at six-thirty in the morning. I was wrong."

"Oh. I'm at Griffin's."

I can picture him nodding. "I should have guessed."

"Why did you—"

"I'd rather say this in person, but my trek across Southern California ate up my time, and I have to get back to the studio, because Cass can only shoot from eight to ten today."

"Cass?"

"She's stepping in for you. It's fine," he adds before I can say anything. "More than fine, because I don't want you to do anything you don't want to do. I love you, Kelsey."

The words slip out as if he's said them a thousand times, and my heart flips over in my chest.

"I love you," he repeats. "And if I have to choose between my perfect vision of the show and you, well, I choose you."

"Wyatt, I—"

"No," he interrupts. "Don't say anything. I'll call you later. And maybe I can buy you dinner and we can talk. Okay?"

"Okay," I say, a little shell-shocked.

"Good," he says. "I love you, Kels." And then he just hangs up.

"What?" Griff demands, sliding the plate of eggs and toast onto my place at the table. I return to my chair, but just sit there, not eating. Not answering Griff's question.

I can't answer. I'm too stunned. Because I love him, too, but I did nothing but run away.

Yet he just sacrificed everything for me. His vision. His work. And all I'm doing is hiding here inside these four walls—

Well, fuck that. *Fuck. That.*

I'm through hiding. I'm through being scared.

Most of all, I'm through believing that fate is my enemy. Punish me? How about reward me? I do something bold and scary and wonderful, then maybe the universe should do something nice for me. Or for the people I love.

I look up at Griffin, my eyes wide.

"What?" he demands again.

"Nia was right. My life's in a box."

"I have no idea what you're talking about."

"That's okay. I know the way out myself." I take a deep breath, and smile. "You're looking at the featured model for a stunning new art show opening in a couple of weeks."

"Am I?"

"Daddy will never let me hear the end of this." I say the words, but this time—for the first time—they're missing the usual dread.

"Dad's in Georgia. And you're here. And the last time I checked, it's your life."

I smile at him. "And I'm going to go start living it."

I'm pacing the studio when he bursts through the alley door. "Sorry, sorry. I got stuck in traffic, and—Kelsey?"

I lift my fingers in a little wave. "Hi."

He hurries to me, his expression a mix of concern and joy. "Are you okay? Where are Cass and Siobhan?"

"I sent them away."

He runs his fingers through his hair, and now his expression looks as if he's trying for patience.

"Baby, I'm thrilled to see you, but I have to get these shots done. I'm down to the wire here, and Cass has a full plate at the tattoo parlor. She's squeezing me in around clients."

"No, she's not."

He takes a step back, then looks me up and down. "What's going on?"

"It's just that you're not really that slammed. You've got at least two-thirds of the images, and the dance is already choreographed."

I watch as he swallows. "Kelsey—baby. Don't tease me."

"I'm doing the show, Wyatt. Me. The pictures. The stage. Nobody's taking my place."

He shakes his head slowly. "We've been over this. It's okay. You don't have to."

"Yeah, I do."

"Why?"

"Because I love you, too. Because I'm the girl. The inspiration. I'm your muse, Wyatt. You told me so twelve years ago. And nobody is pulling that out from under me. Not even you."

I take a step closer. "And I'm doing it because it's right. Your photos—it's like you said. They show a progression. And that's what I need. A path from the old Kelsey to the new. So I'm going to walk the corridor in the exhibit, and I'm going to see my face looking back at me, and I'm going to dance on that stage.

"And the universe won't fall apart," I add. "And nothing bad will happen. I know, because your show is amazing and it deserves all the good things. *And* I know because my father's theory is bullshit hocus pocus and I'm out from under that spell."

I lift a shoulder. "I mean, so long as that's all right with you."

He bursts out laughing. "Are you through?"

I think about it. "Yeah, I pretty much covered everything."

"Good." And he tugs me to him, and I don't even have time

to cry out his name before his mouth is pressed against mine, hot and demanding and so deep it goes on and on, seeping deeper into my body. Keeping me warm. Keeping me safe.

"I love you," I say, when we break the kiss.

"I should get points for saying it first," he teases.

"Fine by me," I say casually. "I don't want points. I just want you."

For immediate release:

After fourteen months as a permanent exhibit at the Stark Center for the Visual Arts, the critically acclaimed photographic exhibition, *A Woman In Mind*, will begin touring the United States and Europe.

The brainchild of W. Royce (aka Wyatt Segel), *A Woman In Mind* presents a provocative view of sensuality that has both delighted and fascinated members of the general public as well as the critics.

Royce and his fiancée, dancer Kelsey Draper, will tour with the exhibit to limited locations. Though eight of the exhibit's photos show an "anonymous" woman as a representation of "every woman," Royce and Draper have made no secret that Draper is the "It Girl" at the center of the show, as well as the performer of the live dance component of the exhibit.

Draper will begin filming *The Far Side of Jupiter*, an adaptation of the Tony Award Winning musical, in the fall.

The Stark Center is pleased to be hosting Royce's upcoming untitled exhibit in the spring.

It began with an unforgettable indecent proposal from Damien Stark...

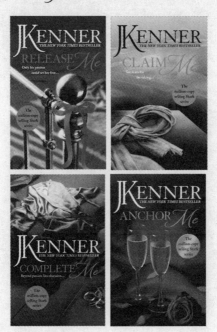

...But only his passion could set Nikki Fairchild free.

The irresistible, erotic, emotionally charged Stark series.
Available now from

A wedding, a honeymoon, a Valentine's Day,
a trip to Vegas and a Christmas
Damien Stark-style means one thing...

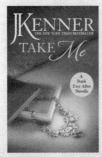
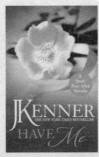
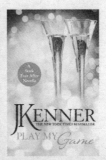

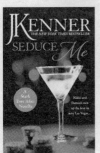
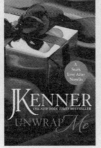
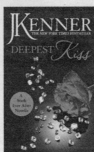
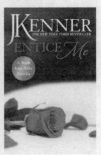

Happy Ever After is just the beginning...

The steamily seductive, dazzlingly romantic
Stark Ever After Novellas.

Available now from

HEADLINE
ETERNAL

Sylvia Brooks never lets anyone get too close.

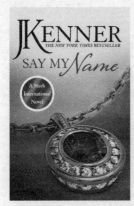 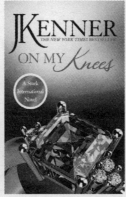 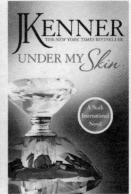

But Jackson Steele is the only man who's ever made her feel alive.

Return to the smoking hot Stark world with the explosive Stark International trilogy.

Available now from

HEADLINE
ETERNAL

It was wrong for Dallas Sykes and
Jane Martin to be together...

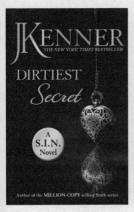 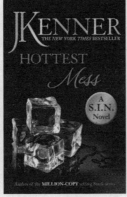 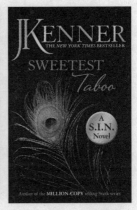

But it was even harder for
them to be apart...

Don't miss the entire deliciously sexy
Stark S.I.N. series.

Available now from

Three gorgeous, enigmatic and
powerful men...

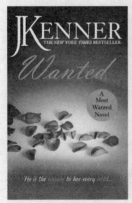 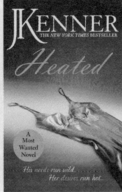 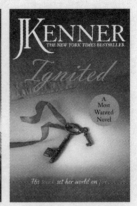

...and the striking women who can bring
them to their knees.

Enthralling and sizzling hot, the Most Wanted series.

Available now from

HEADLINE
ETERNAL

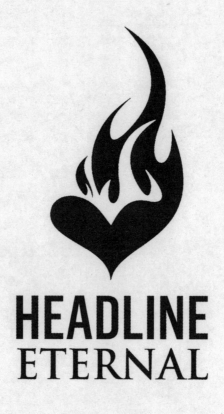

HEADLINE
ETERNAL

FIND YOUR HEART'S DESIRE...

VISIT OUR WEBSITE: www.headlineeternal.com

FIND US ON FACEBOOK: facebook.com/eternalromance

FOLLOW US ON TWITTER: @eternal_books

EMAIL US: eternalromance@headline.co.uk